contents

1. The World of Books..1

2. Cold Winter Days 13

3. Sled Riding 27

4. Staying in at Recess 39

5. Grandpa Glicks Moving Day.......................55

6. Hard Times..71

7. The Auction 85

8. Summer Days...101

9. The Accident 115

10. The Funeral 127

11. Fishing with Marvin 141

12. The Miller Relatives Visit..........................157

13. Potato Soup 171

14. A Lesson Learned 187

15. Washing...201

16. A Visit to Jefferson County........................213

17. A Wonderful Afternoon.............................227

18. The First Day of School 239

19. Grandma Miller Is Sick 253

20. Another Trip to Ohio.................................269

21. Thinking of Moving 281

22. Saying Good-bye...295

23. Settling In 309

24. Starting Anew 323

LINDA BYLER

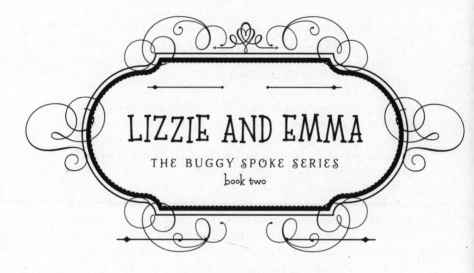

LIZZIE AND EMMA

THE BUGGY SPOKE SERIES
book two

LIZZIE AND EMMA

Copyright © 2018 by Linda Byler

Good Books books may be purchased in bulk at special discounts for sales promotion, corporate gifts, fund-raising, or educational purposes. Special editions can also be created to specifications. For details, contact the Special Sales Department, Good Books, 307 West 36th Street, 11th Floor, New York, NY 10018 or info@skyhorsepublishing.com.

Good Books is an imprint of Skyhorse Publishing, Inc.®, a Delaware corporation.

Visit our website at www.goodbooks.com.

10 9 8 7 6 5 4 3 2 1

Library of Congress Cataloging-in-Publication Data is available on file.

ISBN: 978-1-68099-357-8
eBook ISBN: 978-1-68099-359-2

Cover design by Jenny Zemanek

Printed in Canada

To "Emma"
For Me and Roo

Like seeds
borne on spring breezes,
Memories fade,
but love arises,
renewed,
each passing year.

chapter 1

The World of Books

The wooden porch swing creaked in rhythm as Lizzie pushed one foot against the splintered oak porch floor. Some of the paint was peeling off and stuck to the bottom of her foot. It felt funny, so Lizzie stopped the swing and pulled up her foot. She carefully brushed off the flakes of gray paint, pulling her old black sweater around her shoulders more tightly. She shivered. It was actually too cold to be sitting out here on the porch swing, but as long as she stayed here, she didn't have to help Emma with the supper dishes.

Her feet were cold, and she wished she would have worn socks at least. But she had to sneak away fast while Emma was in the bathroom, or else she would never have been allowed to sit here reading.

Lizzie was eight years old now, so she could read lots of books. There was almost nothing in her life that was more important to her than her books. Every spare moment, she had a book in her hand, biting her lower lip if the story was very exciting.

Lizzie's sister Emma was nine years old. Mandy was only five, and baby Jason was two. They all lived with Mam and Dat, in a big white house in the middle of a small town in Pennsylvania. Dat's name was Melvin Glick, and he had a nice big harness shop on the first floor of the white house. There was a sign hanging outside that said "Glick's Harness and Shoe Shop" with a horse's head painted on it. Lizzie was so proud of the sign, because Dat had painted it all by himself. Dat could do almost anything and it turned out right, Lizzie always thought.

The part where they actually lived in was above the harness shop. They always had to go up a flight of stairs if they came home from school or were playing in the yard. But Lizzie didn't mind. She liked to run up the stairs, sometimes missing a step to see if she could take two at a time. She hardly ever could, because she wasn't very thin.

She was short and round, with brown hair combed back into a "bob" on the back of her head, in the fashion of all little Amish girls. Her eyes were blue and her teeth in front overlapped a bit. Emma said she looked like a rabbit, which hurt her feelings terribly. She told Emma she couldn't help it if her teeth stuck out in front. Emma said they didn't really stick out as much as a rabbit's — they just kind of reminded her of one.

Lizzie thought Emma was prettier than her. She had dark hair, for one thing. It was almost black and it was shiny when it was wet. Her eyes were bright green. Sometimes Emma told Lizzie her eyes looked green, too, if she wore a green dress. So Lizzie figured her eyes would probably turn more green as she got older. If they didn't, she could always wear a green dress to go to the singing, when she was old enough.

Their kitchen had blue and gray-speckled linoleum on the floor and dark, wooden cabinets. There was a table along one wall, with a wooden bench along the back. A blue oilcloth—which was always sliding off—covered the table. Lizzie wished Mam wouldn't use that slippery tablecloth at all, but Mam said it saved the wooden table-top. There was a refrigerator and stove in the kitchen, and a big brown stove that burned coal to keep the kitchen cozy in the winter.

The living room was bigger, with green linoleum and a green sofa and chairs. Dat had given Mam a chair called a platform rocker, with wooden arms that were curved down, like a swan's neck. If you looked closely, there was a swan's head carved way on the bottom. That chair was covered with itchy blue upholstery that wasn't very comfortable if you sat on it too long.

There was a bathroom and three bedrooms along the back of the house. One bedroom was for Dat and Mam, another one for Jason and Mandy, and one that Emma had to share with Lizzie. Emma didn't want to share her room with Lizzie, because Emma was neat and clean and Lizzie was not.

Emma made her bed carefully, fluffing up the pillows and dashing around the bed three or four times to make sure the pink chenille bedspread hung exactly right in the corners. She put her underwear and nightgowns away very neatly after Mam had folded the clean laundry.

Lizzie couldn't see any sense in that at all. What was the use? If the pink bedspread hung exactly right all day, they would just make it crooked again that evening. And who would ever know what a drawer looked like on the inside? Lizzie's drawers held her clothes, mixed with school papers, pens, rocks, feathers, and old candy wrappers. Every once in a while, she found the remains of a half-eaten cheese cracker in her drawer, and that made her feel guilty. She never told Emma, because Emma would tell Mam.

Since Lizzie had learned to read, she had accumulated quite a row of books across the top of their bed. It was a bookcase bed, wooden with two small doors on each side to put their treasures in. Lizzie's side was so full of different things, she had to slide the little door open very carefully so her stuff did not come tumbling out all at once. Emma's side had neat little rows of birthday cards, erasers, tablets, and bits of ribbon and pretty things.

But the row of books was stacked neatly—exactly by size—and Lizzie knew which one was missing if Emma got one. Because Lizzie loved her books so much, she took good care of them. There was one book that she especially loved, because it was about doughnuts. There was a boy named Homer who invented a huge machine that made doughnuts so fast that he became very rich. When Lizzie looked at the pictures of the doughnuts with a bite taken out of one, it looked so good.

But today, sitting barefoot on the porch swing, shivering, with her old, fuzzy black sweater around her, she was reading *Heidi*. It was by far the best book she had ever read. It was so wonderful that Lizzie even forgot she was cold, or that she was supposed to be helping Emma with the dishes.

For one thing, Heidi and her grandfather put big pieces of goat cheese on the end of a long stick and held it over the fireplace. Lizzie thought that must be the most delicious thing in the world—cheese that sizzled over the fire! She had asked Mam if she was allowed to put a chunk of Velveeta cheese on a fork and hold it over the gas stove, but Mam said, "No, of course not!" That really irked Lizzie. What would be wrong with that?

Another thing about the *Heidi* book that made Lizzie long to be Heidi was her little bed made of sweet-smell-

ing hay up a ladder, under the roof. Lizzie could only imagine how much fun that would be. It wouldn't be so ordinary. Just opening her bedroom door and getting into the same old bed was not nearly as exciting as climbing up a ladder and being able to look through a little window and see the stars.

Lizzie had never tasted goats' milk, but when Heidi drank a bowl of sweet, warm milk that came fresh from a goat, Lizzie wished with all her heart she could be Heidi. She could only imagine going up, up, way up to the grassy pastures with Peter and the goats. It must be the most wonderful feeling, to be up so high.

Lizzie tucked her feet back under her skirt and pulled her sweater over her knees. It was cold—so cold, in fact, that she felt a chill go up her spine. She put down her book and wondered how she could sneak into the living room to get the warm blanket that lay across the top of the couch.

She slid off the swing, tucked her *Heidi* book under her arm, and slipped past the kitchen window, bending her back so no one would see her. She crept quietly down the stairs and walked into Dat's harness shop.

Dat was whistling at his sewing machine, but stopped and turned around when the bell above the door tinkled. Lizzie had forgotten about the bell.

"What are you doing, Lizzie?" Dat asked, turning back to his sewing.

"Oh, nothing," Lizzie answered.

"Done with the dishes already?" he asked, putting two pieces of leather together.

"Yes. No. I mean, I think so," Lizzie stammered.

"Weren't you helping Mam?" Dat asked, getting ready to sew the two pieces on the machine.

"Well, Emma was, so I thought they might not need me if they didn't say anything. I waited a while, Dat, really, I did. I actually waited a long time. Nobody said anything, so I, well, I kind of went out on the porch swing with my *Heidi* book," Lizzie explained.

Dat stopped, turned his chair, and looked closely at Lizzie. His blue eyes twinkled down at her and he said, "How can you kind of go out on the swing?"

"Well, I wasn't going to, but . . ." Lizzie pushed some leather scraps with her toe. She looked up at Dat defiantly. "Dat, did you like to read when you were a boy?"

Dat flung back his head and laughed heartily. "Ach, Lizzie, of course I did. But we had lots of chores to do on the farm, and I never had much time to read. But yes, Lizzie, I kind of went to the haymow or down to the chicken house more than once to read my book. I just kind of went, just like you!"

Lizzie held her book tightly to her chest and laughed happily. "You mean, sometimes you . . . you kind of sneaked away to read? Just like me?" she asked.

"Oh, yes." Dat smiled. "I sure did."

Lizzie held up her *Heidi* book. "Did you ever read this book, Dat?"

Dat took the book from her, looking carefully at the cover. "Yes, I did, Lizzie. I kind of remember this book. Is it about an old man and a little girl?"

"Yes, it is, Dat!" Lizzie showed him the cover of the

book. Dat looked carefully at the picture on the cover and flipped through the book. Lizzie put her elbows on Dat's knee and peered over his arm to see what he was looking at.

"And Dat, do you know how many goats Peter drove up the mountain? A whole bunch. And they all wore a bell, and they all followed him the whole way up the mountain and he didn't even lead them with a rope. They just all came when he called. And Dat, another thing. Grandfather—that's Heidi's *doddy*—put goat cheese on the end of a stick and held it over a fire. He toasted it. Mmmm! Do you think that would be good?"

Dat looked down at Lizzie and patted her head. "I think melted cheese would be very good. I really do!"

Lizzie took a deep breath. She smiled straight into Dat's eyes and loved him with all her heart. Dat was a really good Dat, because he always understood exactly how she felt. She didn't tell him, though, because she was ashamed to. But she knew that Dat knew that she really loved him.

"Now I better get back to work, Lizzie. Don't you think you should see if there are still dishes to dry or something?" he asked.

Lizzie sighed. "Yes, I guess."

"Don't you like to help Emma with the dishes?" Dat asked.

"Oh, not really. Especially if I have a book." Lizzie took two pieces of leather and snapped them together. She snapped them again.

"Lizzie!" Emma burst through the shop door. Her

face was red and the front of her dress was soaking wet from standing at the sink washing dishes.

"Lizzie, I mean it! Where were you? You are supposed to come help me with the dishes. Or you *were*. I'm done now. Dat, you have to help me tell Lizzie that she has to help me do the dishes. You know where she was, Dat?"

Lizzie kept snapping the two pieces of leather.

"Stop that!" Emma looked as if she could cry. For some reason, Lizzie wished she would, but then she thought that wasn't nice, so she put down the two pieces of leather.

"Where were you?" Emma asked, glaring at her.

"On the porch swing," Lizzie answered.

"Why?"

Lizzie held up her *Heidi* book.

Emma sighed. "Dat, you have to tell Lizzie she has to stop reading when it's time to do the dishes."

Dat put down the halter he was sewing. "Emma, when did you notice Lizzie wasn't helping?" he asked kindly.

"Well, I didn't really, because Mam was helping and we were learning a new song. We were singing and I kind of forgot about Lizzie. But it still isn't fair if she's allowed to read and I have to do dishes," Emma said.

"What song did you learn?" Lizzie wished she would have been able to help sing.

"I'm not going to tell you!" Emma was still a bit huffy.

"Emma, you tell Lizzie what you were singing, and she'll tell you what she was reading. Then tomorrow evening she'll have to wash the dishes, so she can't sneak out on the porch swing to read her book," Dat said.

"Okay," Emma said.

"I was reading this." Lizzie held up her book.

"And we sang 'Footsteps of Jesus'," Emma said.

"And tomorrow night Lizzie washes the dishes," Dat said.

"Yep!" said Emma.

Lizzie didn't say anything. She tucked her *Heidi* book under her arm and marched past Emma with her head held high. She stomped up the steps, putting her feet down heavily on each step.

It was always the same, Lizzie thought. Things would just never change, because Emma didn't understand how much Lizzie hated to wash dishes. Emma liked to do it, you could easily tell. She stacked everything in perfect order on the countertop before she started washing. The water was always the right temperature, and she never used too much soap, like Lizzie did. Lizzie just knew by the way Emma acted that washing dishes was something she enjoyed doing. And she was always sweeping the kitchen, picking up toys, putting pillows on the couch, or straightening the tablecloth. Actually, Emma was even more particular in some ways than Mam was.

Emma didn't know how it felt to feel so deeply sad when it was her turn to wash dishes. It was such a sad, dreary feeling. It simply ruined her good supper. Lizzie hated it with all her might. But she supposed she would like it better when she was Emma's age. At least she hoped so, because it was too hard to live with all these books to read and having to wash dishes.

She wondered if Heidi put her piece of melted cheese on bread, or if she put it on a plate. She knew Grandfather wouldn't make Heidi do dishes — she guaranteed he didn't.

Lizzie opened the door quietly and sat on the living room couch. She opened her book to the place where she had put her bookmarker and started reading. Soon she was lost in Heidi's world, with Peter and the goats, high up on mountains filled with wildflowers. She forgot about Emma and the dishes, becoming so engrossed in her book that she didn't even hear Emma come into the the living room and sit on the platform rocker.

"Lizzie."

"Hmmm."

"Are you mad at me?" Emma asked quietly.

"No."

"Are you sure?"

"Umm-hmm."

"Lizzie, do you really like to read so much?" Emma asked.

Lizzie sighed. She put down her book, putting her finger between the pages where she was reading.

"Emma, it's okay. I'm not mad. You just don't understand how much I hate to wash dishes. It's awful."

"I know," Emma said.

"So I'll try to do better, if you try and be nicer." Lizzie smiled at Emma, because she kind of felt sorry for her. She couldn't help it that she was so different.

"I'm your friend, Lizzie." Emma smiled back.

"Yep, you are," said Lizzie.

And she meant it with her whole heart.

chapter 2

Cold Winter Days

Lizzie opened one eye, pulled the covers up over her head, and shivered. She moved over closer to Emma. She had awakened because she was so cold, but Emma felt nice and warm, and Lizzie drifted back to a warm, cozy feeling, almost falling asleep.

She remained perfectly still when the door opened and Mam walked quietly into their room. She was carrying some laundry in a basket, which she set softly on their bed. She tried to be quiet, sliding the drawers open carefully and putting in neat stacks of clean clothes.

Lizzie opened her eyes and peeped at Mam. There was something about someone coming into your room, Lizzie thought. They could be as quiet as they possibly could, but something felt like a whisper when they moved. Mam was being very quiet, but Lizzie watched her hang their dresses carefully in the closet.

Mam wasn't very big; she was just right. She felt soft and fluffy when she held Lizzie close, and always smelled like Pond's talcum powder. Her hair was dark, but it was never smoothed down flat like the other women in church had their hair, because, originally, Mam came from Ohio where the women combed their hair loosely over the top of their heads and wore different coverings. Here in Pennsylvania their hair was parted in the middle and smoothed down sleekly with water. That was considered neater, but Mam always combed her hair back a bit more loosely and did not wet it down like the other women did. She always looked more "shtruvlich" than the others, but Lizzie thought she looked nice exactly the way she was, because she was her Mam.

Mam paused and looked toward their bed. Lizzie quickly closed her eyes tightly, but Mam smiled to herself and walked over, gently lifting one of Lizzie's eyelids. "Peep!" she said.

"Mam!" Lizzie hit at her mother with both arms. "I was sleeping!"

Mam grabbed hold of Lizzie's arms and held them tightly. "No, you weren't!" she said with a laugh.

"Good morning, sleepyhead," she said to Emma, as Emma sat up, stretching and yawning.

"Brrrr! It's terribly cold in here," Emma said crossly. "Give me the covers, Lizzie."

Mam sat up. "Yes, it certainly is a cold morning. You probably won't have to go to school, because it snowed all night and the temperature is only a little bit above zero degrees. Dat said he thinks the wind is picking up, too. But just in case you do go to school, you had better get up and get dressed, because Uncle James might take you if there is any school," Mam said.

Emma stuck her face out from beneath the heavy comforter. Her eyebrows were drawn together, and she did not look happy at all. "I guarantee we don't have school, Mam. It's too cold," she growled.

Mam was standing at the window, looking out to the street and the neighboring houses. "Look, girls," she said. "The snow even blew in between the cracks in this old window. You have a whole layer of snow drifted on your windowsill here."

"Where?" Lizzie hopped out of bed in her bare feet.

Sure enough, there was a layer of pure white snow that had blown in from the snowstorm during the night. Lizzie stuck her finger in it, and licked off the snow that stuck to it.

"Ooooh, that's cold! This floor is freezing!" And Lizzie took two flying leaps back into bed. She yanked hard on the comforter, and Emma yelled, "Stop that! It's cold!"

Mam remained standing at the window, her arms crossed tightly around herself because she was cold. She just stood there quietly, watching the snow swirling around the house. Lizzie watched her. Sometimes she pitied Mam, although she didn't know why. Mam's gray everyday apron was frayed at the corner and there was a rip along one of the pleats. Her bedroom slippers were torn along the top and her black-stockinged toe stuck out above the flowered material of her slippers. She looked tired and a bit sad this morning, Lizzie thought.

She remembered hearing Mam and Dat talking late

last evening. Emma had been sleeping for awhile, but
Dat's voice would rise sharply at times, followed by
Mam's soft voice, talking faster than usual. Lizzie knew
something was wrong, but she didn't know what. If she
asked Mam why Dat was in the harness shop so late,
she just said he was busy. Sometimes when Mam rocked
Jason and sang softly, her nose turned red and tears
ran down her cheeks. She would not go on singing—she
just sat there rocking until she had her emotions under
control.

This worried Lizzie immensely. Mam was sad and
Dat stayed in the harness shop. It made Lizzie feel like
something really terrible was going to happen very soon.
She was just about certain the end of the world was
coming any day now.

Or there was going to be a kidnapper on the way to
school. She could just picture it. They would be walking
along in the snow and a really horrible-looking, rusty
old car would stop. The bearded man would grab them
by their scarves and drag them into the ugly car. That
was partly why Lizzie tucked her scarf inside her coat. It
would be much harder for a man to grab her by her bonnet strings, because they were tucked tightly under her
double chin. Emma said Lizzie was dumb, tucking her
scarf in, but Lizzie still thought it was the smart thing to
do.

"Well," Mam sighed, "no use wishing for something
I can't have. It would be nice to have new windows to
help keep this house warmer, though."

"Now come, girls. Time to get up now," she said, letting herself out through their bedroom door.

"Come on," Emma said, resigning herself to her fate. She swung her legs over the side of the bed and stood up. She raised her arms above her head, shivered, and hopped right back in, pulling the comforter over her head until she disappeared. "It's too cold," came her muffled voice.

Lizzie giggled. It certainly was cold, she thought, but they had to get up and go to school, unless the snowplow didn't go at all. So she ran over to the closet, grabbed her green dress from the hanger, and in one quick movement, she shed her nightgown and shivered into her dress.

"The floor is freezing cold, Emma. Come on, you have to get out sometime," Lizzie said.

"I will. Just go on," came the muffled reply.

Lizzie giggled again and yanked the door open, dashing across the living room into the warm kitchen, where she held out her hands to the warmth of the big brown coal stove.

Dat sat at the table holding Jason. He was bouncing him up and down on one knee, and Jason's curls were flopping up and down at an alarming rate. Dat stopped when he saw Lizzie.

"Good morning, Lizzie. Is your bedroom cold?" He smiled.

"There's snow on the windowsill and it isn't melting yet," Lizzie told him.

"Really?" Dat asked.

"Mmm-hmm," Lizzie said, as she sat down on the floor in front of the coal stove to put on her woolen black tights. Emma came running into the kitchen, her hair sticking out in every direction. The buttons on her dress were not closed, and she held her socks in one hand.

"It is not even funny how cold our bedroom is," she said, shivering beside Lizzie.

"Is it that cold in there, Annie?" Dat asked, setting Jason in his high chair.

"It's plenty cold. I don't see how the girls could keep warm," Mam said wryly.

"Oh, that doesn't hurt them. I remember very well in the old brick farmhouse at home, it used to be so cold that water in a glass froze on the dresser. You just have to add lots of heavy comforters, that's all," Dat said.

Mam turned to the stove, expertly flipping pancakes. She said something quietly, which sounded a lot like "Humph," but Lizzie wasn't sure. She just knew that Mam's mouth was in a straight, stiff line, and she said almost nothing all through breakfast. Dat was teasing Jason, but Mam told him to stop, because he wouldn't eat. Dat sighed and ate his breakfast silently.

It was a good breakfast, as usual, because everything

Mam made was delicious. They had warm golden pancakes that were done to perfection, slathered with soft
yellow butter, and syrup poured on top of the butter.
Besides the pancakes, Mam served a platter of fried eggs
that had a nice amount of soft yellow "dippy." Toast
was done in the broiler of the gas stove, which turned it
crispy and buttery at the same time. They almost never
had bacon or sausage, because it was too expensive
to buy from the meat man. But that was alright with
Lizzie—she liked "dippy" eggs and pancakes better
anyway.

But when Dat and Mam were not happy, like this
morning, the pancakes stuck in Lizzie's throat. She cast
furtive glances at Mam, wishing she would smile at Dat
so her pancake would taste better. She dipped a piece of
toast halfheartedly into her "dippy" egg, but she really
didn't feel much like eating.

Jason was trying to get out of his high chair. Mam
smacked him hard on his hands, and Jason screamed
and cried. Dat looked at Mam, but said nothing.

Mandy said, "Jason, you have to stay sitting if Mam is
grouchy!" Mandy was only five years old, with straight
brown hair and huge green eyes. She didn't go to school
with Emma and Lizzie, but she would in another year.
Sometimes, if Emma was working too much or acted too
bossy, Lizzie had more fun playing with Mandy, even if
they only played childish games.

"There goes the snowplow, girls!" Dat said brightly,
trying to set a better tone to their silent breakfast table.

"Does that mean we have to go to school?" Emma

asked.

"Oh, yes, I would say so," Dat replied.

"Then we'd better get moving," Mam said sharply, getting up and starting to pack their lunchboxes.

They were all ready to go, their warm coats and sweaters buttoned, bonnets tied securely, and their bright red mittens pulled snugly around their fingers when Uncle James pulled up beside the house.

"Bye! Bye!" yelled Emma and Lizzie, as they opened the door and raced down the stairs. It was so cold when they stepped outside that it took their breath away. The snow was blowing in every direction and stung their faces. Lizzie squinted against the bright light and held a mittened hand over her mouth.

"Good morning, girls!" Uncle James said. He held their lunches as they struggled to place their feet carefully on the high iron step. They tumbled into the buggy, clambered over the front seat, and squeezed in beside Lavina Lapp, who was a sister to Uncle James.

"Hi!" Lavina smiled. "It's really cold!"

"It sure is," Emma said.

"Yep!" Lizzie agreed.

Uncle James settled himself in the front seat, clucked to the horse, and they were off. He was driving the old market wagon that swayed and lurched, rattling terribly if the horse went fast at all. A market wagon was a bit heavier than a regular buggy, and it rattled more because you could lift up the whole back to set heavy things inside. Lizzie just loved to go home from school in Uncle James's market wagon when it rained.

Once, Uncle James's sister Nancy had brought them home in the pouring rain, and her little horse ran as fast as he could. Nancy couldn't hold him back too well, and the old market wagon rattled and swayed so badly, it felt as if the wheels weren't even round. They had giggled and laughed until the tears ran down their faces, because the little horse was so funny.

But Uncle James wasn't driving that little horse this morning. He was driving his big black one, and he was not going fast because he had to be very careful because of the blowing snow.

"I can hardly see a thing," he muttered. "Guess I'll have to open my window, girls, so I can see where I'm going."

Lizzie peeped worriedly over the back seat. She swallowed hard. It looked so dangerous, because sometimes there was only a solid wall of whirling whiteness. When the wind let up a tiny bit, she could see the shape of trees or houses. The snow swirled into the buggy, and Lizzie shivered, partly with fear.

"Maybe we should have stayed at home," she offered in a very small voice.

"We'll be alright," Uncle James assured her.

But Lizzie felt a tight knot of fear in her stomach. She just had a feeling something was going to happen today, mostly because Mam and Dat weren't happy. It was too cold for kidnappers, and Lizzie didn't think the end of the world would come in a snowstorm, but then, you never knew. Her mittened hand clutched the back of the seat tightly and her eyes opened wider in alarm.

"Hang on—here comes the snowplow!" Uncle James said loudly. "Don't know if Rusty will like this or not!"

Lizzie pulled in her breath sharply. A sob tore at her throat. Emma grabbed Lizzie's arm, pulling her over toward her side of the buggy.

"Lizzie, don't cry! Now I mean it. Everything is going to be . . ."

"Whoa!" yelled Uncle James. His shoulders moved back and forth as he struggled to control the skittish horse.

"Whoop! Whoa! Whoa there!" Uncle James pulled back on the reins as hard as he could, but there was not much he could do. Up, up came Rusty until Lizzie could see only his broad black back with the harness flapping and his tail blowing in the whirling snow. Lizzie choked, trying to keep back the terror she felt.

But when the horse seemed to topple backwards and Uncle James yelled again, a loud scream broke from her throat. Emma screamed, too, and Lavina Lapp cried out in a strange, hoarse voice. It seemed as if Rusty was falling now, straight back into the window. Uncle James was half standing, fighting to keep control of his horse, while staying out of the snowplow's direct path.

Suddenly there was a horrible lurch, and Lizzie banged her head sharply against the back of the seat. She screamed again, and Emma held her tightly as her head hit the back, throwing them against the side of the buggy.

Snow swirled in through the open window as Rusty came down on all fours. He hit the ground running, taking great, leaping strides in his urgent need to run away from the snowplow that had terrified him.

They tore down the snowy road at a pace Lizzie hadn't thought was possible. She wondered if they were going to have a real accident, because Rusty was running away. Wasn't this how bad accidents actually happened? The buggy wheel could fly off and they would all fall out on the road. She squeezed her eyes shut very tightly, just waiting until the whole buggy flew apart.

But it didn't. Slowly, Uncle James regained control, and Rusty trotted with only a small amount of fear. His ears still flicked back and forth and his head was held high, but he was not running away. Lizzie sighed.

"Boy, that was scary!" Lavina breathed.

"It sure was," Uncle James said with a laugh.

Lizzie couldn't understand how Uncle James could laugh about it. It wasn't even one bit funny. She fought back tears of fear and frustration, and mostly she felt like crying because it seemed as if the horse had wanted to kill them all. Lizzie was really angry at the horse.

She dug into the pocket of her dress to find her handkerchief and wiped furiously at her nose, sniffing loudly. It was so hard to think that a horse could actually get so fierce. They should never do that, especially not in a snowstorm!

Lizzie loved horses and ponies, and it had never occurred to her that they would ever be quite that dangerous. So she wiped her eyes hard with her handkerchief, sniffed, adjusted her bonnet strings under her chin, and frowned. They never should have come to school, that's what, she thought. The weather just was not fit. Now she wasn't even sure if she liked horses or not. Ponies were smaller, and their pony, named Dolly, had run away once, but it hadn't been as horrifying as this. And when a horse reared up that far, he looked as big as an elephant. Bigger, actually.

When they pulled up to the school yard, the gate stood open and there were children huddled on the porch. Uncle James threw open the door of the market wagon and asked the children if the teacher was there.

"Yeah, she's here," Reuben Zook told him.

"Alright, then. Out you go," Uncle James said, hopping down into the swirling snow.

Lizzie grabbed her lunchbox and tumbled out of the buggy. She struggled through the snowdrifts and up the steps of the porch, followed by Emma and Lavina. They burst through the door and into the warm, cozy classroom. Teacher Katie hurried across the room, putting her hand on Emma's shoulder.

"My goodness, girls! Your Uncle James is a brave man! I cannot imagine how hard it must have been for him to keep that buggy on the road! Didn't you meet a snowplow? I sure hope that is a horse that doesn't shy away from heavy vehicles," she said.

Lavina and Emma both started talking at the same time, explaining to Teacher Katie how frightening their ride to school actually was. Lizzie couldn't get a word in at all, so she took her lunchbox back and set it on the wooden shelf beside the water bucket. She was thinking very serious thoughts about Uncle James and Rusty, blinking her eyes as she unbuttoned her heavy black coat.

"Lizzie!" Her best friend, Betty, rushed over to greet her.

"What?" Lizzie looked up from unbuttoning her coat and shrugged it off her shoulders, turning to hang it on a gold hook that had a piece of adhesive tape above it saying "Elizabeth Glick."

"Lizzie, it isn't e-even funny how windy it is!"

"Oh, I know," Lizzie answered gravely.

"How did you come to school? Surely you didn't walk!" Betty exclaimed. "No," Lizzie said, shaking her head. "Uncle James brought us with his horse, Rusty. It was *awful!*"

"Why? What happened?" Betty asked, leaning forward in anticipation.

Lizzie shook her head and rolled her eyes toward the ceiling, taking a deep breath for emphasis. She hung her bonnet and long, woolen scarf on the hook, turning to Betty and saying, "We almost ended up in the hospital with an ambulance."

"Really!" Betty's eyes opened wide, and she put both hands up to her mouth in dismay.

That really made Lizzie feel important, so she launched into the whole story, waving her arms to accentuate the exciting parts.

Later, when she sat at her desk listening to the teacher read the Bible story, she felt a bit guilty. She had told Betty the truth, though—except maybe the horse didn't quite fall back on the buggy. He may as well have, as scary as it looked. She bet he actually did touch the top of the buggy, at least his blowing mane and tail.

chapter 3

Sled Riding

After the wind died down, the sun shone on a glittering world of pure white. The snow was compacted from the steady force of the wind, which made conditions perfect to go sledding.

So one day at school, just before it was time to dismiss the children, Teacher Katie announced that the next day they would have classes till lunchtime, then they would go sledding on Stoltzfus's hill the remainder of the day. They should be sure and pack extra food in their lunchboxes, and bring a Thermos with a drink, and a pair of extra warm socks in case their feet got too cold.

Lizzie was so excited. She clapped her hands together without actually hitting them against each other. Betty gave her a gleeful look and bounced up and down in her seat. They were not allowed to be noisy, so they just quietly acted out their excitement.

That evening, Mam made whoopie pies. Lizzie thought that besides doughnuts, whoopie pies were the best thing to put in your lunch. Mam didn't make them very often, because she was helping Dat in the shop quite a lot lately.

But tonight, because they were going sledding, she made whoopie pies. She beat sugar, oil, and eggs, adding cocoa powder and flour until she had a smooth, creamy dough which tasted absolutely delicious. Lizzie put her finger in the soft, chocolaty dough so often that Mam said she would get sick if she didn't stop it right this minute.

After the cookies were baked, Mam put creamy white frosting on the bottom of one cookie, putting another one on top to make a little sandwich. Then she wrapped each one individually in little squares of plastic wrap. Emma was allowed to help wrap them, but Lizzie wasn't, because she had eaten too much of the dough.

The next morning, Lizzie was up bright and early to pack her food in her lunchbox. She went straight to the pantry and arranged five whoopie pies on a plate, carrying them over to the table where their lunchboxes stood side by side. She carefully placed them inside hers, being very concerned that she wouldn't smash them too tightly against each other.

Mam came over with their bologna sandwiches and peered into Lizzie's lunchbox. "Lizzie, how many whoopie pies did you put in there?" she asked.

"Five," answered Lizzie.

"You can't have five, Lizzie. Now take two of them out. Three are even too many," she said briskly, hurrying over to the sink to mix orange juice in a pitcher.

"No, Mam—you just don't understand. One is for first recess, and two for dinner. Then if we go sledding I'll need one for a snack, and one for on the way home 'cause I'll be so tired," Lizzie explained.

Mam tried to hide her smile, but she was smiling broadly when she looked into Lizzie's upturned face. Lizzie's eyes were very serious, and she was terribly concerned about having enough to eat on this strenuous outing.

"Ach, Lizzie, you're going to be as round as a little barrel if you keep on eating so many whoopie pies. That's just too many," she sighed.

"I can give Betty one, okay?" Lizzie bargained.

"Alright," Mam said, giving in.

But Lizzie was already thinking about not giving Betty one, or else she wouldn't have enough. But she didn't tell Mam what she was thinking, because there was no sense in it. Besides, maybe if Mam would make them more often, Lizzie wouldn't be so hungry for them. So really, if you looked at it that way, it was Mam's fault.

The whole way to school, the girls chattered happily about going sledding. Lavina had a big, long, wooden sled with steel runners, and Emma and Lizzie had a smaller one to share. They put their sled upside down on top of Lavina's big one and set their lunchboxes inside. Lizzie didn't have to carry her lunch that way, so she swung her arms and skipped along behind Emma.

"Lizzie, watch out. You're going to fall on a patch of slippery snow. Stop skipping," Emma said.

So Lizzie walked carefully, even if she felt like skipping. It was a wonderful, sunshiny day. Cold, but not so cold that it hurt your nose like it did sometimes. Lizzie's mittens were soft and dry from hanging on the wooden rack by the coal stove during the night. Her boots were dry, too, because Mam had made sure the tops were turned down when they were put by the stove in the evening.

It seemed like the forenoon was twice as long as usual. Lizzie tried hard to concentrate on her arithmetic lesson, but she just couldn't think as well as usual. Emma had told Lizzie some time ago that third grade was harder than second, and it was. Especially arithmetic.

Lizzie propped her head on the back of her hand and worked on some problems. David Lantz walked past her desk and slapped at her elbow. Her hand flew away from her face, and, for a second, it felt like her head would fall off, till she snapped it up to save embarrassment. She glared up into David's laughing face, batting her eyelashes with righteous anger. Some of her classmates snickered, and David walked hurriedly on down the aisle. The teacher had not seen any of the commotion, because she was correcting answers in class.

Boys were so ignorant, Lizzie thought. Half of them smelled like a cow stable when they came to school, and most of them hardly ever brushed their teeth. They ate green apples, too, which made Lizzie's mouth pucker just to watch them. And one day Mosie Fisher told Emma he could eat a whole apple—the core, seeds, and everything. Even that thing you twirled on the top! And he did. Lizzie told him she guaranteed he felt like throwing up, but he told her the seeds were the best part.

Finally, the clock showed half past eleven, and Teacher Katie told them all to put their books away, clean off their desks, and put on their warm coats, scarves, and boots. There was a lot of noise, although nobody spoke because it was still school hours.

Lizzie pulled on her boots, her face red with exertion. She yanked on her coat and reached into the pocket for her mittens. They weren't there! She searched every corner of her coat pocket, but they simply were not in there. She looked on the floor, checking inside her desk, but her mittens were gone.

She raised her hand, needing permission to go back where her lunch had been. The teacher was busy helping the first graders with their boots and didn't see Lizzie's hand. She shook her hand, coughing, so the teacher would notice, but she still didn't look. Lizzie was just sure everyone would leave without her, and panic rose in her throat. She shook her hand again, clearing her throat loudly.

"Lizzie!"

Oh, good, Teacher noticed! she thought.

"I can't find my mittens," Lizzie said, almost in tears.

"You may go check the lunch shelves. Are you sure they weren't left outside?" she asked.

Lizzie hurried back to the shelves, searching frantically for the lost mittens. She cast a quick glance back at the other pupils, who were all dressed and waiting, their lunchboxes on their wooden desks. Her panic increased, and she felt hot tears prick at her eyelids. She just couldn't cry now, she thought wildly.

Suddenly Emma was beside her, touching her coat sleeve with her hand, whispering, "Lizzie, I think you left them in the bathroom at recess."

"Oh," was all Lizzie could manage without bursting into tears. She dashed madly out the door, and, sure enough, there in the bathroom lay her bright red mittens. Running back as fast as she could, she thought about how she must say thank you to Emma for remembering.

They were all put in pairs of two for their march to the Stoltzfus's hill. Lizzie walked with Emma, and they took turns pulling the sled.

"Emma, I'm so glad you remembered where my mittens were!" Lizzie said sincerely.

"Well, Lizzie, you were almost crying, weren't you? I pitied you so much, because I know how that feels if everyone is watching you, and they're all waiting to go. Oh, that makes me so nervous," Emma said.

"Me, too!" said Lizzie, and she meant it with all her heart.

When they reached the hill, the big boys unloaded wood from one of the sleds and started a fire. First they put newspapers and scraps on a small pile, lit a match, and held it to the paper, adding very small slivers of wood, until a crackling flame licked steadily higher. Then they added larger pieces of wood, and soon Lizzie could feel the soft warmth of the bonfire on her face. They pulled the sleds in a circle, making a cozy ring around the fire. Then the teacher told them all to bow their heads and they said their usual lunch prayer. "God is great and God is good, and we thank Him for our food."

After the prayer, everyone opened their lunchboxes and ate the good food their mothers had prepared. They all laughed and talked excitedly, because after dinner they could go sledding for a long time.

Lizzie sat on her sled and ate her bologna sandwich first. Mam had bought fresh, sweet bologna from the butcher truck. It tasted extra good today, because of the cold winter air and the cozy fire crackling in the middle of the sled ring. But the best part of all was her two whoopie pies. The crumbs stuck to her hands, they were so moist and soft, and the creamy vanilla frosting made a mess on the plastic wrap. Lizzie licked up every sweet bite, then looked at Betty. She looked at the two whoopie pies in her lunchbox, and looked at Betty again.

Slowly she closed her lunchbox, because she knew how hungry she would be from sledding. She stole a glance at Emma, but she was talking to her friend Rebecca. No one would know if she gave Betty a whoopie pie. Mam would say God did, but Lizzie didn't suppose it mattered that much to God. He probably wouldn't mind, especially not if she gave her one tomorrow.

Teacher Katie stood up and said in a clear voice, "Now, everyone listen carefully. We have two hours to go sledding, and I'll blow the whistle when it's time to return to school. No more than two on a sled, and everyone has to take turns so the little ones get to ride as well. You may go now, and please be careful."

With whoops and yells of excitement, the sleds lined up and started down as fast as they were filled up. Lizzie watched the big boys as they flung themselves on their

sleds, two to a sled, and flew down the hill. Little wisps
of snow drifted from beneath the speeding runners, and
the boys' cries of elation sent chills of nervousness up
Lizzie's spine. The hill looked so long and steep, she
wasn't sure if she dared go down with Emma or not.
Some of the boys were pushing each other, going so
closely, side by side, that Lizzie held her breath, biting
down on her lower lip—it scared her so much.

"Lizzie, do you want to ride with me?" Katie Lapp
bent down to look at her kindly.

"I-I guess," Lizzie stammered.

"Okay, I'll lie on the sled, and you lie on top. Hold on
to the sled on each side of me, and don't let go, because
if you do, you could slide off. Don't be afraid, because I
did this a whole bunch of times. It's really, really fun,"
she said in her loud voice.

So, with her heart hammering in her chest, and her
mouth dry with fear, Lizzie plopped down on Katie's
back.

"Here, put your hands right here," Katie said, guiding
her hands to a round piece of wood that ran along the

side of the sled. "Ready?"

"Yes," came Lizzie's small reply.

"Here we go!"

And they were off. The air hit Lizzie's face with little bits of snow biting her cheeks. The pressure of it took her breath away, and for a short time Lizzie panicked, because she thought she wasn't able to breathe at all. Her eyes just wanted to close, and even when they opened she could hardly see anything except a blur of white. Katie was soft and not very solid, so Lizzie always felt as if she was rolling off either to one side or the other.

They went so fast that Lizzie could do nothing but scream. She screamed loud and long, half laughing and half crying, but screaming nevertheless. Katie laughed and laughed, telling Lizzie to hang on, which she was doing with all her strength.

When the sled slowed at the bottom of the hill, Katie heaved underneath her, and Lizzie rolled off into the cold white snow. They lay on their stomachs and laughed helplessly, gasping for breath.

"You have . . . have a whole pile of snow in your hair!" Lizzie gasped.

"Look at yourself!" Katie said, laughing.

"Oh, that was *so* fun! Let's go right up as fast as we can and come back down again!" Lizzie said.

So they ran up the hill till they were out of breath, then they walked along, shouting to each sled that whizzed past. Lizzie thought she had never had a day as wonderful as this one in her whole life. The sky was so bright blue that it actually hurt her eyes, and the snow sparkled and glistened, making everything seem unreal. Lizzie had never gone so fast on a sled ever before in her life. She decided that day that she loved speed, and the faster the sled went down the hill, the better.

Emma and Lizzie even took a sled completely on their own, and Lizzie ran alongside, pushing Emma to give them a fast start.

Some of the older children starting sitting on their sleds and steering them with their feet. That looked too dangerous to Lizzie, and she and Emma decided they would try that next year, maybe, when they were older.

They were walking back up the hill, slowly now, because they were getting so tired. Emma said this was the best day she ever had in school, and Lizzie said she loved her teacher so much that she was going to bring her a whoopie pie tomorrow for taking them sledding.

"Why don't you give her one today?" Emma asked, pulling off her mitten and shaking it against her knee. "My mittens are soaked."

"Why don't you put them in your lunchbox, Emma? They're too wet to keep your hands warm, anyway," Lizzie said.

"Put them in your lunch, because mine is full of stuff," Emma said.

"What stuff?"

"Just stuff. Little containers, and I didn't eat all my food," Emma answered.

"What do you have left?" Lizzie asked.

"Everything."

"You mean all your food? Everything?" Lizzie asked.

"Lizzie, don't tell anyone, okay? But . . ." Emma lowered her voice. "I was so terribly afraid of going sledding that I . . . well, Lizzie, don't tell anyone—promise?"

"I promise," Lizzie answered solemnly.

"Cross your heart?" Emma asked worriedly.

"Cross my heart."

"Okay. I was so scared that when I tried to eat my bologna sandwich, I almost threw up. Really, I had to take a drink and put my sandwich away."

Emma stopped and looked squarely at Lizzie. "And Lizzie, I don't really like to go sledding very much, because it still scares me terribly. Don't tell anyone, but I'd almost rather sit at my desk and do my lessons".

Lizzie's eyes squinted as she looked out over the sparkling white hill. She watched as the boys tried to push each other off their sleds while they were going down at quite an alarming rate. Then she turned to look at Emma, who looked back quite solemnly at Lizzie.

"Emma, that doesn't matter one bit," Lizzie said staunchly. "I will not tell one single person ever that sled riding scares you if you don't tell one single person that I put five whoopie pies in my lunch this morning."

"Five?" Emma was horrified. "Why five?"

Lizzie looked carefully over her shoulder and whispered to Emma, "Because. And I'm not even giving one to the teacher!"

When Teacher Katie blew her whistle, she looked at Emma and Lizzie, their heads thrown back in laughter, and thought how much they must love sledding.

chapter 4

Staying in at Recess

The weather remained cold, with snowfalls almost every week. Lizzie trudged to school every day with Lavina and Emma, carrying her little tin lunchbox.

Lizzie loved school, but it was getting to be a bit boring. She was tired of playing "Duck, Goose, and Tramp" in the snow, which she always thought was a dumb game in the first place. Besides, the boys played too rough, and if Lizzie got in their way, sometimes they pushed her rudely to one side to get past on the narrow snow trails.

Teacher Katie had just tapped the bell to dismiss the pupils after they had eaten their lunch. Lizzie and Betty pulled on their coats, tying their scarves securely under their chins. Lizzie pulled on her mittens and ran through the door.

"Lizzie!"

Lizzie jerked to a halt and turned around.

Teacher Katie stood beside her desk, her eyes glaring

at Lizzie. Lizzie's heart skipped a beat and her mouth felt dry as she picked at her coat button nervously with her mittened hand.

"What?" she asked, meeting the teacher's displeased stare.

"How many times do I have to ask you to stop running in the schoolroom? Can't you ever slow down to a nice, normal walk like the rest of the pupils do?" Teacher Katie asked.

"I . . . I guess I can," Lizzie stammered. She could hardly meet those piercing eyes, so she scuffed her toe against the wooden floor, looking very hard at the different-colored splinters in the wood.

"Thank you," Teacher Katie said, turning to the blackboard.

Lizzie walked slowly over to the door, and Betty tiptoed out beside her. There was a lump in Lizzie's throat, and she felt so much like crying, but she knew she couldn't because she was too big. *I wasn't even running more than a few steps anyhow*, she thought.

"Boy!" Betty said, emphatically.

"I was hardly even running," Lizzie said, slipping her arm under Betty's.

"She's just grouchy today. Did you hear her at lunchtime?" Betty asked.

"You mean telling Amos to pick up the waxed paper from his sandwich?" Lizzie asked.

"Yes," Betty replied. "She said it so loud and angry. I almost pitied Amos."

"Oh, well," Lizzie shrugged. "Maybe she's tired of

teaching school and wishes she could get married."

"She doesn't want to get married. She said so," Betty said.

"Oh," said Lizzie.

There was a group of children standing on the playground having a loud discussion. Mose Fisher was waving his arms and yelling, and Rebecca yelled back just as loudly. Lizzie stopped to listen to the conversation, scooping up a handful of snow with her mittened hand. She stuck her tongue into the frosty mound scooping up a mouthful. The snow slid down her throat almost before she had a chance to chew or swallow. That was just how snow was, Lizzie thought. It covered everything in sight and if you tried to eat it, it was really nothing. She flung the rest of the snow into the air, and watched as it settled on top of the other snow. She clapped her mittened hands together to shake off the remaining snow, scuffed the toe of her boot into a snowdrift, and sighed.

She was too little to speak her mind with the big children, but she just couldn't see any sense in school, at recess especially. It was just so awfully boring, because nobody wanted to play anything fun. All the boys ever wanted to do was throw snowballs as hard as they could.

Lizzie was scared of the boys throwing snowballs, so she stayed far away from their forts. Teacher Katie warned them not to hit the little ones or to throw the snowballs too hard, because it could be dangerous. They had all promised they wouldn't, but Lizzie didn't really believe them. You just never could tell, with boys.

"I don't care what you say!" Rebecca shouted. "It

simply isn't fair!"

The boys all waved their arms and walked off, saying something about there not being enough room on the playground. Rebecca sat down in the snow and all the big girls crowded around her. They were talking quietly, Rebecca looking as if she could burst into tears.

"Lizzie, let's do something, because it's almost time for the bell. We didn't even play anything yet today," Betty told her.

"Well, what?" asked Lizzie.

"'Duck, Goose, and Tramp?'" Betty asked hopefully.

"No," Lizzie answered firmly. "I'm too bored with that."

Rachel joined them. "You know what we could do?" she asked.

"What?"

"At home in our yard, we made a big trail, and we have little roads going everywhere, and we all have our separate house. We have real little furniture and our refrigerator is dug into the snowbank. Our drinks stay really cold!" she said with a giggle.

"That would be fun!" Lizzie shouted.

"I'll say!" Betty agreed.

"Let's do it!" Rachel was excited. "First you take tiny little "peepie" steps through the snow to pack down the trails. Then we all decide where our house will be, and everyone makes their own house."

"Like this?" Lizzie asked. She started off, shuffling her feet to tramp the snow down sufficiently.

Betty watched carefully, twisting her scarf with her

bright-colored mittens. She lifted her head and laughed out loud. "You look really funny!"

In a moment the three of them were shuffling their feet, moving steadily through the snow in a corner of the playground. It seemed as if they had just started when Lizzie was startled by the loud clanging of the old cast-iron bell on top of the gray-shingled schoolhouse roof.

"Uh-oh," Betty groaned.

"Ach, my!" Lizzie agreed. "Let's keep going a little while yet till the others are all in, then we'll hurry up and run in as fast as we can. We can still make a few more trails till second bell."

Teacher Katie always rang the big outside bell once and allowed the children two minutes to put their clothes away and get settled in their seats. Lizzie thought it really wasn't enough time if you needed to use the restroom, but she always managed to slide into her seat before the two-minute tap bell.

Lizzie went shuffling along in the snow, thinking she could get a little more done. Everything seemed strangely quiet on the playground, and when she looked up, Betty and Rachel had already left.

She broke into a run, racing against that dreaded two-minute tap bell. Just as her mittened hand grabbed the slippery doorknob, she heard the familiar "Ding!"

She squeezed harder on the doorknob, but her wet mittens slid off again. Desperately, she used both hands to turn the knob, and the latch clicked reassuringly. She slipped inside, breathing heavily, just as Teacher Katie announced, "Now it's storytime, and I'll start to read as soon as Lizzie sits in her seat."

Lizzie's face flamed. She felt hot all over, and carefully turned her back to the classroom to take off her coat. She was even more humiliated when big chunks of half-melted snow dumped on the floor from her wet mittens. She struggled to open the knot in her head scarf, but she could not loosen it. The classroom was so quiet that the sound of her own breathing roared in her ears.

She picked helplessly at the tight, wet knot under her chin, but she could absolutely not open it. If only she had a fork, she thought wildly. Mam always used the prong of a dinner fork to open shoelaces that were too tight.

In despair, she tried slipping the head scarf down backward, over her bob at the back of her head. But now her scarf was off her head, but still around her neck, the knot as secure as ever. She grabbed hold of the knot and yanked it up over her face, where it stuck just above her eyes at the hairline.

"Lizzie, come here." Teacher Katie was looking at her, displeasure all over her face. Lizzie blinked miserably, but walked bravely up the wide middle aisle to the teacher's desk, the fringes of her green scarf bobbing on each side of her head like a rabbit's ears.

Snickers and giggles rose like horrible creatures to taunt Lizzie. Tears pricked her eyelids. When she reached Teacher Katie's desk, the teacher slid the scarf off Lizzie's head and opened her drawer. She inserted a pen into the knot and pulled. Lizzie swallowed her tears as the knot gave way, and turning quickly on her heel,

she walked hurriedly to the back of the room. She flung
the dreadful scarf onto her clothes hook, and with her
head bent low, biting hard on her lower lip, she scuttled
to her seat.

Teacher Katie cleared her throat and began to read.
Lizzie put her arms on top of her wooden desk, turned
her face to the wall, and let the tears come. They formed
a puddle beside her nose and ran into her mouth. She
tasted the salt from her tears, and her nose started to
run, so without looking up, she quietly fished around in
her huge pocket on her dress for her handkerchief. She
wiped savagely at her leaking nose, and honked loudly
into her handkerchief, glancing at Emma. Emma pulled
her eyebrows down and shook her head at Lizzie as if to
scold her for daring to blow her nose.

Suddenly all the pent-up shame and anger of the past
few moments rushed to the surface, and Lizzie lifted
her head defiantly, glaring back at Emma. She stared
straight at her and, without thinking, stuck out her
tongue. Emma recoiled in horror, and to Lizzie's dismay,
she heard a sharp "Lizzie!"

Lizzie's head snapped to attention.

"You may put your head on your desk and keep it
there for the remainder of storytime," Teacher Katie said
sternly.

Lizzie obediently lowered her head, a sob tearing
at her throat. This just wasn't fair; there was no doubt
about it. The only thing she had done wrong was come
in a tiny bit later than usual. It was not her fault that the
knot stuck. It was not her fault that she had stuck out

her tongue at Emma, because Emma never should have looked at her so angrily. Well, maybe it wasn't right to stick out your tongue—actually, it was very wrong at home. Mam said only snakes stick out their tongues, and snakes are not pleasant creatures. But how else could she have let Emma know how angry she was? She could have wrinkled her nose, or opened her eyes and glared back at Emma, but that would not have been forceful enough.

Oh, she just knew she was going to be punished somehow. The awful misery of it flooded Lizzie's heart, and a fresh flow of tears ran down her cheeks. It just wasn't fair.

As the teacher's voice droned on, Lizzie listened half heartedly. It was the same dumb story she had been reading all week, and today Lizzie couldn't stand how she stopped to swallow in between sentences. Teacher Katie was just so bossy, and those strange habits irritated Lizzie.

The teacher closed the storybook with a clap, then opened her drawer and put it inside. She stood behind her desk and announced the afternoon's classes.

"And Lizzie, you may stay in at recess. I think I need to talk to you."

Lizzie lowered her head as far as it would go. She twisted her soaked handkerchief in her fingers and swallowed hard. Her breath came in shallow gasps and her heart beat rapidly. Now she was going to get it; she just knew it. And Dat told the girls if they got disciplined in school, they would be at home, as well. Lizzie wondered if you could get spanked twice and still be alive. Probably not, if it was with a stick both times. Well, if she would not live after two spankings, then everyone would at least pity her. She knew Mam and Dat would feel awful, and Teacher Katie would be so terribly sorry that it would take her a long time to get over it. That was the only thought that cheered Lizzie even one bit. So she bravely got out her English book and looked over the afternoon's lesson.

The lesson looked easy, so she got out her yellow pencil. The tip was dull, but she was not going to walk the entire length of the classroom to sharpen it, either. Everybody would look at her and not pity her one bit, so she thought it was much better to stay in her desk. She pulled out her plastic pencil box to look for her small pencil sharpener that was shaped like a little globe. When she pulled it out, her whole box of crayons came flying out of her desk and clattered loudly to the floor, scattering crayons everywhere.

Lizzie quickly slid out of her desk onto her knees on the wooden floor, and started to pick them up as fast as she could. Betty and Emma bent down to help her, and Lizzie glanced hurriedly at Emma. Her sister put a finger to her lips to ask Lizzie to please be quiet, and without one comment from Teacher Katie, the crayons were restored to order in the box.

Lizzie bent over her English book, swinging her legs nervously. She chewed on her fingernails, biting them down in little crunches that actually hurt her teeth. She wished recess would come so her punishment would be

over, but at the same time she also wished recess would
never come. She wished with all her heart she would
have stayed at home in bed. That's what made life so
uncertain, so scary. When you got up in the morning
and were happy and everything was going well, you just
never knew what all could happen in a day.

She guessed she would have to start saying an extra
prayer in the evening. Maybe that was why so many
scary things happened to Lizzie, because Emma knelt
beside her bed faithfully to say her little German prayer,
and Lizzie hopped into bed and said it under the warm
quilts. And often, Lizzie didn't really say her prayers
right. She felt silly, or sometimes she felt like God didn't
hear her say them. How could He hear it if she just
thought her prayer? And yet, she felt silly to say it out
loud. When Mam helped them say their prayers, she
didn't feel silly; that felt just right, because God heard
Mam—Lizzie was positive of that. He heard Emma,
too, because Emma was a good girl. She was always
straightening up the living room or sweeping the kitchen
floor, and she loved to wash dishes. Lizzie just didn't feel
comfortable with God yet. And now her life had come to
this—staying in at recess.

"Put your books away!" Teacher Katie's voice seemed
to boom out much louder than usual.

Lizzie jumped nervously and quickly put her pencil
box and tablet in her desk. She clasped and unclasped
her fingers in her lap, looking straight ahead, even when
Aaron passed the waste can much too fast, and she did
not put her wastepaper into it. When the dismissal bell

was tapped, Lizzie stayed in her seat, trying hard not to cry. The lump in her throat was so big that she couldn't swallow, and her mouth was as dry as paper. She licked her lips fitfully and wiped her hand across her brow.

The other children were all pulling on their boots and buttoning up their coats. As the last person clattered noisily out the door into the crisp, sunny afternoon, Lizzie's throat constricted with fear. With downcast eyes, she noticed every pencil mark in the wood of her desktop.

When everything remained quiet, Lizzie dared to peek at Teacher Katie. She was checking papers nonchalantly, as if nothing in the world bothered her. She stood up, and Lizzie thought wildly, *Oh, here it comes — she's going to get her stick.*

Her fears were put at rest when she walked quickly to the back of the room where the lunchboxes stood in an orderly row on wooden shelves. She reached up and brought her lunchbox to the table, and, finding a large yellow apple, she closed her lunchbox and came striding back to her desk. She sat down on her chair and wheeled it up to her large metal desk. She took a big bite of the apple and sighed. She looked long and hard at Lizzie, and Lizzie met her gaze unflinchingly.

"Lizzie, why were you five minutes late coming in when the bell rang?" the teacher asked sternly.

"I . . . I really don't know. Rachel had a good idea about packing down the snow to make trails and houses, and I just wanted to do a little bit more. When I looked up from tramping down snow with my feet, Rachel and

Betty were already inside."

"Whose idea was it to stay a bit longer to tramp down snow trails?" Teacher Katie asked, her piercing blue-gray eyes never leaving Lizzie's own worried face.

Lizzie shrugged.

"Whose was it?"

"I guess mine."

"You guess."

Lizzie nodded miserably.

"Don't you know when we have rules, they are meant to be kept without exception, especially the two-minute time to get to your seat. There's just no excuse for a seven-minute timing," the teacher said.

Lizzie did not know what to say. There was nothing to say, because if she tried to explain how engrossed she had become in making those trails, the teacher would not believe her anyway. So she said nothing.

"And, Lizzie?" Teacher Katie asked.

"Hmm?"

"Whatever possessed you to stick out your tongue at your sister?"

Lizzie shrugged.

"Why did you do it, Lizzie? Answer me," Teacher Katie said, very sternly.

The lump in Lizzie's throat was growing at such an alarming rate that there was no way she could talk without bursting into tears. So she sat there in her desk, looking miserable, and wanting this whole awful ordeal to be over.

"Lizzie," Teacher Katie said, with just a tinge of kindness in her voice. The little touch of pity was Lizzie's undoing, and she dropped her face into her hands and began to cry with an alarming force. She shook with heartbroken sobs, gasping and sniffing for her breath.

It was too much for Teacher Katie's kind heart, and she got up quickly, moving to Lizzie's desk in one quick glide. She knelt, bending her head low, putting her arm over Lizzie's heaving shoulders.

"Shhh, shhh, Lizzie. Don't cry like that. My goodness, please, Lizzie—it's alright," she soothed.

The teacher's kindness only fueled Lizzie's despair, and she kept crying until she was feeling exhausted by the force of her sobs.

Teacher Katie wisely remained quiet, patting Lizzie's shoulders and waiting out the storm of weeping. After Lizzie drew a long, ragged breath and soundly blew her nose, Teacher Katie returned to her desk.

"Come, Lizzie," she said kindly.

Lizzie walked slowly to her desk, her head bent, knowing that now was the time the teacher would spank her as hard as she could. She crossed her hands behind her back, as if to ward off the pain of the spanking.

"Lizzie, did you know that only snakes are supposed to stick out their tongues?" Teacher Katie asked.

Lizzie nodded.

"Do your parents allow it at home?"

Lizzie shook her head, sniffling loudly.

"Then you must never, ever do it in school, either. It is very rude, and God does not like it when His children are rude or disrespectful. Emma surely did not do anything to make you so angry, Lizzie," she finished.

Lizzie shook her head again, dutifully. There was no use explaining her anger. The teacher wouldn't understand anyway. *Maybe I'm not like other people; maybe I'm just not good enough to even go to school,* she thought.

"So, for your punishment, you may write on this lined piece of paper until it is full: 'I will not be disrespectful.'"

Lizzie was so relieved that the teacher had a bit of mercy and did not give her a spanking that she looked steadily up into her blue-gray eyes with a big smile of gratitude. It warmed the teacher's heart so quickly that tears sprang to her eyes and she smiled back warmly. An overwhelming feeling of love flooded her heart, and she seemed to really see Lizzie for the first time. *What a complex little mischief,* she thought. *She drives me to distraction, but who can hold it against her?*

Teacher Katie pushed back her sleeves and grasped the apple with her long, slender fingers. She crunched into it with her white teeth and chewed methodically.

Lizzie was transfixed. She had never seen anything that looked so classy, so natural and effortless. She loved her teacher with her whole heart and youthful soul, knowing that her goal from here on was to push back her sleeves, grasp an apple with long, thin fingers, and eat it exactly like Teacher Katie. She grasped the edge of the desk and watched with unwavering adoration until Teacher Katie became quite unnerved.

Then Lizzie's smile lit up the whole classroom, much like the brilliant sun after a thunderstorm, the teacher thought.

"Thank you for not giving me a spanking," Lizzie whispered.

"You're welcome," Teacher Katie whispered back, her head bent to Lizzie's level.

And they giggled together like two classmates, until Teacher Katie thought her heart would burst, and Lizzie knew, without a doubt, that someday, somewhere, she would be a teacher just like Teacher Katie, pushing back her sleeves and eating a yellow apple.

Grandpa Glicks' Moving Day

The Glick family was all snuggled into the freshly washed buggy, with Red clipping along at his usual fast pace. The air was still cold, but Dat said it had the scent of spring. There was still snow on the ground, but only in patches, and Mam had stopped to marvel at the little green shoots pushing through the earth in her flowerbed beside the concrete sidewalks.

Lizzie always felt the same about the snow melting. It was sad, partly because she loved the snow so much, and partly because of the mud that followed. When they walked to school, Lizzie always had to walk in slippery mud when a car passed them, and she would have much rather walked in snow.

Today they were all on their way to Grandpa Glicks, who were moving to another farm about ten miles away from the old homestead. Lizzie had asked Dat why Grandpas were moving, and Dat had said he really didn't know, except that Doddy Glick was not going to milk cows anymore. He was going to raise beef cows and pigs. Emma asked Dat what beef cows were, and Dat told her they were cows that you raised for their meat and not for their milk. Lizzie asked what happened with the beef cows' milk. Dat said they only had milk when they had a baby calf, and the calf drank all the milk. Lizzie told Emma, "No wonder the calves grow so fast—that's a lot of milk for one baby!"

As they turned in a drive, Lizzie pulled herself up to peer between Dat and Mam's shoulders. *This farm is really different*, she thought.

"Dat, is this where they're going to live?" she asked.

"Looks like it," Dat said.

"It all kind of hangs on a hill, doesn't it?" asked Mam.

"Yes, it really does," Dat said with a laugh. "But maybe that's why he didn't have to pay more for the property. It will be good land for pasture, no doubt."

They arrived at the house first. Lizzie strained to take in all the sights—the horses and buggies, moving vans, trucks, and people scurrying around in every direction. Lizzie wondered if Grandma Glick was going to have chicken corn soup at this moving like they did when Dat and Mam moved to the new harness shop.

"I can't wait to see Marvin and Elsie!" Emma said excitedly.

"Me, too!" Lizzie agreed.

They stopped, and Dat held Red's bridle while Mam clambered out, reaching back in for Jason. She put her diaper bag over her shoulder and reached for the carrot cake under the seat. "Let Emma carry the cake, Annie,"

Dat said.

"Oh, I'll get it," Mam said, already on her way to the house.

Emma, Lizzie, and Mandy tumbled out of the buggy and were instantly besieged in one noisy whirl, which was Marvin and Elsie.

Marvin pumped their hands up and down eagerly, followed by Elsie doing the same, saying, "Hello! Hello! Oh, it seems so long since we saw you!"

The girls giggled, grasping their aunt and uncle's hands firmly. Marvin and Elsie were a little older, but were actually their real aunt and uncle, because Dat was the oldest in Doddy Glicks' family, and Marvin and Elsie were the youngest of fourteen children. They were a very special aunt and uncle.

"This seems so different," Emma said.

"But it's so fun," Marvin said. "We have huge hills and a pond at the bottom of the biggest one. Can you imagine how much fun that will be next winter, taking our sleds way up on top of that long hill, then coasting down and flying on the pond?" He waved his arms in the direction behind the barn, and twirled his finger to show how the sleds would spin on the ice.

Lizzie giggled, and Mandy stood aside, staring at Marvin with her large green eyes. Emma shook her head doubtfully, a worried expression on her face. "That sounds too dangerous, Marvin," she said.

Marvin's curls bounced up and down as he waved his arms again. "Ha, ha! That's not dangerous. There's nothing we could hit! You would just slide right on the pond and go *TWIRLING* around!"

"Let's go look around," Elsie said. She was always the practical one, keeping Marvin in line with her bossy, worried expression. Marvin never worried too much about what Elsie said, but between the two, they balanced each other. Lizzie and Emma thought they were absolutely perfect and admired everything they did. They even ate things that Marvin told them were good. He had informed them on a previous visit that he had just discovered how good it was to eat pretzels with water. First you took a big bite of a hard, salty pretzel, then you drank a sip of ice-cold water. When it mixed together in your mouth, it was the best thing he had ever tasted.

So whenever Lizzie ate a bite of pretzel, she drank water. Emma and Elsie said chocolate milk was better with hard pretzels, but Lizzie sided with Marvin. Actually, she never told anyone, but chocolate milk *was* better—she just wanted to agree with Marvin.

"Do you have pigs and beef cows already?" asked Emma.

"Dat said you aren't going to milk cows anymore," Lizzie added.

"Nope, we're not. Come on, let's go look at the barn, then we'll go through the house. The barn is bigger than our old barn," Marvin said.

So they all ran to the barn, Emma taking Mandy's hand protectively. The interior of the barn was stone and concrete, smelling a bit dark and dank. The part where Doddy Glick unhitched his horses had a big stone watering trough, and rows of sturdy lumber nailed to the wall, where the big workhorses' harnesses hung.

Next to this area was a high fenced-in part, where the heavy, lumbering beef cows milled around. Much to Lizzie's consternation, the pigs were in the same pen with the huge, fat cows.

"Why don't the cows tramp on those little pigs?" she asked in horror.

"I don't know. They just don't, I guess," Marvin said.

"Do they eat the same food?" Emma asked.

"You mean 'feed'," Elsie corrected her.

"Whatever," Emma said.

"How do you know when these cows' meat is ready?" Lizzie wanted to know.

"Who butchers them?" piped up little Mandy.

Elsie bent low, and told them the cows were sold at an auction like the auctions Dat went to when he bought ponies. Then whoever bought them had to have them butchered at a place where they do that kind of thing, she guessed.

Marvin took them to the new chicken house, where a flock of about fifty brown hens were pecking at a long, narrow trough that had finely ground feed in it. Lizzie loved to watch the chickens eat, because they took a mouthful and their beak worked almost faster than you could see. While they were eating, their perfectly round eyes blinked, but their eyelids were on the bottom—or that's how it seemed. Lizzie was never sure if a chicken's eyelids came up from the bottom or the side, and she never remembered to ask Dat.

There was a row of metal cabinets on the side of the chicken house that had holes in them and a wooden perch all along the front. That was where the chickens went to lay their large brown eggs. There wasn't much room for them, Lizzie thought, so probably that was why they were so grouchy when they sat in there.

"When do you have to get the eggs?" she asked.

"Not now. They were just moved in here, so they didn't have much chance to lay an egg yet," Elsie said.

"Why do a chicken's eyes close from the bottom up?" Lizzie asked.

"They don't," Marvin snorted, laughing at Lizzie.

"They do."

"No, they don't. That's dumb!"

"I think they do."

"I never heard of such a thing," Marvin argued.

"Well, watch them once."

"I'm going to catch one and I'll show you. Now be quiet, so I can catch one," Marvin said.

He charged straight into the line of chickens that were peacefully pecking at their feed. The flying frenzy that followed was one squawking, dusty whirl of chickens, and Mandy screamed while the girls all rushed madly for the door. Elsie fumbled with the latch, and Lizzie coughed as they fell into the chicken yard. Mandy started crying, and Emma put her arm around her shoulders while her little sister hid her face in Emma's apron.

Marvin came out of the henhouse, triumphantly carrying a chicken upside down by the legs. Lizzie had never seen anyone carrying a chicken, and it looked as if the poor creature was quite dead.

"Marvin!" she scolded angrily.

"What?"

"You killed that poor chicken. You're not funny."

"No, he didn't. That chicken isn't one bit dead. Look at its eyes. That's how you carry chickens," Elsie said indignantly.

"Oh," said Lizzie.

"Now watch," Marvin said.

He held up the frightened chicken, tucking down the wings with his hands, holding it firmly against his stomach.

"Now watch!"

They all bent to peer closely at the chicken, which was so terrified that her eyes were blinking in rapid movements.

"Get back!" Marvin said, clearly impatient.

"Well, we can't see if we don't look closely!" Elsie said.

They all watched in total silence, intently staring at the chicken's eyes.

"See?" Lizzie said.

"See?" Marvin interrupted her. "They come from the top down."

"No, they don't!" Lizzie was very angry at Marvin. He just always thought he knew everything, and he didn't. Those eyelids went up from the bottom—she just knew they did.

"Hey!"

They all jumped and whirled around, their eyes wide, feeling very guilty because they all knew Marvin should not have been chasing those chickens. It was Uncle Samuel, who was older than they were, and who Marvin respected and tried to imitate all the time. Samuel was tall, with very curly black hair, and he always treated Marvin as if he needed to be growing up and behaving himself. Emma and Lizzie were a bit in awe of Samuel and Raymond, because they were older and did not have much time for their pesky little nieces. Samuel was holding a box, and he looked at Marvin with a patient expression.

"What are you doing with that chicken?" he asked, shifting the heavy box.

"We're checking its eyes, to see if they close from the top or the bottom," Marvin told him, quite seriously.

Samuel burst out laughing. "Marvin!"

"What?"

"Now go put that poor chicken away. Mam was looking for you because it's time for coffee break, and they made hot chocolate," Samuel said, turning to put the box in the buggy shed.

The girls ran to the house, while Marvin put the chicken back and locked the door. In the kitchen, the warm, chocolaty smell embraced them. They put away their coats and bonnets, moving in among the crowd of adults who were all talking at once, or so it seemed. Grandma Glick was hurrying between the stove and her big kitchen table, which held steaming mugs of coffee and hot chocolate. Mounds of cookies and homemade glazed doughnuts were piled on her green Melmac trays. There were different kinds of bars; some were chocolate and others had a coconut or nut topping.

Lizzie could not decide which looked better—a glazed doughnut, or a thick, chewy coconut oatmeal cookie to dip into her mug of hot chocolate. Marvin had already chosen a doughnut and was sitting on the sofa, talking to Grandpa Glick.

Elsie took Lizzie's hand and said, "Come, Lizzie, do you want to sit here on the bench?"

Lizzie nodded, but was detained by a hand on her shoulder.

"There's my Lizzie." Grandma Glick's kind face beamed down at her, as she shook Lizzie's hand in welcome. "I haven't seen you yet today. Are Emma and Mandy in for break, too?" she asked.

"They're here somewhere, Mommy," said Lizzie. "Marvin and Elsie were showing us the new barn and the chicken house. You have lots of hills here!"

"Yes, we do," Grandma said with a smile. "It will be something to get used to. Did you see the big hill beside the house? My garden will be a bit lower than the driveway. Hello, Emma! How's little Mandy?" She bent down to pat Mandy's head and say a few words to Emma, and then she was rushing off again.

The aunts all took turns fussing over Lizzie, Emma, and Mandy. Mam beamed as she helped Jason with his large, sticky doughnut. Lizzie loved when the aunts teased her. They always stopped what they were doing to say hello and joke about something with them. She liked them all, and there were lots of aunts, because Dat had nine sisters. Some of them were married, and some were planning on being married soon. To Lizzie, it seemed as if they came in all shapes, sorts, and sizes. But Elsie was their favorite, by far, because she was their own age.

After everyone had enjoyed their coffee break, the work resumed. The men carried in huge pieces of furniture, grunting and groaning, joking and yelling if someone pinched a finger. A few uncles were doing plumbing work or connecting the propane gas stove and refrigerator. Grandpa Glick was giving directions, managing the placement of different articles. His wiry gray hair stuck out in every direction, and his piercing gaze didn't miss anything. He was short of stature and very bowlegged. Lizzie often wondered why Doddy Glick's legs were like that. She thought maybe he rode horses too much when he was little, and asked Mam once. Mam said it was just the way God had made Doddy Glick, but Lizzie never quite understood why anyone would have to have legs like that. She kept careful watch on her own legs, hoping fervently they wouldn't go crooked like his.

She broke her coconut oatmeal cookie in half and dipped it into her hot chocolate. The cookie broke, and she grabbed a spoon, rescuing the soaked cookie. *Mmmm*, she thought, *this is almost better than shoofly and cocoa.* She finished her cookie and reached for a doughnut. She took a huge bite of it and held it away to look more closely to see if it looked like one of Homer's doughnuts in her favorite book. It looked like a perfect doughnut and was so delicious. She finished it off in a few more big bites, reaching for another.

"Lizzie, how many doughnuts did you have?" Emma asked, looking at Lizzie with a worried expression.

"One," Lizzie answered sourly.

"Are you sure?"

"Of course, Emma. I had only one. Why can't I have another one?"

"I guess you can; just don't let the aunts see you or they'll tease you. I know they will," Emma said.

"That doesn't matter."

"Well, okay then," Emma muttered, lifting her hot chocolate cup and drinking carefully, because it was so hot.

"Emma." Lizzie leaned over and whispered, "I could eat five doughnuts!"

Elsie smiled and said, "What are you saying?"

Lizzie put her hand over her mouth and giggled. She

leaned over past Emma and said quietly, "I could eat five doughnuts."

"Really?!" Elsie's eyes opened wide.

"I bet I could—should I try?" Lizzie meant to try it.

"Mam, Lizzie is going to eat five doughnuts. Tell her she isn't allowed to," Emma said in desperation, catching Mam's apron as she walked past with a heavy box of dishes to put in the kitchen cupboards.

"Lizzie! Of course not. You'll get sick," Mam said, hurrying past without even glancing in Lizzie's direction.

Elsie and Emma giggled, but Lizzie's feelings were hurt. That was just like Emma, the bossy thing. Lizzie slid off the bench abruptly and stalked off, her head held high. Well, if that's how they were going to act, Emma and Elsie sticking together and not letting her eat doughnuts, they could just play without her. She looked all over for Marvin, but he was nowhere to be found. She looked in the living room, but it was full of aunts, cleaning, arranging things, and chattering among themselves.

She walked into the bedroom, which was already set up, clean and shining, the bed made perfectly. She wandered on, through the kitchen without even glancing at Emma and Elsie, and found a door beside the kitchen cupboards. It was a heavy door, but more narrow and not as high as most doors. Lizzie pulled it open slowly, peering into a tiny little room. It smelled like water and was damp and cool. The walls were made of gray stones, but were covered with a very shiny coat of silver-colored paint. It was so sparkling that it looked almost like aluminum foil.

Lizzie blinked and stepped carefully inside. It seemed a little spooky, because there was only one small window up high that let in a thin beam of light. There was a low stone trough that had cold water in it. Lizzie dipped her finger into it hesitantly, pulling it back out with surprise. The water was icy cold, and she noticed there were gallon jars of milk submerged in this freezing water. There was also a machine in this little room that looked as if it wasn't good for anything—it was just something that made no sense. Lizzie touched it, and it was as cold as the water. She shivered. This little room definitely gave her the creeps, and she turned to go back out into the warm kitchen.

She grasped hold of the latch to lift it and open the door, but it would not budge. She used both hands, jerking the latch until her hands ached and were freezing. She stopped and looked around. Surely she was not going to be stuck in this horrible little room. She would freeze, she thought.

Lizzie turned back to the narrow door and resumed pounding on the latch, wondering if she should call out for someone to find her. Turning around, she noticed there was another door in an adjoining wall. *Good*, she thought, *maybe this one will open easier*. She took both hands and pulled on the latch as hard as she could, and it sprang up, the door creaking open immediately.

Warm air rushed into her face as she found herself in the area where Grandma Glick would do her laundry.

She stood in the doorway and blinked, surprised to see where this door opened. Before she could close the door behind her, Marvin came dashing in, holding two small boxes.

"Lizzie, shut that door. What were you doing in the cooler room?" he asked bluntly.

"I don't know," answered Lizzie, feeling immensely relieved to be out of it, whatever kind of room it was.

"Shut the door," Marvin said again, impatiently.

"What is this cold little room for?" Lizzie asked, closing the door firmly.

"Don't you know?" Marvin set down his boxes and came over, pushing the door open. The little room didn't seem half as frightening when Marvin was there, so she relaxed as he showed her what everything was for. The cold machine was called a separator. He showed her where the milk was poured in, and how you turned the handle, and the cream collected in one part, and the milk ran out into another.

"Then," Marvin finished importantly, "we put different containers of milk and cream in that ice-cold water to keep it cold. Anyhow, Lizzie, you're not really supposed to be in here, because it has to stay really, really clean."

"Well, how was I supposed to know?" Lizzie snapped.

"You didn't, of course not. But stay out now." And with that, Marvin picked up the two boxes and continued on his way. Lizzie wanted to ask him where he was going and what he was doing, but she didn't, because she kind of felt like crying. Everybody was just so bossy, and this moving day was not very fun. She wished it was time to go home, because she felt so sad.

She pushed open the screen door and stood outside against the brick wall. The sun felt warm, but the air was cold enough that she turned to get her coat and head scarf.

"Hey, Lizzie!"

Lizzie turned to see Uncle Samuel with Nicky, Grandpa Glicks' fast pony, hitched to the shining black cart. "Get your coat and *kopp-∂uch* and you can ride along over to Ben's farm to get a cable. Tell your mom," he said.

Lizzie's heart beat rapidly, and her breath came in gasps as she hurried to tell Mam. She flung her coat over her shoulders, holding her scarf in her teeth as she buttoned her coat frantically. Elsie and Emma rushed into the washhouse and asked where she was going.

"Uncle Samuel said I may ride along to Ben's farm," she panted.

"We want to go, too," Emma said.

"Ask him if you may," Lizzie answered, dashing out the door, slamming it in Elsie's face.

"Samuel, we want to go, too," Elsie begged.

"There's not enough room," he said. "I'll give you a ride when we get back, alright?"

So there was nothing for them to do but stand back as Nicky took a flying leap, scattering gravel in every direction as they started off. The cold air hit Lizzie's face, and she clutched the metal rail around the back of the seat with all her strength. She had never in her

life seen a pony go as fast as Nicky. Samuel was holding back as hard as he could on the reins, but the pony
arched his neck, lowered his head, and ran faster than
Red. His little hindquarters flopped up and down, in
staccato rhythm, and in spite of herself, Lizzie giggled
out loud. She hadn't meant to, because she was ashamed
of Samuel, but she had to do something for the sheer joy
she felt.

Samuel glanced down at Lizzie and laughed. "Does he
go fast?" he shouted.

Lizzie's eyes shone with pure elation as she looked up
at Samuel and said, "Faster than Red, I think!"

Samuel laughed again.

That night, when Lizzie snuggled under the covers,
she knew the only part of moving day she would never
forget was the taste of the doughnuts and her wonderful
ride with Samuel and Nicky.

chapter 6

Hard Times

The warm spring sunshine slanted through the window as the Glick family sat down to their supper. It had been a lovely day, with warm breezes stirring the apple blossoms on the trees in the yard.

Mam opened the kitchen window, just enough to smell the apple blossoms. She returned and sat down with a tired sigh. She swept the loose strands of hair away from her forehead before she folded her hands in her lap, bowing her head in prayer before they started their meal. When the silent prayer was finished, Mam raised her head and sighed again. The atmosphere was strangely quiet, so Lizzie cleared her throat nervously.

Dat looked at the big white bowl in the middle of the table. "Potato soup again, Annie?" he asked hesitantly.

"Yes, Melvin, it's potato soup again. My groceries are running very low and our money is . . . well, you know," she said quietly, ladling the creamy potato soup into everyone's bowls.

Dat looked very unhappy, but he sighed, looking hopefully at Mam. "It'll get better, Annie—you wait and see. That man from northern Pennsylvania will pay real well for all the fancy harnesses he ordered."

Mam looked steadily down at her bowl. "But Melvin, you should not have bought that large amount of saddles. We'll never be able to sell them; you know we won't." Mam's voice rose sharply, and a hot stab of fear shot through Lizzie's stomach. Were they going to starve? She thought they must be awfully poor if they had only potato soup, two evenings in a row.

"Annie, you're always looking on the dark side of everything. Of course those saddles will sell, and at a good profit, too. Just not right now, today or tomorrow, but in the future," Dat told her.

Jason threw a boiled potato in Emma's direction. Mam whirled around, smacking his fingers hard, and he yelped in pain and surprise.

"Stop that, Jason!" she snapped.

Jason yelled, hurling another potato in Emma's direction. Dat looked sternly at Jason, getting out of his chair and picking him up. Mam looked at her plate, her face a mixture of anger and despair. Dat disappeared into the bedroom with Jason, and Mandy started to sob quietly, her head held in both hands.

Lizzie tried to act as if nothing was wrong, taking a big spoonful of creamy potato soup. She chewed carefully, avoiding looking in Mam's direction, wishing with all her heart they would not have to be so unhappy today. Emma bent her head and buttered a piece of bread, making sure the bread was covered evenly with butter and jelly. Emma was like that, Lizzie thought. She could sit in the middle of the most nerve-racking things and be calmly thinking about something else. Right at this moment, she was more intent on making sure the jelly touched every crust of her bread than in the troubled atmosphere of the supper table.

Emma cleared her throat, cutting the piece of perfectly spread jelly bread in half. She lifted one part and bit off a perfect "U."

"Mmmm!" she said, and smiled at Lizzie.

"Can I have the other half?" Lizzie asked.

"I guess."

Dat returned to the table, putting Jason in his high chair. Jason continued to cry, and Lizzie pitied him with all her heart. It must be awful to have such a headful of curly hair, or rather, woolly hair. It was so thick and full of curls. When he cried, he reminded Lizzie of a sheep with its mouth wide open when it cried for its mother. Of course, Lizzie never told anyone, not even Emma, because she always felt bad about it, but she always thought Jason was not one bit cute like other babies and toddlers. She loved him and played with him almost more than Emma or Mandy, but she was so glad her own hair didn't look like Jason's.

"Pass the soup, please," Dat said, stiffly.

"Just give me your soup plate, and I'll fill it," Mam said, just as stiffly.

Dat sighed and looked at Mam pleadingly, but Mam avoided looking at Dat. Instead she got up and went into the bedroom.

Oh dear, thought Lizzie. *Now Mam is going to cry, and Dat will feel so bad.* She laid down her spoon and swal-

lowed hard, because the potatoes stuck in her throat.
She looked over at Dat, who sat at the end of the table,
looking as if he could burst into tears himself. He caught
Lizzie's eye and smiled at her, even if it was only a small
lift of the corners of his mouth.

"Eat your supper, girls, then we'll drive Dolly awhile,
okay?" he asked.

"I'd rather drive Teeny and Tiny," Lizzie said.

"Maybe later, if we have time," he said.

"When can Emma and I drive them ourselves?" Lizzie
asked.

Dat didn't answer as he carefully took a bite of bread.
He kept his eyes downcast and looked unhappy for a
moment while he chewed and swallowed.

"I guess I may as well tell you now, girls," he said
quietly.

"What?" Emma asked innocently.

But Lizzie's heart sank way down with a sickening
thud. She knew. She knew exactly what Dat was going
to say, because she had overheard Mam trying to per-
suade him to sell Teeny and Tiny, along with the glossy
black spring wagon with the golden pinstripes along the
side.

"We are going to have to sell Teeny and Tiny," he said
solemnly.

"Why?" Emma asked, stopping halfway with a bite of
potato soup.

"Because we really need the money soon, and because
it costs too much to feed three ponies, Mam thinks it
would be best. I do, too, of course, but I wish we could

keep them; I really do," he finished.

Lizzie was heartbroken. It was just unthinkable, selling their miniature ponies. They were pint-sized little animals, a perfectly matched team of coppery-colored ponies with blond manes and tails that Dat had made a little wagon for. The girls just loved when Dat hitched them to this wagon, clipping down the road with their heads held high. They didn't even have them very long, Lizzie thought sadly. And just when Dat was about ready to let them drive alone.

"Are we going to have to sell Dolly, too?" Emma asked.

"No, not Dolly," Dat said. "We need her to get milk at Uncle James's farm, don't we?"

"We sure do. I'd hate walking so far and carrying that huge milk jug," Emma said, relieved.

"When do we have to sell Teeny and Tiny?" Lizzie asked.

"Oh, I thought about this and decided we'd sell them at Harrison's Auction in Taylorsburg. That's a horse auction where they sell horses and ponies under a big tent about every six weeks. So what we'll do is I'll teach you and Emma to drive them by yourselves, so you can drive them in the ring at the auction. Do you think you can?" he asked.

Emma shrugged her shoulders. "We probably could."

Lizzie's eyes shone, because that sounded so exciting! Imagine driving Teeny and Tiny around and around under a huge tent with hundreds of people watching them. She wiggled around on the bench and swung her feet furiously under the table.

"You think we should?" she asked nervously.

"We'll see," Dat said, getting up and grasping Jason under his arms, throwing him into the air. Jason giggled with pleasure. "There you go, Jase," Dat said, setting him on the floor, and he promptly toddled into the living room to find his toys.

"Girls, you had better get busy here and clear off the table," Dat said, looking in the direction of the bedroom door. "I'm going down to the shop now, and after you have the dishes done, we should drive Teeny and Tiny if we're going to sell them."

He clattered down the steps, and Emma looked over at Lizzie. Lizzie looked straight back at Emma, and they did not say a word. It was almost as if they knew, at that moment, that things were not good, but they didn't know how to express their feelings.

"Where's Mam?" Emma asked wearily, older than her years. She scraped Lizzie's uneaten potato soup into her own bowl and added the crusts of leftover bread.

"I don't know," Lizzie said, shrugging her shoulders.

"What's wrong with Mam and Dat?" Emma asked.

"I think we're very, very poor," Lizzie said slowly, gathering a handful of silverware and heading to the sink.

"Why are we so poor?" Emma asked. "I mean, Dat and Mam are always busy in the harness shop. Dat makes lots of halters and harnesses, and the little bell above the door rings an awful lot lately."

"I know," Lizzie said. "But, Emma, they argue all the time."

"No, they don't, Lizzie. Mam and Dat really like each other and don't argue all the time, either," Emma answered defensively.

"I don't care what you say, Emma. I heard them."

"When?"

"One time."

"Lizzie, you stretch your stuff. Everything you say is not nearly as bad as you make it sound."

"Well," Lizzie sighed, grabbing a washcloth and wiping furiously on the plastic tablecloth. There were little rips and holes in the cheap fabric, and Lizzie caught her washcloth in one. "See, if we weren't so poor, we wouldn't have this pitiful-looking, old torn tablecloth on our table."

"Lizzie, you should be ashamed of yourself. Lots of Amish families have torn plastic tablecloths on their tables. When I get married, I'm not going to go buy a new tablecloth just because it has a hole in it. Everybody has holes in their tablecloth," Emma said.

Lizzie drew herself up to her full height and said vehemently, "Emma, I don't care what you say. Anyone that has a torn plastic tablecloth on their table is poor. If they weren't, they'd buy a new one. When I'm married, I am not going to keep mine that long. It looks sloppy and makes you look like you're poor, anyhow."

Emma added dish detergent to the hot water in the sink. "Well, I pity Mam."

"Why?"

"I don't know. I just do."

"I pity Dat."

"I pity Mam most, because she's always working in the harness shop and it's just a fright how sloppy this house looks," Emma said.

"Why don't you clean it up?" Lizzie asked, swishing her hand in the warm rinse water. She made a wave with the back of her hand, and water sloshed over the sink.

"Stop that!" Emma barked.

"Girls, what's wrong?" Mam came up behind them, turning to the stove to help clean up the pots and pans.

"Oh, nothing," Emma said quickly.

Lizzie wiped dishes, quietly remembering to dry each piece properly. Emma washed just as quietly, while Mam cleaned the stove. There wasn't much to say, because Mam was not her cheerful self, and they were afraid of saying the wrong thing. When Lizzie could stand it no longer, she blurted out, "Mam, why are we poor?"

"Ach, Lizzie, you're too little to ask such questions. We're not really poor—we still have our house and food to eat, even if it's only potato soup. We're just having a hard time because of the large amount of inventory we have that isn't selling," she said wearily.

"What's inventory?" Emma asked.

"New things to sell in the harness shop. Saddles, blankets, shoes, and all those things we need to sell faster," Mam replied, swiping at the countertop.

"Did you know we're going to learn to drive Teeny and Tiny?" Emma asked.

"Oh, are you? Well, they're another thing we need to sell. I don't know why we still have those expensive little ponies. They just aren't worth a thing, and I mean it," Mam said sharply.

"No, we're going to learn to drive them because Dat is going to let us drive them in the auction ring when he sells them in a couple of weeks," Emma said importantly.

Mam froze. She looked at Emma, hard. "When did he tell you that?" she asked.

"At the supper table."

"Oh, my!" Mam threw up her hands and sat down on a kitchen chair. "I wonder what made him change his mind?"

"Do you think we can, Mam?" Lizzie asked.

"I don't know. I just don't know. Ach, I feel sorry for Melvin in a way, but it simply makes no sense keeping them. We simply cannot afford them," she said, as if she were talking to herself.

"We're done with the dishes, Mam. Can we go now?" asked Emma.

"Mm-hmm," Mam said, as if she wasn't aware that they were even in the kitchen.

So Emma and Lizzie ran down the stairs and into the golden evening sunshine. Robins were noisily getting ready to settle their babies for the night, and bluebirds were flying through the air in search of one more insect for their families.

It was hard to be troubled on such a beautiful evening, and the girls forgot their problems when Dat appeared at the barn door. He pulled out the little black spring wagon, pushing it aside while he whistled for Teeny and Tiny.

They trotted to the gate of their stall, nickering in reply, eager to see if they would be allowed to run this evening. Dat opened the gate and they rushed out to the water trough together, bending their heads in unison to take deep, long draughts of cold water. Dat brushed their coats, while Emma and Lizzie took turns combing their manes and tails.

Dat had taught them to stand to the side when they brushed their tails, just in case the ponies kicked out the back unexpectedly. Ponies could be caught by surprise, or frightened easily, as skittish as they were, so the girls had to be careful and listen to what Dat told them.

After their coats glistened to Dat's inspection, the harnesses were brought from the long wooden cupboard that hung from the wall. He placed them on each pony's back, fastening buckles and straps, until everything was in the right place. He put on the bridles last, because that was just the proper way to harness a pony.

Lizzie often wondered why the bridle was put on last, but she suspected it was to keep the ponies from suffering longer than they had to. She could not imagine having a bit in her mouth and those horrible blinders on each side of her head. But Dat said you had to have those so the ponies couldn't see what was beside them, or something that came up unexpectedly behind them.

Dat led the ponies out and Lizzie held their bridles while he fastened the tongue to their collar straps. They pranced in anticipation and tried to throw their heads up, but Lizzie hung on to their bridles, saying, "Whoa," quite well, she thought.

"Now," Dat said. "You and Emma sit on the seat and I'll just kneel on the back behind you. Emma, you may drive first, since you're the oldest, and I'll be back here, in case you can't handle them. And remember, keep a firm grip on the reins, keeping your hands away from your body so if they rear back with their heads, you still have control. And don't be afraid; just make yourself boss, and they'll listen."

Lizzie smiled to herself. Dat always said that when they drove ponies. *Make yourself boss, and they'll listen,* she thought. They were never allowed to show fear of ponies, or Dat would scold them. To him, you were not able to drive a pony well as long as you were afraid of it.

Dat went to the ponies' heads, and Emma and Lizzie hurried up into the seat. They settled themselves nervously, and Dat handed the reins to Emma.

"Here you are! Ready?"

Emma nodded her head, biting her lower lip.

Lizzie glanced at her nervously, but she didn't say anything. Dat climbed on the back, while Emma eased the reins forward a tiny bit.

"C'mon, giddap," she said, in a shaky little voice.

Teeny lunged forward, pulling Tiny along, and they zigzagged a bit, until they straightened out their gaits. As they pulled onto the road, they were stepping out together as if they were one animal instead of two. Their coats glistened in the evening sun, and their blond manes and tails streamed out behind them, as their little black hooves pattered daintily on the macadam. The neighbors stopped their work and waved at Dat, calling out to him or shaking their heads in wonder at the size of these miniature ponies. Lizzie tilted her head back to see Dat's face, and he was smiling and waving. He was so proud of this matched pair of ponies, and the little spring wagon he had made all by himself.

Emma was starting to relax as the ponies trotted out of town and past the green, rolling hayfields. Lizzie was thrilled to be able to sit on that seat, up so much higher than the ponies, and feel the power of their sturdy little bodies. There was just something about driving ponies that made Lizzie so happy that she smiled to herself without even thinking about it. Dat said he loved it, too, so that was why she felt that way.

Lizzie was allowed to drive on the way home. Her hands held firmly to the reins, and she sat as tall as she possibly could. She had a notion to let the reins loose

completely, just to see how fast they would go, but she
knew Dat would not allow it. So she held back smoothly, her little arms held out straight in front of her.

"Let them go a little, Lizzie!" Dat said.

"Should I?"

"Sure!"

So she let loose on her grip of the reins slowly, and
immediately the ponies surged forward. Their gait
increased until Dat, Emma, and Lizzie all burst out
laughing, filled with the sheer joy of the moment. Teeny
and Tiny were so little and funny, and if they ran as fast
as they could without breaking into a gallop, their legs
looked like they were whirring instead of actually stepping.

As they pulled into the gravel driveway, Lizzie said
to Dat, "We should get lots and lots of money for these
ponies and never be poor again, ever—right?"

"Yes, Lizzie, you're right," Dat agreed.

But Lizzie wondered how Dat could have been laughing so much one minute and sound quite so sad the next.
She thought he was probably as sad as she was to be at
home so soon after that ride.

The Auction

Emma and Lizzie were dressed in their best robin's egg blue Sunday dresses, with a black school apron pinned around their waists. Mam hadn't thought it was a good idea to wear their Sunday dresses, but they had begged her, because their school dresses were getting old since school was almost over. Mam finally gave in, but warned them to take very good care of them, since they had only worn them to church once.

They had just started wearing black aprons pinned around their waists, because they were turning nine and ten years old. Little girls wore a black apron that was like a sleeveless pinafore that you buttoned in the back at the top. Now, since they were getting older, they wore the type of black aprons the big girls wore.

Lizzie felt older now, and bigger. The only thing that caused her any unhappiness about her belt apron was her size. Lizzie was chubby. Actually, Mam said she looked just fine—she was just as round as a little oak tree—and she smiled when Lizzie lifted the pot lids of cooking food on the stove. Lizzie was always hungry and loved to eat good food, so her waistline was not

as small as her classmates'. But then, Emma was a bit
chubby, too, and Lizzie always thought Emma looked
nice.

Their hair was freshly combed, rolled back at the
sides, and pinned securely into a "bob" at the back of
their head. They had long hair, but Mam brushed, twisted, and rolled until it was all done up neatly in the style
of all little Amish girls. Mam pulled horribly on the hair-
brush, and when she wet down their hair to roll it, water
landed on Lizzie's shoulders, making her feel wet and
uncomfortable. She always grimaced and scrunched her
dress together in the wet area, wishing Mam would not
be in such a hurry and get her all wet. Sometimes she
grumbled, and Mam would always say she was sorry,
but she had to hurry. It didn't help one bit to grumble or
complain, so Lizzie had learned to stand still and not say
anything. That was just how Mam was, and her friend
Betty said her Mam was exactly the same.

This was the day they were selling the miniature ponies. Mam said she would stay at home because a horse
auction was no place for Mandy and Jason. But she was
happy and gave Emma and Lizzie each two dollars to
buy a hot dog and french fries for their lunch, in case
Dat was busy. They were allowed to spend it all, even
on candy or ice cream, and they certainly were excited.
Emma told Lizzie that they weren't near as poor as
Lizzie said, or else they would never, ever have been allowed to have two dollars each to go to the auction with
Dat. Lizzie solemnly nodded her head in agreement,
because, really, two dollars was a lot of money.

Lizzie had a lump in her throat, though, because she was sad about selling Teeny and Tiny. Thankfully, as Emma wisely said, at least they still had Dolly. But it was hard for Lizzie, because she loved Teeny and Tiny so much.

There was a huge crowd of people at the auction. A large yellow tent rose above the brightly colored throng, and in the outlying areas there were trailers, trucks, and different types of vehicles that were all used to transport horses or pones.

Everywhere Lizzie looked there were horses. She had gone to horse auctions before, but never to one this size. There were huge draft horses, or workhorses, which the Amish used in the fields to pull a plow or a wagon load of hay. They looked so gentle, their soft eyes looking straight at Lizzie, as if they knew her almost. Sometimes Lizzie felt like she should wave to them, or at least say, "Hello," because they looked so friendly.

There were nervous, prancing horses, white ones, jet-black ones, and lots of plain dark brown horses, with a black mane and tail. There were sorrel horses like Red, and blond ones that Dat said were called palominos. There were horses that were sort of red or gray with splotches on their hindquarters, almost as if someone had splattered their rump with paint; these horses were called Appaloosas, Dat said. Lizzie asked him why no one ever drove an Appaloosa horse in their buggy, and he said it was because they were made for riding, like quarter horses. Lizzie told him whenever she was as old as Teacher Katie, she was going to buy an Appaloosa and try to hitch him to a buggy, because she couldn't see why that wouldn't work. Dat just smiled, saying nothing.

Dat told the girls he must go register Teeny and Tiny, then he would be back. So they waited outside the building into which Dat had gone, their backs against the brick wall, in the warm spring sunshine. It was interesting, standing there and watching the people milling around them.

Lizzie was getting hungry. She looked at Emma to ask her if she was hungry, too, but she was afraid Emma would laugh at her. It probably was still morning, but she wished she could spend her two dollars on ice cream and candy. She watched a short, heavyset man walk past with a cup of coffee in one hand and a doughnut in the other. Lizzie's mouth watered and she swallowed.

"Emma, are you hungry?" she asked, no longer able to bear the thought of her empty stomach.

"A little, maybe. But it's not even close to dinnertime yet," Emma answered.

"I know." Lizzie fell silent, knowing Emma was right, as always. But she wished so much she could have a doughnut.

"Emma, we could get a doughnut, then not buy so much candy this afternoon," she ventured hopefully.

"Lizzie, you don't even know where to go to buy one. Besides, how do you know they even have doughnuts here?" Emma asked.

"'Cause a man walked past eating one. It looked so good," Lizzie pleaded.

"He might have brought it from home, you know," Emma said, always the practical one.

"I guarantee he didn't," Lizzie said. "Why wouldn't he eat his doughnut at home and then come to the horse sale?"

"Come, girls!" Dat came walking briskly, his eyes shining with excitement. "We're going to be selling the ponies just soon. They're going to be one of the very first ones sold. Come and we'll hitch them up a while to get used to the crowd and the noise. Emma, you have to be very quiet with them, because they'll be so nervous, okay?" he said, snapping his suspenders with quick movements as he walked.

Lizzie ran a bit to catch up, listening to every word Dat said. Dat was really nervous himself, Lizzie could tell, and Emma looked a little pale and scared. Her stomach felt funny, and she forgot all about wanting a doughnut to eat. She wondered if Emma would let her drive, or if she had to let Emma do all of it.

Teeny and Tiny were tied to the rail fence, munching on a block of hay someone had put there for them. They didn't look excited, nickering quietly as they saw the girls approaching.

Lizzie pitied them with her whole heart. She really couldn't even think about it, where they would go, and with whom. Who would be their new owner, and would he treat them right? For one wild moment, Lizzie thought she could not bear the thought of leaving these adorable little ponies. She thought if she could only grab Dat's hand, begging him not to do this, he might not.

But then she thought of that awful supper table when Mam cried and smacked Jason, and Dat looked so troubled, and she stopped herself.

"Dat," she whispered, after Teeny had pushed his nose into her hand, and she felt how velvety soft his little nose actually was. She would just mention how she felt; she wouldn't beg him.

"Hmm?"

"Do we have to do this?" she asked in a low, choked voice.

"What did you say?"

"Do we . . . I mean . . . do we have to, really have to sell Teeny and Tiny?" she asked, raising her eyes in misery.

"Ach, Lizzie." Dat's face softened, and for a minute, Lizzie knew Dat felt exactly the same way. Emma stopped brushing Tiny, resting her hand on his back, to listen. Dat didn't say more, and Lizzie waited expectantly, brushing back Teeny's forelock. His hair was so soft and blond, and . . .

"We have to, Lizzie. We need the money, and that's all there's to it," Dat said gruffly.

"Oh," said Lizzie, knowing deep down that Dat was only saying what she knew all along. It was just so hard to give them up. She sighed and felt hot tears prick her eyelids. She kicked at some loose gravel and clasped her hands behind her back, clenching her teeth in the effort not to let the tears tumble down her cheeks. Maybe she wouldn't feel so sad if Emma would have allowed her to go buy a doughnut. That was just the trouble, always

having to listen to Emma. A doughnut would definitely
help her feel much better.

"Emma!" Lizzie kicked at more gravel, raising her
head to glare at Emma.

"What?" Emma asked, looking at Lizzie with a surprised expression. You could never tell with Lizzie, she
thought. One minute she was good as gold, and the next
she was mad about something.

"Why didn't you let me have a doughnut?" she asked
loudly.

"Well, you don't even know if they have any to sell,"
Emma said defensively, glancing at Dat as she spoke.

"What are you talking about?" Dat asked, lifting the
harness onto Teeny's back.

"Oh, she wanted a doughnut, because she saw a man
walking past eating one, and I don't even know where
they sell them," Emma explained.

Lizzie sniffed self-righteously. If she couldn't have
Teeny and Tiny, at least she could have a doughnut.

A loud voice spoke on the speaker system, urging all
owners to bring their ponies to the large yellow tent.

"Hurry up, girls! Here, take this rag and make sure
the wheels on the spring wagon are clean, Emma," Dat
said, slipping the bridle on Teeny's head. Emma ran to
polish the wheels, and Lizzie fastened the rein to the
bridle, as Dat hurried to lift the tongue of the wagon
to hitch them to it. The ponies pranced a bit, lifting
their heads higher than usual, and a nervous pang shot
through Lizzie's stomach. Suppose the ponies ran, terrified, out of that tent?

"Dat!"

"What?"

"Are you sure Emma and I can do this? What if they get all scared and go running away?" Lizzie asked worriedly.

"I'll help you get started, and I'll be right there in the ring, watching you all the time. So don't be afraid—you know you'll be fine, both of you," Dat assured her.

He finished hitching the ponies to the glistening black cart, the wheels shining with every turn as he brought it to the right position for the girls to climb up on the seat.

"You may drive, Emma," he said, knowing she was the levelheaded, steady one, who would keep her head about her when excitement ran high. So Emma picked up the reins, clucked to the ponies, and they were off at an easy walk, with Dat at their heads.

People turned to stare, and "Oh!" and "Look!" were quite common. Lizzie loved every minute of the attention they received. She sat up a bit straighter, smoothing back the loose strands of brown hair the wind had tugged out. She adjusted her black apron, making sure the pins were all straight, and waved at a little boy who was waving both arms and yelling at her.

After they reached the yellow tent, Dat hopped off the back, going to Teeny's bridle. The loudspeaker was so noisy here, and the miniature ponies were prancing nervously, tossing their heads with impatience. Dat stroked their necks, talking softly to them, quieting them with his expert hands.

"Lizzie, do you want to drive them in the ring?"

Emma asked unexpectedly.

"I don't know, Emma. Why don't you want to?"

"My knees are shaking."

"Are they?"

"I'm just so nervous, Lizzie. You drive, okay?"

Lizzie looked over at Emma and felt sorry for her, because her face was drawn and pale, and she actually was shaking. She bit her lips together to keep her teeth from rattling.

"I will," Lizzie said, knowing from somewhere deep inside of her that she could. Emma's nervousness made her feel suddenly very strong, and she knew, without a doubt, that she could drive those ponies around that ring.

Emma scooted over when Lizzie stood up, and Dat turned to the girls immediately. "What? Aren't you driving, Emma?" he asked.

"No, Dat. I'm just too scared," she answered quietly.

"That's okay, Emma. Lizzie can. Right, Lizzie?" Dat

asked, looking carefully into her face for signs of her usual fear.

"Yes," answered Lizzie firmly. "I can drive them."

"Good!" Dat said. "Now, as soon as you hear them announce these ponies, just start them nicely, down to the left. Keep going on the sawdust. It may pull a bit hard at first, and keep a firm hand, because they're excited. If anything goes wrong, I'm watching every move you make, and I'll be right there. Now make yourself boss, and don't be afraid."

"I will," Lizzie said, holding the reins firmly, one in each hand, leaning forward for better control.

They waited as the auctioneer's voice boomed over the speaker. He was selling a white pony which had a nervous gallop, the whites of its eyes showing fear. The rider on the pony's back struggled to keep it in check, but Lizzie thought it looked as if he could barely stay in the saddle.

Dat was using his handkerchief to polish the ponies' bridles, checking the girth on the harness, and double-checking the straps that held up the tongue of the little spring wagon.

"Two hundred five, two hundred five, anybody gimme ten?" the auctioneer's voice boomed, begging the buyers for five more dollars. He knocked the wooden gavel on the stand in front of him and shouted, "Two hundred five it is. Gone to the green hat. Number six hundred ten."

The auctioneer turned to wipe his brow and take a drink from his can of soda, talking quietly away from the microphone to his assistant. Another man handed him papers and he read, "What have we here? Miniatures! Miniature ponies. A perfectly matched pair."

"Go!" Dat said to Lizzie.

Lizzie sat up straight, loosened the reins a tiny bit, and said quietly, "C'mon, Teeny. C'mon, Tiny."

Dat stepped back and patted Emma's arm, giving them a nervous smile, and they were off.

The ponies seemed to sense the importance of this moment, and, holding their perfect little heads high, they trotted together as one. Lizzie felt calm and strong, guiding them along the narrow ring covered with sawdust.

The crowd went wild. People stood up in their seats, clapping and cheering, smiling and waving their hats. The auctioneer could barely be heard above the thunderous applause. He laughed, put his microphone down, and waved his white cowboy hat. Emma and Lizzie looked at each other and laughed.

Around they went, back to where Dat was standing, shaking his head and laughing, although Lizzie thought he looked as if he could cry at the same time.

"Keep going, Lizzie!" he yelled.

The ponies kept trotting, holding their heads nicely, picking up their dainty little hooves, scattering the sawdust as they pulled the shining black spring wagon with gold pinstripes.

"What am I bid?" the auctioneer started. No one was bidding; they were still applauding this well-behaved little team of ponies. The auctioneer laughed again, and gave up trying to sell them until they had made another circle.

"Stop them, stop them!" he motioned to one of the workers. Lizzie saw what he wanted her to do and pulled back on the reins slowly, so as not to scare them with a harsh jerk on their mouths. They rolled to a perfect stop and stood quietly.

"Ladies and gentlemen, this is unbelievable. I have not seen anything like this in quite some time. These girls are not very old. How old are you?" he gestured to Lizzie with the microphone.

"I'm eight," she answered.

"You're eight—and your sister?" he asked.

Lizzie punched Emma's ribs with her elbow and Emma promptly told the auctioneer she was nine years old. Then she punched Lizzie back, because she was insulted that Lizzie thought she couldn't speak for herself when someone asked her a question.

"These matched miniature ponies are, no doubt, very well trained, driven by these young ladies. Would the owner step up here and give us a word for them?" the auctioneer asked.

Dat walked up behind them and was handed the microphone. Lizzie was so proud of her Dat when he talked about Teeny and Tiny, recommending them for children, and saying he had made the little spring wagon himself. After he finished, he handed the microphone back and told Lizzie to take them around a few more times.

As Lizzie eased up on the reins, Teeny stepped forward first, tugging Tiny along. For one heart-pounding moment, Lizzie thought Tiny wouldn't cooperate because of the noise and tense atmosphere, so she called his name in a steady voice, "Tiny, come boy," and his hindquarters lowered as he dug in his hooves to pull his share. Lizzie's heart swelled with love for these wonderful little horses. Surely they were the best in the world, and she hoped with all her heart no one would have enough money to buy them. For one moment, she longed to drive them straight out the wide yellow canvas door of that tent, across the field with rows of vehicles glistening in the sun, and never return. But she knew better, and the desire to leave was replaced by a willingness to obey Dat and Mam, because they really did need the money.

The auctioneer opened the sale of the ponies at five hundred dollars. It was lowered to three hundred, and Lizzie dared hope that maybe, after all, Dat could not get a good price for them and they would be taken back home. But after the low price of three hundred, the bidding escalated so fast and at such a confusing rate, with the auctioneer talking so fast that his words were a blur as well as the kaleidoscope of color and action, that Lizzie just drove them steadily before stopping them in front of the auctioneer's stand.

Now Lizzie could hear the amount. "Emma!" she whispered. "One thousand dollars!"

"That's a lot, isn't it?" Emma smiled at Lizzie, wringing her hands nervously in her lap.

Dat ran over to hold the ponies' heads, patting their necks as he spoke to them.

"Eleven hundred dollars!" yelled the auctioneer. "Do I hear eleven twenty-five?" A pause and a resounding, "Sold!" with a whack of his gavel, and the ponies were officially sold to buyer number 520.

Dat looked at the girls, a broad smile on his face, but there were tears in his eyes. Lizzie and Emma smiled back, but Lizzie's smile felt funny, as if it could slide downhill and pull the tears along down, like melting ice cream off a cone. She loved Dat and she loved Teeny and Tiny, so it was a mixture of smiles and tears.

As Dat led the ponies out of the ring, Emma told Lizzie she had done a really good job of driving Teeny and Tiny.

"I know I did," Lizzie agreed. "I really don't know how I did it, Emma."

"You were good, anyway," Emma said, squeezing Lizzie's hand.

When they met the new owner, Lizzie felt better instantly. He was an older gentleman, with a small beard and mustache, his hair shining like a white halo around his head. He wrung Dat's hand over and over, congratulating Lizzie and Emma on their horsemanship at their young age. The girls just smiled shyly, saying nothing. Lizzie kicked at the loose gravel, and pleated a corner of her apron with her hands. She felt awkward when someone congratulated her, and never knew what to say. She had often heard English people say "Thank you!" after a compliment, but that would be acknowledging the fact that she was a good driver, and that would be too bold of her. So she said nothing. When there was nothing else to do but say their final farewells to Teeny and Tiny, Lizzie tried very hard to feel the same as she had before entering the ring under the tent. Dat was talking to the new owner and blinking his eyes rapidly. Lizzie walked over and laid her head on Tiny's back, while the tears flowed freely. She watched as Emma hugged Teeny's neck, through a fresh wave of sadness.

"Come, girls," Dat said firmly, and they walked away, Dat in the middle with Emma and Lizzie on either side, looking straight ahead, and none of them looked back — not once. There was simply no use.

chapter 8

Summer Days

After the sale of Teeny and Tiny, the days became longer and sunnier. School was over and the summer weather was upon them with a vengeance that year. Instead of the usual spring rains, the wind blew steadily from the west, and there were weeks of no rain at all.

The soft green grass turned in color, becoming a different shade of green, and it tickled Lizzie's bare feet to walk on it. During the day, the sun shone hotly, and the girls sat on the porch swing, dangling their legs down over the side, saying nothing and swinging slightly to catch a tiny breeze.

It was hot. The heat waves shimmered above the road, making it seem as if the road was moving up and down. If you tried to walk on the road, the black, sticky tar bubbles welled up and were so blistering hot that they hurt your feet. So Lizzie and Emma did not walk on the road because of that.

Because their living quarters were above the harness shop, it was frightfully hot in the house in the afternoon and evening. Mam helped Dat every afternoon, making halters and harnesses, waiting on customers, and

keeping cooler than the house would have been. So
Lizzie and Emma had to watch Jason and Mandy, but
really, Mandy was getting so big that she didn't need to
be watched, just Jason. They always had to do dishes,
sweep the kitchen, and pick up the toys. Mam even let
Emma help with the laundry, teaching her how to sort it
properly and help put the clothing through the wringer
of the gas engine-powered washing machine. Sometimes
Lizzie had to help hang it on the line, but she couldn't
reach it very well and had to stand on the wagon. That
was really scary, because if Emma became impatient,
she would pull on the handle and the wagon would lurch
forward, causing Lizzie to lose her balance.

But on most afternoons when it was so hot, they sat
on the porch swing, Lizzie reading and Emma pushing
the swing slightly with one foot.

Emma glanced over at Lizzie, frowning. *She looks
terribly sloppy*, she thought. *As long as she has her nose in a
book, she couldn't care less what she looks like.* Lizzie's dress
was torn under one arm, and a button was missing, and
instead of at least putting in a small safety pin, Lizzie
just let it hang open. Her hair looked awful, that was all
there was to it. Emma wondered when Mam had last
taken a brush thoroughly through her sister's hair. In
the summertime, Mam would braid their hair and make
a bob with the braid, and that stayed longer. But Lizzie
had bits of hay sticking out of her unkempt braids, and
there was a brown line on Lizzie's forehead that was just
plain dirt. Emma decided it came from wiping her forehead up toward her hair with her dirty hands.

Emma's eyes narrowed and she watched Lizzie more closely. She was eating again, something that looked like cheese curls, and her fingernails were black under the rims, with the tips of her fingers covered with bright yellow cheese from her snack. Lizzie was definitely getting chubbier, too, Emma decided. She was always sitting around reading her books and snacking on something salty. If they didn't have pretzels or other snacks, she would spread peanut butter on saltine crackers, which Emma thought were dry and disgusting.

"Lizzie, what are you eating?" Emma began.

"Cheese curls," Lizzie answered, absentmindedly.

"You should stop eating so much, Lizzie. Your dresses are getting tight."

"Of course they are—they're old."

"Mine are, too, and they're not tight."

No answer, so Emma pinched her mouth into a straight line and said, "Lizzie."

"Hmmm?"

"Stop eating those sickening cheese curls."

"They're good," Lizzie said defensively.

"Where did you get them?"

"In the pantry."

Lizzie put down the book, looking squarely at Emma. "Anyway, I can eat these cheese curls if I want to, and it's none of your business. They're stale. I love stale cheese curls, and I left the bag open overnight on purpose, 'cause I like them that way." She popped another one into her mouth and chewed, making a stale, squooshy sound.

"Eww, Lizzie!" Emma said.

"They're good. Here, try one," Lizzie said, handing over a greasy little bag filled with the stale snacks.

"I don't want any. Lizzie, you shouldn't just sit around and read; you're getting fat, for real," Emma told her bluntly. "And why don't you wash your face? It's dirty."

Lizzie shrugged her shoulders and smashed her teeth down on another cheese curl. Emma watched her yellow teeth demolishing the disgustingly stale food.

"Why don't you get up and do something? I'm thirsty, so why don't you go make a pitcher of Kool-Aid?" Emma asked.

"You go."

"You're probably thirstier than I am, eating like that."

Lizzie slammed down her book. "Oh, all right. Stop pestering me when I'm reading, Emma. You just do it to disturb me; you know you do. I'm going to go make Kool-Aid and I'm taking some to the shop for Mam and Dat, and you can just come up to the kitchen and make your own, 'cause I'm not giving you any."

"Lizzie, you have to let me have a glassful," Emma whined.

Lizzie slammed the screen door and walked across the kitchen into the bathroom. She took a really good, long look at herself, turning sideways and pulling in her stomach. What did Emma mean? She was not getting fat. She looked the same as she always did. She put her face up against the mirror and smiled. She wasn't either dirty, not even a little bit. She couldn't understand what Emma meant, because there was no dirt anywhere on

her face. She decided Emma was fussy; she was the same with her as she was with sweeping the kitchen and straightening the tablecloth.

Lizzie got a stool and climbed up to the kitchen cupboard, selecting a packet of cherry Kool-Aid. She moved the stool over and grabbed a two-quart pitcher, ripping open the packet of Kool-Aid and dumping it into the bottom of the pitcher. She let the water run into it till it was full, then ran over to the refrigerator for a tray of ice. She dumped the ice cubes into the Kool-Aid and set the empty tray on the counter. Mam always told them to refill the ice cube trays whenever they took some out, but Lizzie never did, because it took too long. She did feel guilty sometimes, though, but as long as Mam didn't scold her too hard, she didn't bother filling it.

She found two tall glasses and filled them carefully with Kool-Aid, putting ice cubes in each one. She grabbed one with each hand and started carefully down the steps to the harness shop.

She paused in the doorway, watching Mam and Dat at work. The sewing machine was clicking steadily with Dat bent over it, sewing a piece of leather for a harness. Mam was sorting rings and keepers, which were little steel and plastic accessories that were put on fancy

harnesses. They both looked tired and warm, not saying anything, just bending over their tasks in the stifling
heat.

Lizzie suddenly felt shy for unexplainable reasons,
but she stepped forward and said, "Do you want a cold
drink?" feeling self-conscious. She really hoped they
would like the Kool-Aid.

Mam smiled down at Lizzie. "Why, Lizzie, that was
really nice! Did you make this all by yourself?" she
asked.

Lizzie clasped her hands behind her back and rocked
on her heels, beaming at Mam.

"Mm-hmm."

"Good! Melvin!" She tapped Dat's shoulder and he
looked up. "Lizzie brought us some Kool-Aid."

"She did?" He turned off the sewing machine, swiveled on his stool, and came
over to the counter.

"Why, thank you,
Lizzie!"

"You're welcome,"
Lizzie said, and turned
to go back to
Emma and her
book on the porch
swing. She couldn't
resist looking back
to see if they liked
the Kool-Aid, only
to see Mam take

a long swallow and make a horrible face. Dat burst
out laughing, bent over double, as Mam struggled for
breath. They both looked toward the door where Lizzie
had just gone through, as if to make sure she didn't see
them.

Lizzie felt terrible. She ran up the steps, her cheeks
burning with shame and humiliation. What in the world
could have been wrong with the Kool-Aid? They definitely did not like it, there was no doubt about that at
all. They hated it.

Lizzie flung herself down on the hot, itchy sofa, turning her face to the back, and cried as if she would never
stop. When Emma came in for some Kool-Aid, she
heard muffled sobs coming from the living room. She
stood in the doorway to find Lizzie crying loudly, her
face bright red and perspiration soaking her dirty hair.

"Lizzie!"

Lizzie sat straight up, her dress tangled about her
knees, her hair sticking out worse than ever and her eyes
swollen from crying.

"Emma, you go away right this minute, and I mean
it! If you wouldn't have made me make that Kool-Aid, I
wouldn't be crying. Go away!" she shouted miserably.

Emma wisely turned her back, smoothing down her
dark hair as she entered the kitchen. That Lizzie. It was
hard to tell what brought that on. Oh well, at least there
was still Kool-Aid in the ice-cold pitcher beaded with
condensation.

Mmm, it looks so refreshing, Emma thought, pouring
some into her favorite cup. She took a long swallow,

coughed, and stuck out her tongue, running to the sink
to let it all drain out of her mouth.

"Lizzie!"

Lizzie appeared at the doorway, looking so miserable
and disheveled and so warm and uncomfortable that
Emma couldn't be mad at her.

"Lizzie, you forgot to put sugar in this Kool-Aid! It
tastes absolutely awful. Did you take this down to Mam
and Dat?" Emma asked.

"Yes."

Lizzie grabbed a dish towel and wiped her face.

"Lizzie, don't use a dish towel. Go to the bathroom
and wash your face," Emma said, opening the canister of
sugar and carefully measuring some into the remaining
Kool-Aid. With her back turned, she asked, "Is that why
you were crying? Dat and Mam didn't like the Kool-
Aid, did they? Lizzie, you could have put sugar in it."

"You just be quiet right this minute, Emma!"

"Well, why are you so touchy about it? You can't
drink Kool-Aid without putting sugar in it—you should
know that," Emma fussed, stirring the sugar and ice,
tasting a tiny sip before drinking more.

"I'm little, Emma. I'm a lot younger than you. How
was I supposed to know?" Lizzie defended herself.

"You're not very little. Didn't you ever make Kool-
Aid before?"

But there was no answer, because Lizzie was running
water in the sink in the bathroom.

Emma wandered into the pantry, feeling a bit hungry,
but not really knowing what she wanted to eat. It was so

warm, and she felt sticky and uncomfortable. She lifted
the lid on the cookie container, but there were only a
few broken pieces of stale chocolate chip cookies on the
bottom. She found the bag of cheese curls that Lizzie
had left open during the night because she liked them
stale and squooshy. She rolled up the bag and stuck in
the clothespin that was lying beside it and sighed. There
was nothing good to eat, except maybe some brown-
speckled bananas. She broke one off and peeled it
halfheartedly, flopping down in a kitchen chair, taking a
large bite of the overripe fruit.

Lizzie was still splashing around in the bathroom.
Mandy stirred from her nap on the recliner, tossing her
leg over the arm, swiping at her warm forehead with
a sticky arm. Emma watched her, wondering how she
could sleep on that prickly chair in this warm weather.
Mandy muttered in her sleep, settled herself, and resumed her long afternoon nap.

Mandy was not very strong, Emma thought. She was
so thin and pale, never having much of an appetite, and
Mam said she just wasn't as hale and hearty as Emma
and Lizzie were, whatever that meant.

Emma wondered why the water was still running in
the bathroom. It was taking her a very long time just to
wash her face. "Lizzie!" she shouted, above the sound
of running water and all the splashing. There was no
answer. "Lizzie!"

The water ran on. Emma was becoming irritated,
because she knew Mam would not like Lizzie to run the
water so long. Besides, she probably had everything wet

in sight. She stalked over to the door, her hands on her hips, glaring at Lizzie.

Lizzie was wet all over her head, her shoulders, and her sleeves, and even the hem of her dirty dress was dripping on the shaggy blue bathroom rug. She was taking a wet washcloth and squeezing it over the top of her head, water making little rivulets down her face. She stopped when she saw Emma, looking guilty, but so much cooler, and, in spite of herself, Emma had to admit she looked a lot cleaner.

"Lizzie, I mean it. I'm going down to the harness shop right this minute, and I'm going to tell Mam and Dat what you are doing," Emma said firmly, turning on her heels and marching away.

"Emma, no—don't!" Lizzie ran after Emma, grabbing at her sleeve with her wet hands. Water was dripping on the living room floor, which only made Emma angrier and more determined to tell her parents.

"Emma, please don't tattle, okay? I'll go clean everything up and put on a clean dress. I'll wash the dishes tonight—I'll wash them for a whole week if you don't tattle," Lizzie pleaded, standing in front of Emma, soaking wet and looking so desperate that Emma had to try really hard not to laugh.

"Please, Emma!" Lizzie gave her the most pitiful, repentant look Emma had ever seen, and she had seen Lizzie try lots of faces to help save herself many times. This look was more than Emma could bear, and she burst out laughing, giving Lizzie a shove to move her away. Lizzie looked so relieved, and giggled along with

Emma, saying, "I'll go clean up," and hurried off.

When Lizzie returned, her arms raised up over her shoulders to button her dress down the back, she looked at Emma and gave her a sheepish grin. Then she hurried into the bathroom, and Emma heard her grunting with the effort it took to clean up the wet bathroom floor. She heard Mam's heavy footsteps coming up the back stairway, and cast a hurried glance toward the bathroom, but didn't say anything, because there was no time. Mam walked into the kitchen, smiled at Emma and said it was high time to start supper.

"I had better clean up first," Mam said, holding up her blackened hands. She turned, spotting Mandy on the recliner and bent to tuck a strand of hair behind her ear, murmuring to her about how warm she looked. She reached the bathroom door, stopped, and put her hand on her hip.

Emma watched nervously, because she was just sure the bathroom was a horrible mess. Mam just kept standing there, not saying a word, but Emma could tell by her stiffened shoulders that she was angry.

"Lizzie Glick!" Mam did not often raise her voice, but this was one time when she was very, very upset. Emma looked carefully between the door frame and Mam, almost afraid what Lizzie would be doing.

Lizzie was putting the shaggy blue bath rug into the bathtub because it was dripping wet. It was too heavy to do it quickly, so half of it hung out, dirty water running steadily across the already wet floor.

In one swift movement, Mam put the whole rug into

the tub, catching Lizzie's upper arm at the same time.

"What do you think you're doing, Lizzie?" she asked in an awful tone of voice.

"I . . . I just spilled water, Mam. I'll clean it up. Honest, I will," Lizzie implored.

"Why is this whole bathroom covered with water? You did not spill it, Lizzie," Mam said, still using that same tone of voice.

"I was just so warm, Mam," Lizzie said, starting to cry. "And I splashed some water on my head!"

"Don't you ever think of playing with water in the bathroom again. You're old enough to know better. Eight years old! Emma, why did you let her? Didn't you know what she was doing? Lizzie, you go sit on that platform rocker and stay there till Emma and I have supper ready," she scolded.

Mam marched into the kitchen, taking a corner of her dirty gray apron to wipe her face. She sank into a kitchen chair, raised both hands, and waved them in front of her face. "It is so warm up here in the kitchen," she said wearily. "What am I going to make for supper?"

Lizzie was sitting on the platform rocker, sniffling and tracing the swan's head on the handle with her fingers. As usual, life just wasn't fair. It really wasn't her fault the bathroom was so wet. She just didn't realize she would splash quite as much as she did. How was she supposed to know? She could hear Mam and Emma start supper, talking together and sharing their day. Emma walked into view, straightened the old torn tablecloth, and set the plates neatly and properly in their place. *Oh, that's really nice. What a good girl Emma is being again, while I get yelled at,* Lizzie thought.

She traced the wooden swan's head again, and wished they were real swans that would go peck Mam and Emma. She knew it was naughty, and she should not have such thoughts, but only for a minute she thought it would be nice.

Then she helped Mandy play a game of Chutes and Ladders until Dat came up the stairs for supper.

chapter 9

The Accident

Selling Teeny and Tiny, the miniature ponies, must have made a difference for Mam and Dat, because they were much more lighthearted again, laughing and joking with the girls. Mam did not work in the harness shop quite as often, so she had more time for her housework, which made a difference for Emma and Lizzie, too.

The heat continued steadily. Every morning the sun rose in a red ball, flaming in the bright blue sky, and by mid-morning everyone felt warm and tired, before the day had hardly begun.

Sometimes Dat set up the sprinkler at the end of the garden hose, and all the children—even Jason—dashed through it until they were soaked with the ice-cold water that came up from the well. If they ran through the sprinkler on days after Mam had mowed the grass, their legs were almost covered with grass. Jason even had grass in his curly hair, but Emma said the grass was clean so it really didn't matter.

Lizzie wished with her whole heart they could have a place to swim. She wanted to learn how to swim, like real people did in the books she read. She could not

imagine being able to kick your arms and legs in deep
water and stay up there. She asked Dat if he could
swim, and he said he could, but not very well, because
he was actually afraid of the water. Mam said she never
even tried, and no, she couldn't swim one tiny bit and
never cared to try.

So Lizzie didn't say anything more, but she thought
Dat and Mam were just terribly unexciting. She hoped
when she was married her husband would dig a pond,
because he would have lots of money, and she would
go swimming every day, in warm summer weather
like this, anyway. She asked Emma why Amish people
didn't have swimming pools like English people did, and
Emma said it was too worldly. That really irked Lizzie,
because that was no explanation at all.

This morning Lizzie was really wishing she could
swim, partly because it was so warm, and partly because
Mam and Emma were doing the Saturday cleaning. She
sat on a stool in the harness shop beside Dat and asked
him again why Amish people couldn't have swimming
pools.

"Lizzie, you really are getting annoying," Dat said,
wiping his forehead with his blue handkerchief. It was
very warm in the shop—even with both doors wide open
there was scarcely a breeze.

"Well, how am I ever going to learn how to swim?
I have to do that, you know. Sometime, Dat," Lizzie
stated seriously.

"Ach, Lizzie. You're a little Amish girl, and Amish
girls shouldn't go swimming, anyway. It's not very lady-

like, you know," he said, tucking his handkerchief into
his pocket.

Lizzie didn't answer. She was thinking how unfair it
was. After all, boys went swimming all the time, because
Marvin said so. "Why do boys go, then?" she asked.

"Because," Dat said, bending over a piece of leather
he was getting ready to sew.

"I would go swimming in my dress, Dat. That
wouldn't be unladylike at all."

"Who would go with you?"

"Just me and Marvin."

"In Doddy Glicks' dirty pond?"

"It isn't dirty, Dat."

"There are huge snapping turtles in there, Lizzie.
They eat baby ducks and geese, coming up from underneath and grabbing their little legs, swallowing them
whole. How would you like to be happily swimming
and have a snapping turtle grab your foot, because he
thought it was a baby duck?"

"My feet don't look one bit like a baby duck's, Dat!"
Lizzie said, punching him hard in the arm.

Dat laughed. He bent down and peered at Lizzie's
brown bare foot. "Why, sure they do!"

Lizzie bent down to look, just to make sure her feet
were normal. They were a little flat and wide, but they
looked like people feet, not a duck's.

"They are a bit flat," she said slowly.

Dat laughed about that, and his laugh was so funny
that Lizzie laughed with him.

Just as Dat turned to continue his sewing, they were

both shocked to an absolute standstill, hearing the sound of desperately screeching brakes, followed by the most sickening thud Lizzie had ever heard.

Dat's face turned pale, and his blue eyes seemed to darken as he listened carefully. Lizzie stood very still, somehow feeling as if something extremely serious had happened.

"That wasn't very far away. Just down the road, it seems like," Dat said, hurrying out on the porch. Lizzie ran along, and they both stood very still, listening, yet almost afraid of what they would hear, or had heard.

The sun beat down on their heads with the same fierce intensity of the previous weeks. The air was so still, not even a leaf turned on the tree beside the harness shop sign.

"Wonder if I should walk out the road?" Dat mused.

"Can I go along?"

"No, you stay here. You go up to Mam, Lizzie. I'll go see what happened," he said, starting to walk out the road at a fast, nervous pace.

Lizzie wrapped her arms around the dark green steel pole that held the harness shop sign. She looked at her bare feet against the concrete and spread them out as flat as she could. She really did have wide, flat feet. She tucked a strand of brown hair behind one ear, twirled around the pole, and wondered what had happened that a car's brakes screeched like that.

A few cars passed, a truck with wooden racks flopping loudly, sounding as if they could fly off any minute. Lizzie was glad she wasn't on the road with a horse and buggy, because things like that really scared most horses, even worse than big tractor trailers. *He should fix his sloppy wooden racks*, she thought.

It was terribly hot on the concrete sidewalk, but Lizzie didn't really want to go into the house, mostly because Mam and Emma were cleaning. But Dat had told her to go up to Mam, so she turned to start up the gray wooden steps that led to the kitchen.

The kitchen door opened, and Emma appeared, holding a dust mop carefully in one hand. She began shaking it vigorously, just as Lizzie was halfway up the steps.

"Emma, stop that!"

Little bits of dust and dirt were swirling all around Lizzie. Emma stopped shaking the dust mop, and said, "Oh, there you are, Lizzie. Mam wants you to come take out the garbage."

"Emma, did you and Mam hear that sound on the road? Dat walked up to see what is going on. There was a loud, screeching sound of someone's brakes, and then, Emma—it isn't even funny—I just know something bad happened."

The air seemed to be split into two parts by the sudden wailing of a siren. The shrill rhythm was earsplitting, and Lizzie held her hands to her ears, as she turned her frightened eyes to Emma's face.

"My, that's close!" Emma shouted.

Mam came out on the porch, her face beaded with perspiration. Her eyes opened wide at the nerve-shattering, insistent sound of the siren. "That's not far away," she said, listening closely.

As the siren wound down to a slow stop, another one started up, piercing through the air with its eerie wail. Lizzie hated that sound. It always made her feel helpless, because she didn't know why the sirens were blowing, or where they were going, or what had happened. It really bothered Lizzie if she had to give up and go on with her play, without knowing exactly what had happened to make them use those awful sirens.

They all stood together silently in the warm, sultry summer air, their breaths abated, wondering why the sirens were so close. There was a thump on the lower step, and Dat's white, terrified face appeared below them. He was hatless, his hair blown back over his wide forehead from running, his upper lip beaded with sweat.

He ran up the steps and took Mam in his arms, something Emma and Lizzie very seldom saw him do. He started crying, tears coursing from his blue eyes, and Mam patted his arms as he struggled for control.

"Annie, Annie. It's just so awful. I'll never forget this as long as I live," he choked brokenly.

"What, Melvin. What?" Mam asked, in tears herself. Dat searched in his pocket and found his big blue handkerchief. He blew his nose and wiped his eyes, looking up the road as if reliving the horror of what he had seen. He took a deep, shaking breath.

"Annie, it's the Beiler girls."

"Oh, Melvin!"

"They . . . they were on the road with the pony and cart, just clipping along, and a car came up over the crest of that small, steep hill, close to Paul Hoovers!"

"Yes. Go on, Melvin," Mam said, wiping her eyes.

"He was going too fast, Annie," Dat broke down again, covering his eyes with his handkerchief.

"Oh my, Melvin. How bad is it?" Mam asked.

Dat sighed. "Bad. Susie was killed. Malinda was taken to the hospital with the ambulance."

Lizzie would never forget this moment. Susie! Her classmate in school, and a good friend. She was very quiet for one long moment as the hard, horrible truth clung to her senses like an awful creature. She wanted to shake it off and make it go away, because it was choking her. She looked at Emma, who was sobbing with Dat and Mam, and wondered why she couldn't cry. She just stood there, while her mind thought other things, like the color of the threads in the dust mop at her feet, and why the mop wasn't put away after Emma was finished with it.

"You know how some people mount those silver decorative horses or airplanes on the hood of their car? Well, this guy had a rocket, and when he hit the pony cart, the rocket went through Susie's back, killing her instantly," Dat said, shuddering at the thought.

Jason and Mandy wandered out on the porch, and Jason reached for his father, fussing happily in his baby language. Dat reached down and picked him up, burying his face in Jason's curls. Mandy started crying, just because everyone else was. Mam bent down and held her tightly, explaining in a soft voice that something had happened and that they would be alright, because Mandy was so little and skinny, so easily afraid of anything.

Dat sat down wearily on the porch swing, holding Jason and swinging gently. Mam moved over and he made room for her on the swing, Mandy climbing into Mam's lap.

Emma sat on an old green lawn chair, leaned back against the webbing, and crossed her arms over her stomach. She was still sniffling, and tears welled up in her eyes as she looked over at Lizzie.

Lizzie stood against a porch post, her mouth in a grim line, her eyes staring at nothing. Emma wondered why Lizzie didn't cry with everyone else, because she always cried easily, especially if she wanted her own way.

Dat sighed. Jason put his head against his shoulder, and they rocked quietly. On the street below, cars went past as usual, but not for very long, because a police car stopped and parked across from the harness shop. As they all watched, the policeman got out of his car and donned an orange vest. He stood in the middle of the road, directing cars in another direction to avoid the accident. He blew his whistle occasionally, waving his right arm or holding up his left, to stop cars or to let them turn into the other road.

"Why is he doing that?" Mandy asked, her big green eyes shining in her upturned face.

"Oh, there's been an accident, and there are too many people and cars on the road, so these other cars are supposed to use another route," Mam told her gently.

"Mam, what happens to Malinda in the hospital?" Emma asked.

"It all depends on how badly she's hurt," Mam answered.

"Do you think she's hurt really bad? I mean, do they have to operate and everything?" Emma asked, sitting up straight and swinging her legs nervously.

"Emma, I don't know how badly she's hurt," Dat said seriously. "We'll soon know."

"Melvin, I feel so helpless. What is the first thing to do when someone dies?" Mam asked, looking over at Dat.

"Let's wait an hour or so, at least till Amos and Sadie find out and are at the hospital. Then we'll go to their house and help get ready for the funeral."

"What's a funeral?" Mandy asked.

Dat looked helplessly at Mam. Mam looked back at Dat, and they agreed in one look to tell Mandy.

"It's when someone dies, Mandy," Mam said.

"Who died?" Mandy asked innocently.

"Susie Beiler. A little girl who went to school with Emma and Lizzie," Dat said.

"Is she dead?"

"Yes, she was killed when a car hit their pony cart."

Mandy thought about this, swinging her legs and looking at Mam.

"Melvin." Mam got up from the swing and stood at the screen door. "I'm going to bake a cake and a few custard pies to take along to Amoses. I can't just sit here and do nothing." That was Mam's way. When she became upset or nervous, she worked fast with her hands, because it helped ease her worries.

Dat looked lovingly at Mam, knowing she would work through the shock and sorrow by doing some baking for the family who had lost a loved one.

Emma jumped up. "I'll help you, Mam."

Dat got to his feet. "I really don't want to, but I'll walk up to the accident again to see if there's anything I can do."

Lizzie was grinding her teeth without thinking. She stood against the post, thinking about helping Mam bake, and she couldn't stand the thought of that stifling kitchen. She wished this accident hadn't happened, because it made her feel awful. She couldn't cry, because she was too angry. Not really angry, just upset. She was, in fact, so miserable that she didn't know what to do, so she just stood there.

She wondered if Susie Beiler was really and truly dead. How did anyone actually know, and who said it if she was? Where was the man who drove into them now? What would happen to him? Mam always said you go to Heaven when you die, so why was everybody crying if she just went to Heaven? And if she did go to Heaven, then why were they having a funeral at Amos Beilers' house?

There were so many unanswered questions, and Lizzie's head hurt from trying to understand everything. She pushed away from the porch post and carefully made her way down the stairs so the policeman would not see her. You couldn't really trust policemen, because they had the power to put you in jail, as far as Lizzie knew.

She wandered across the warm brown lawn, under the apple trees, across the gravel driveway, and into the barn. The barn was much cooler, and the familiar horse and pony smell reminded Lizzie of a much happier time, when Dat helped them hitch up Teeny and Tiny.

Dolly popped her head up over the gate, and whinnied to her. Lizzie petted her nose, but Dolly kept on nickering in soft little rumbles.

"You're thirsty, aren't you?" she asked. "C'mon."

Lizzie opened the gate, and Dolly pushed past her to get to the water trough. Lizzie ran after her, in case she decided to run out the door. But Dolly only wanted a drink, that was all, and Lizzie put her arms around her neck as she took long, deep gulps of cool water. Dolly seemed so big compared to Teeny and Tiny. Lizzie still missed them, but not as much as before. Sometimes she even forgot what they looked like. She guessed Susie Beiler was the same. She would forget about her, too. Maybe when Teeny and Tiny died, they would be in Heaven with Susie and they would all wait for her.

But what if she lived to be an old, wrinkled *mommy*

and couldn't even hitch them up? The thought was so cruel, it welled up in her throat in a hard lump, and she gave up trying to swallow it. She simply buried her face in Dolly's mane, and cried great tears of grief for Susie, for Teeny and Tiny, for growing old, for not knowing, for things that happened in your life that you could do nothing about, and for the deep feeling that there was a God up in Heaven — she just couldn't understand Him yet.

The Funeral

The days that followed the accident were long, sad, confusing days. Lizzie tried hard to be a very good girl, because it seemed as if it was a time when she really needed to be on her best behavior. But it was hard. She just couldn't keep quiet and act sad all the time, she decided.

Emma told her she should not laugh too much, because it wasn't being respectful to Susie Beiler, or the accident, or even to her sad parents. Lizzie nodded her head in agreement, but didn't say what she was thinking, because Emma was older and wiser. Lizzie wasn't sure what *respectful* meant, really, so she guessed it meant sitting still and being very quiet without laughing at all.

The first day, Dat and Mam both went to Amos Beilers' place to help prepare the home for the funeral. As is the Amish custom, the family stayed at the house, and friends cleaned everything thoroughly, cooked meals, and helped with preparations for the large funeral which was to be held there. They supported the grieving family members, showing their love through kind words, kind deeds, and helping hands.

Loaves of freshly baked homemade bread, chocolate layer cakes, nut cakes, plastic containers of chocolate chip cookies, cupcakes, and all sorts of different pies were heaped in the Beiler pantry. Stainless steel kettles of chicken corn soup, vegetable soup, jars of applesauce, pears, peaches, and cherries also found their way to the grieving family. The food was all accepted with a quiet nod of acknowledgment by the people who were taking charge, shouldering the burden for the family members.

The men worked together, cleaning the shop and building a temporary addition, using lumber and clear plastic as a shelter for the huge crowd of mourners. This was where the funeral service would be held the following day.

The neighbor girl, Fannie, came to stay with the Glick children, because they had to stay at home until evening, when Mam and Dat would come home to get them all dressed up for the viewing. Lizzie didn't know what a viewing was, although she knew it was to look at poor Susie Beiler. She didn't want to go, not really, because what if she saw Susie lying in her coffin and she felt so awful she would burst into tears?

She sat on the couch, her legs curled under her, chewing on her lower lip, trying to read her book. Her mind kept going to the dreaded viewing, until she could contain herself no longer. She put down her book, and went to find Emma. She found Fannie in the kitchen, taking big, plump raisin oatmeal cookies off a hot cookie sheet with a metal turner.

Fannie smiled at Lizzie, and she smiled back shyly.

Lizzie really didn't know Fannie very well, so she felt shy of her, not knowing what to say. She walked over to the sink and got a drink of warm tap water, pretending to take a long drink, so she could get up the courage to talk to Fannie. Turning, she cleared her throat, tapping her bare feet self-consciously.

"Do you like raisin oatmeal cookies, Lizzie?" Fannie asked, trying to warm up to her.

Lizzie nodded. "Mm-hmm."

"Even if they have raisins in them?"

"I like raisins."

"Good. I'm glad you do. Not very many children like raisins," Fannie said, her eyes twinkling at Lizzie.

"I even eat raisin pie," Lizzie said proudly.

"Really?"

"Mm-hmm."

Lizzie watched Fannie take a teaspoon of cookie dough and drop it expertly onto the emptied sheet. Her hands flew fast and she never made one cookie too big or too small. Lizzie didn't know what to say anymore, so she sat on the bench and watched awhile, until she became uncomfortable, because it seemed as if she should be talking to Fannie.

"Where's Emma?" she asked.

"She's rocking Jason in the bedroom, because he cried for me. I just couldn't do anything with him. Maybe I'm not a very good babysitter," Fannie said with a laugh.

Lizzie didn't know what to say, because she didn't know if Fannie was a good babysitter or not. But just to make her feel good, Lizzie assured her she was a good one, or else she wouldn't know how to make cookies.

"Were you in Susie Beiler's grade in school?" Fannie asked.

"Yes."

"This is all really, really sad. She was so young. I just hope her mother and father can bear up under this. I suppose, as everyone says, her time was up and God took her home. Another rose in His bouquet in Heaven," Fannie said, clucking her tongue sympathetically.

"Mm-hmm." Lizzie bit her lip, looking down at the cookie crumbs on the brown linoleum. What did they mean by saying her time was up? Did they mean everybody had a certain amount of time to live here on earth, and that was all? She couldn't understand it, really, because it was too hard to think about things like that. God could just pick the time when you would die, Lizzie supposed, and then you died.

Lizzie did not want to die anytime soon. She could not imagine leaving Dat, Mam, Emma, Mandy, and Jason, and never seeing Doddy and Mommy Miller or Marvin and Elsie again. The thought made her feel so lonely and sad, she couldn't stand it, so she got up and went into the bedroom to find Emma.

Emma was rocking furiously, holding Jason with his blanket, humming loudly. She didn't look happy, and Jason did not look one bit sleepy. He sat straight up and pointed a finger at Lizzie, laughing happily because he thought Lizzie would rescue him from his naptime.

Emma scowled. "Lizzie, go out!"

"He's not sleepy, Emma," Lizzie said, holding out her arms for him.

"Then you put him to sleep," Emma said.

"Why does he have to have a nap if he isn't sleepy? Come, Jason." Lizzie held him and Emma stood up.

"He would have gone to sleep if you wouldn't have come in," she said.

"Did Fannie say he has to sleep?"

"No."

"Well then, let's let him play awhile yet. We could take him outside on the swing," Lizzie said.

"Okay."

So the girls took Jason through the kitchen, informing Fannie they were letting him play awhile, because he wasn't sleepy yet. She said it was alright, but to be very careful because of the road.

"There's a fence around our yard," Lizzie told her.

"I know. But watch him anyway," Fannie said, bending to open the oven door to check a sheetfull of cookies.

Jason toddled off to the sandbox, happily chattering to himself. Emma and Lizzie sat on the swings, slowly swinging, not saying anything at all. Lizzie wondered if Emma knew what it meant when people said someone's time was up.

"Emma?"

"Hmm?"

"Why do people say Susie Beiler's time was up? It just sounds like when we have an arithmetic test at school and the timer goes off."

"Why?"

"Well, Emma, think about it. How long do you think we're going to live?"

"Ach, Lizzie, I don't know. Why do you think such things?" Emma asked, clearly wishing she would be quiet.

"I don't know."

They swung their swings, digging their bare toes into the loose dust. The grass was growing really high around the metal legs of the swing set, but Lizzie guessed Mam didn't have time to trim it with the grass shears. The sun was uncomfortably warm again, but Lizzie knew they would not be allowed to run under the sprinkler today with Fannie being here.

"Emma."

"Hmm?"

"Do you want to go to the viewing? I mean, do you really want to see Susie if she's dead?"

"Not really, Lizzie. But we have to go. Do you want to?" Emma asked quietly, looking closely to see if Lizzie really was serious about this conversation.

"Well, it's just not fun to think about somebody dying. Especially if it's your friend. I don't know why it happened; do you, Emma?"

"No. I don't, either."

They swung in silence, watching Jason play in the sandbox. A bumblebee droned under the wooden eaves of the washhouse, reminding Lizzie of a little helicopter. She was afraid of bumblebees, but only if they sat down. When a bumblebee was flying, it usually didn't bother anyone unless they tried to slap it, and Lizzie never tried to swat at a bumblebee. She wondered why it hurt so bad when you got stung, as little as they were.

"Do we have to wear a *halsduch* to go to the viewing?" Emma asked.

"Emma, look at that bumblebee. He looks as harmless as a fly, but, boy, does it hurt when they sting!" Lizzie squinted her eyes to watch it more closely.

"Lizzie, you're not listening to me. Do you think we have to wear a *halsduch* this evening?" Emma insisted.

"What? I don't know. Did you know a bumblebee stung Marvin in his eye once, and it swelled so badly he couldn't even see out of it for days and days and days?" Lizzie asked.

Emma narrowed her eyes, looking at Lizzie. There she went again, stretching everything. She made little things seem so much bigger, and often it was only half as bad. Mam had often told Lizzie to be careful, because it was as bad as telling a lie.

"It was not days and days, Lizzie," Emma huffed.

"Well, long."

"I remember. It was once when we saw him, and the next time it wasn't swollen one bit. Lizzie, you have to stop stretching things."

"Girls!"

They turned at the sound of Mam's voice, answering

her in unison.

"Come now, we have to eat a bite of supper and get ready for the viewing," Mam called.

Emma ran to get Jason, and Lizzie hurried up the stairs to start getting dressed for the dreaded viewing.

Later that evening, so many buggies went past their house, Lizzie could hardly hold still long enough so Mam could comb her hair, straining to see who was in every buggy.

They wore dark navy blue with black capes and aprons pinned over their dresses. Their white coverings were pinned securely on their sleek hair, with the strings tied loosely beneath their chins. Mandy still wore a pinafore-type black apron, but Emma and Lizzie had to wear their *halsduch*, which is a cape, with their apron pinned securely around their waist.

They all walked together soberly, dressed in dark colors. Mam wore a black dress, because she was older, and everybody who was not a child wore black.

The sun was sinking behind the row of houses as they made their way up the street to Amos Beilers' house. It was still very warm, but Mam said she was thankful the viewing was held in the evening, because it was cooler.

There were so many people dressed in black, you could hardly see the house. Lizzie wondered where these people all came from and if they even knew who Amos Beilers were. The buggies could not all find room to unhitch, so some of them had to wait beside the road. Dat and Mam shook hands with lots of people Lizzie didn't know, so she had to shake hands as well.

Lizzie wished it was over, because her apron was
pinned too tightly and it was so warm and uncomfortable. She was used to going barefoot in the summertime, so her shoes pinched her feet horribly. Her black
stockings dug into her leg below her knee, making it
feel like someone was squeezing her leg. Lizzie thought
shoes and stockings were just not necessary, even if you
dressed up in the summertime.

They entered the house, and Dat talked to a sober-
faced man who directed them to the living room where
the Amos Beilers' family and their relatives were sitting.
Lizzie peeped around Mam's skirt to see, and was suddenly overcome with pity for all of them.

Amos looked so tired and sad, and there was a strang-
er crying with Susie's mother, who was wiping her eyes
with her wet, wrinkled handkerchief. Susie's sisters
looked so warm and tired, shaking hands and saying
things to the seemingly endless row of people.

Mam and Dat slowly made their way through the
kitchen, shaking hands, acknowledging acquaintances
with a nod or a smile, Emma and Lizzie following politely.

When they came to Susie's parents, Mam hugged
her mother, and they cried together, while Dat's face
worked with emotion as he talked in low, serious tones
to Amos. Emma fished around in her pocket for her
handkerchief and cried softly because Mam was crying.
Mandy watched the women carefully with her large,
solemn green eyes, while Lizzie just became steadily
warmer and more nervous, casting anxious looks at the

closed door where she saw small groups of people enter.

A tall, bearded man told them to come this way, and he opened the door to the room where Lizzie supposed Susie lay. Her heart started beating rapidly, because she was so nervous. She had never seen a dead person before, so she did not know what to do or how she would feel.

The room was empty except for a small brown wooden coffin in the center. It was lined with pure white cloth, with part of the coffin being closed. At first Lizzie thought there was no one in it, because everything was so white and blurry, but when Mam put a hand on Lizzie's back to gently prod her forward, Susie's face came into view.

Lizzie glanced desperately at her mother, who was softly wiping tears, and Emma had her handkerchief stuffed tightly against her nose, sniffling quietly. There was nothing left to do except stand close to the coffin and look at Susie, which brought such an unexpected rush of emotion that Lizzie didn't even have time to stifle her sob. Mam put a protective arm around her shoulders, while she turned her face into Mam's apron and cried.

Susie looked so real, almost as if she was asleep. Lizzie could not grasp the fact that she would never go to school with her again, and that her soul was supposedly in Heaven with God. She turned her face to look at Susie again and quickly turned away, because it just hurt too much.

Dat and Mam both commented on how natural she

looked, and how she didn't suffer, as death had been instant. They talked about the innocence of children, and again, the dreaded phrase of the fact that her time was up.

Walking slowly home in the warm summer evening, Dat said they were all so blessed to have each other.

"Yes," Mam agreed. "We just don't realize what a blessing we have every day, just having all of us together."

"But now Amos Beilers' have one rose in Heaven, which, actually, is one step ahead of us," Dat said.

Mam nodded solemnly, squeezing Mandy's hand.

"How can they be ahead of us?" Lizzie blurted.

"Well, we all want to go to Heaven, Lizzie, and one of their family is already there before them. Meaning, they have one ahead of us," Dat explained.

"Oh," said Lizzie, but she really didn't know what he meant. Why, if it was so sad, were they one step ahead? This whole death thing just made no sense. Lizzie felt confused and irritable, because nothing made any sense. She guessed she didn't have to understand any of it, really, since she was only little.

When they arrived at the house, Lizzie kicked off her shoes, pulling off her black stockings as fast as she could. She untied her covering, tossing it on the kitchen table, and was rapidly removing pins from her tight apron belt when Mam started making a pitcher of iced tea.

"Mam?"

"Hmm?"

"How can Susie be in Heaven when she's lying in her coffin?"

Mam laid down the long-handled wooden spoon, kicked off her shoes, and untied her covering. She looked closely at Lizzie's troubled face, and knew, as naturally as every mother knows, it was more important to answer Lizzie's questions than to make iced tea.

She sat down in a kitchen chair and pulled Lizzie over against her. She helped her remove her *halsduch* and apron, folding it neatly on the table because she would need it for the funeral tomorrow.

"Lizzie, you look so warm," Mam said tenderly, brushing at a stray hair with her hand.

"It is warm, Mam."

"I know, but it's summer." Mam sighed and watched Lizzie closely. She was chewing her lower lip and her eyebrows were arched high, showing her anxiety.

"Lizzie, when someone is killed like Susie was, or if they die because they're sick, or whatever the reason, their bodies stay here—the natural body we live in—but their souls go to be with Jesus in Heaven."

"I know."

"Okay. I think a soul is like a breath, which is actually your spirit that becomes like an angel when it gets to Heaven."

"Oh."

"It's hard to grasp when you're only nine years old, Lizzie, but that is actually true. We believe that Jesus died for us, you know, in the Bible story where He hung on the cross?"

"Mm-hmm."

"Well, because of that, our sins are forgiven, then when we die, we can go to Heaven."

"Are you sure?"

"Not perfectly sure, because we live by faith, and not by sight."

"See?"

"What?" Mam asked.

"You just said we aren't sure. So how do you know where Susie is?" Lizzie challenged.

"All children go to Heaven, Lizzie. Their sins are forgiven without asking, because they are innocent children."

"Are you sure?"

"Yes, I am very sure," Mam answered.

"Well, good. Because it worries me."

"What worries you?"

There was a long pause as Lizzie struggled with asking her mother about why some people have to be lost, as the preachers say. But she only shrugged her shoulders and said nothing, because it was too dumb to ask Mam that question, even if it often bothered her.

"What?" Mam asked.

"Nothing. Is the iced tea all done?"

Mam stood up and pulled Lizzie against her, wrapping both arms around her shoulders. Lizzie laid her head against Mam's *halsduch*, feeling as if she never needed more reassurance than the safe, warm haven of her mother's embrace. Mam smelled like talcum powder, laundry detergent, and iced tea, but she felt even bet-

ter than that. Nothing had ever come as close to being
perfect in all of Lizzie's short life as knowing Mam could
help when she needed it—the feeling that she would
not need to lie in bed at night worrying all alone about
scary things, because all she needed to do was ask Mam,
and Mam would really know for sure how things were.
At least most things. Someday she would ask her about
what the preachers meant when they said someone was
lost.

chapter 11

Fishing with Marvin

A few weeks before it was time to go back to school, Dat asked Mam if she wanted to go to Grandpa Glicks for a Saturday, just to spend the day. Maybe he could help Doddy with his work, while Mam visited with Grandma.

Lizzie waited anxiously, clutching the corner of the wooden bench with her fingers. She wanted to go so badly, but she knew if she begged too much it wouldn't help one little bit, especially if Mam was not in the mood to go.

"Let's do!" Mandy sang out.

Jason clapped his hands and yelled, just because Mandy was excited.

Emma, always the careful one, asked if they could get all the laundry, cleaning, and yard mowing done on Friday if they went away all day Saturday.

"Oh, Emma, you're always so worried about the work. I suppose we could go if you girls helped me extra

good on Friday. We just won't work in the garden or
trim around the flower beds this week, because I should
bake something to take along," Mam mused.

"Good! Oh, goody!" Lizzie whooped. "We can go
fishing with Marvin and Elsie!"

Dat smiled widely, looking closely at Mam to make
sure she really wanted to go. Because she lived so far
away from her own family he sometimes felt guilty if
they spent all their spare time with his own. Mam told
the girls it was just a part of her life, not being able to
spend time with her own family, because of the distance.
Lizzie thought Mam was brave, but sometimes she was
grouchy to Dat's sisters, the aunts. When Mam's nostrils
flared and the color in her face heightened, Lizzie was
sometimes embarrassed, because Mam said things that
sounded sharp. But that was just how Mam was.

All day Friday, Lizzie tried to be a good helper. But
things just went as they always did, she thought wryly.
Everything went well for a while. Mam was doing
laundry, while Emma and Lizzie got a clean rag, furniture polish, broom, and dust mop, and started cleaning
bedrooms. Emma started sweeping, while Lizzie sprayed
furniture polish on the soft, clean rag.

"Not so much!" Emma said loudly.

"That's not much."

"Stop it, Lizzie. I'm going to tell Mam."

"I didn't even spray much on the rag." Lizzie went on
spraying till Emma grabbed the can of polish.

"You just do that to make me angry!" Emma shouted.

"I do not."

"You do!"

So Lizzie was quiet, moving the dust rag around the doilies.

"You have to take the stuff off the dresser, Lizzie! Put everything on the bed—don't just dust *around* the doilies."

So Lizzie obediently dumped everything on the bed and sprayed more furniture polish on the dresser top.

"Not so much!" Emma yelled.

Lizzie stopped spraying, wiping halfheartedly while she looked at herself in the mirror. Her brown hair was a mess, because Mam didn't have time to comb it back in neat rolls this morning. Her eyes were blue—well, not really, Lizzie thought. Kind of gray. Her nostrils were way too long and slanted, which was the only thing Lizzie didn't like. She wondered why—if her nose was not big, or had a bump like Marvin's—it had such oddly shaped nostrils. She pushed on the end of her nose, but it only made her nostrils look worse. If she lowered her head, she could hardly see them, so she thought she'd practice keeping her head down so no one could see them very well.

"Come on, Lizzie. Hurry up!" Emma said.

Lizzie looked in the mirror and could see only Emma's

backside sticking up beside the bed, because she was
on her knees, sweeping out from under it, making loud,
clapping sounds with the broom. Lizzie examined her
nostrils again, wondering vaguely how Emma could
tell if she was getting the dusting finished if she had her
head under the bed.

Emma is so strange, Lizzie thought. *Always sweeping or
worrying if the toys are scattered over the living room floor.*

. . . . .

On Saturday morning, after a very good breakfast of
pancakes with syrup and scrambled eggs and toast, they
all piled into the buggy. Dat rolled up the gray canvas
part in the back, so the girls could see out the window
and the breeze would blow through the buggy.

The girls wore short-sleeved everyday dresses, although they picked out the best ones, being careful all
the buttons were on and no rips or patches could be
seen. They pinned on their black belt aprons, but they
didn't need to wear shoes, because bare feet were a lot
more comfortable.

Emma's dress was dark green, Lizzie's was royal
blue, and Mandy wore a lavender one. Mam had baked
molasses cookies, and they were tucked under the front
seat, along with the horse's halter and neck rope.

Red was as ambitious as always, starting off at a brisk
trot. Dat had to hold back with both arms, because if he
didn't, Red just ran at a speed that was actually dangerous. Mam always worried about Red being too tired, or
the sun being too warm, or that he would become thirsty
before they reached Grandpa Glick's farm.

But Red was still trotting briskly as they turned in the drive. "This still seems different," Mam commented.

"It sure does," Dat agreed.

They said that because Doddy Glicks had moved from the dairy farm not too long ago. This was a farm, too, except they didn't milk cows. Lizzie liked this farm almost better because of the hills and the pond where they were going fishing.

Marvin and Elsie were thrilled to see them, as were the aunts and Doddy and Mommy Glick. Lizzie always felt so welcome and everything seemed cozy, and, well, she thought very hard how she felt in Doddys' kettle house, but she didn't really have a word for it. It just seemed good.

Their kettle house was the first room you walked into when you went in the front door. It was attached to the kitchen, so one wall was brick like the exterior of the whole house. The brick wall was painted with glossy blue paint, so they could wash it off when they spring cleaned. The floor was concrete, but that, too, was painted with shiny gray paint. There were hooks for clothes, racks for shoes, chests where buggy blankets were kept, the wringer washing machine with double steel tubs, a sink and stove, and even a little sink with a mirror above it to wash your hands. The windows were lined with pots of violets and ivys, all dark green and shades of purple, because Mommy Glick loved houseplants and always kept them healthy.

Lizzie asked Elsie why they had double rinse tubs at their washing machine, and Elsie said they rinsed their laundry twice. Lizzie just said, "Oh," because she wasn't going to tell Elsie they only rinsed theirs once. That was why Mam said Mommy Glick was very clean and particular about her work. Mam always shook her head, saying she didn't know how Mommy did it, raising fourteen children and being so meticulous about everything. But then, Mam helped Lizzie cut out her paper dolls or colored a picture in her coloring book, and she couldn't imagine Mommy Glick doing that. Lizzie did secretly wish Mam would rinse her laundry twice, so she wouldn't have to say just, "Oh."

The grownups were soon settled around the long kitchen table, having cups of tea and coffee, along with Mam's molasses cookies and a pan of freshly baked cinnamon rolls. They smelled so warm and cinnamon-y that Lizzie's mouth watered. She eyed the one panfull and wondered if that was the only pan Mommy had baked, because it looked like a very small pan of cinnamon rolls, according to all the people taking one. Just when Lizzie was sure she would not get one, Mommy went to the pantry and brought out two more pans. One of them was covered with caramel icing, Lizzie's favorite. Then she poured tall glasses of ice-cold tea, made from tea leaves she grew in her garden, for the children.

Lizzie took a long, cold drink of tea and bit into a soft cinnamon roll covered with caramel icing and smiled at Marvin and Elsie, thinking this was one of the best days of her life.

Mommy passed a bowl of stick pretzels, saying they were to take the sweet taste out of their mouth. Lizzie put a handful in her lap and couldn't decide which was more delicious, cinnamon rolls with tea, or stick pretzels with tea.

"Lizzie, you better not get up before you eat all those pretzels," Doddy Glick teased.

"I won't," Lizzie said, smiling back at him.

He asked Emma about Susie Beiler, if she had been in her grade, which turned the conversation to a very serious subject. Everyone was asking questions, with Dat and Mam answering them, relating in detail how it had all happened.

Marvin got up, saying it was time to get started if they were going to go fishing. "Did you bring your fishing poles?" he asked.

"We don't have any," Emma said matter-of-factly.

"Doesn't your dad ever go fishing?" he asked.

"No, he doesn't like to fish," Lizzie replied.

"Well, we have a few extra. You can use my old one, Lizzie, 'cause you probably won't catch any, anyhow," he said.

"Boy!" Lizzie said, insulted.

"Well, you're always talking and moving around. How are you going to fish with all those pretzels?" he asked, nodding toward the pretzels clutched in her fist.

"Don't worry about it, Marvin. I'll eat them on the way down to the pond," Lizzie huffed.

"All right, then. Elsie, I'll carry two poles and the can of worms, but you have to carry the other poles. And we really should have a jug of water, because we're going to get thirsty," he said, sizing up the length of the poles.

"I know. I'll ask Mam for tea, and get a bread bag of pretzels," Elsie said, opening the door to the kitchen.

With Marvin in the lead, they all started off, through the pasture gate, equipped with four fishing poles and a blue Maxwell House coffee can containing dirt and earthworms. Emma carried a metal Coleman jug of tea, while Lizzie clutched a plastic bag filled with stick pretzels.

Flies droned in the morning heat, sounding like quiet little airplanes. Small white butterflies hovered above the swampy spaces, darting and chasing each other above the grasses. The sun was already high in the sky, its warmth spreading across the pasture. They had to be careful where they walked, because the cow dung was scattered everywhere, and Elsie said sometimes horse-flies sat on it and they could bite almost as hard as a wasp.

"Wasps don't bite, Elsie—they sting," Marvin snorted.

"What's the difference? They both hurt. You know how bad it hurts when a horsefly bites you," Elsie re-torted, bending low to swat at a mosquito on her leg.

"A wasp's stinger comes from its backside. That's a real sting. A horsefly just bites, like a dog, with its mouth," Marvin said.

"How do you know? Did you ever see it?" Elsie asked.

"Of course."

"You didn't."

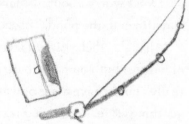

"You can *easily* see it when they bite," Marvin said, swatting at a horsefly with his straw hat.

Lizzie walked behind everyone else, thinking how Marvin always knew everything. He really did, too. Lizzie knew that he probably had seen a horsefly bite and a wasp sting. Marvin was like that, because he watched everything around him on the farm and in the woods. He also read a lot in books, like Lizzie did.

When they arrived at the pond, Elsie spread out an old blanket and they put the tea and pretzels in the middle. Elsie made sure the pretzel bag was closed securely, so the ants wouldn't crawl inside. Marvin took the coffee can of worms and started baiting hooks.

Lizzie looked out over the glassy surface of the pond. There were little swirls of tiny flies in some areas, and in others huge dragonflies skated on the surface, as if the pond was a mirror. They were pretty, green and blue with silver-veined wings, but when Lizzie told Elsie they were pretty, Elsie looked shocked.

"They're not, Lizzie," she said.

"Why aren't they?" Lizzie asked.

"Because they're snake doctors. When a snake gets sick, they make it better, and besides, they're poisonous, I think."

Emma's eyes opened wide. Lizzie watched the dragonflies uneasily. "Do they bite?" she asked.

"I think."

"Marvin, do dragonflies bite?" Lizzie asked worriedly.

"No. They're not dragonflies—they're snake doctors."

Lizzie shivered. That sounded so awful. Snakes gave

her the creeps, and she could just imagine how awful a
dragonfly could be. She wished she wouldn't have come
fishing because of the snake doctors.

"Here, Lizzie. Here's a pole with a worm on the hook.
Do you want to cast? I'll show you how," Marvin said.

So, with Marvin showing her which buttons to press
and how to throw the line out, Lizzie soon felt like a
real fisherman, even forgetting about the horrible snake
doctors. She sat in the tall grass, her pole resting on the
ground, her chin in her one hand, waiting. She thought
surely the worm must be quite drowned, but she waited
longer, not saying anything, and certainly not moving
around, so she could prove to Marvin that she could
hold still and not talk at all.

Marvin yelled and jerked on his fishing pole. He
started winding the little handle on his reel furiously,
being very careful not to let his fish get away. "I got one!
It's a big one, I can tell!" he shouted, bracing his feet
and turning the reel handle. The tip of his fishing pole
bent down in an arc, so Lizzie thought he must have a
huge fish.

"Marvin, you have a huge fish! Look at your pole!"
shouted Elsie.

"I know!" Marvin panted.

"Can I help you?" Emma asked, concerned that Marvin would get too tired with all that weight on the end of
the line.

"No, I'll get it," he breathed, working anxiously with
the reel. Lizzie watched carefully, to see what was on the
end of Marvin's line. A dark round head appeared, and

at first Lizzie thought it was a snake. Elsie saw the head at the same moment, and she put her hands up to her mouth and screamed. She just kept screaming as Marvin pulled up a huge brown snapping turtle. The hook was imbedded firmly in its lower lip, and it was hissing grotesquely, its mouth wide open to reveal a huge pink abyss.

Marvin yelled hoarsely, clearly panicking at that huge face with the gaping mouth. Elsie went on screaming. Emma started to cry, and Lizzie was dumbfounded. She wanted to scream, but nothing came out of her mouth except dry little horrified gasps.

"Let it go!" screamed Elsie.

"I can't. He'll drag away my fishing pole!" shrieked Marvin hoarsely.

"Cut the line! Cut the line!" howled Emma.

"I don't have a scissors!" Marvin was still pulling on the line, and the turtle was still hissing and resisting the pull of the hook. Marvin's face looked white and terrified, but he was still resolutely pulling on the fishing line.

"Go get Samuel!" yelled Marvin.

"Lizzie, run and get Samuel," Elsie said, running desperately toward her.

"By myself?"

"Yes, just go!"

So Lizzie took off as fast as her legs would carry her. She dodged cow dung, horseflies, bumblebees, and wasps, tripping over a clump of grass, but she got up and ran blindly on. Her breath came in painful little gasps, and her side hurt fiercely, yet she ran on. When she came to the pasture gate, she clambered up over the top, dropping to the ground on the other side. She was gasping for breath, but her legs churned determinedly up the gravel drive and across the well-kept lawn. She tore open the kettle house door and squawked hoarsely, "Somebody come!"

Instantly everyone got up from the table, Mam's face a picture of horror.

"What happened?" they all cried, as if one voice.

"M-Marvin! He . . . he . . . he has a snapping turtle on his fishing line!" she gasped, clutching her aching side as she struggled for breath.

Everyone sat down weakly, and Grandpa Glick said, "Whew!" Grandma Glick took Lizzie's hand and helped her to a chair, while Mam brought her a drink of water.

Samuel and Malinda raced out the door, chattering about those turtles that were going to take over the pond.

"I want to see what Samuel's going to do!" Lizzie said, sliding off the chair, running into the kettle house, and banging the door behind her. She couldn't catch up with Samuel and Malinda, but she kept running and walking fast until she reached the pond.

"Marvin, you must have used an awfully huge hook!" Samuel said.

"I did, I guess," Marvin panted.

"Here, give me your pole."

They all stood in a group, watching with wide eyes as Samuel hauled the angry turtle up on the grassy bank.

Lizzie could see its yellow eyes, unblinking and angry, as the boys tried to cut the line.

"Why don't you have a pocketknife?" Samuel asked, keeping a wary eye on the turtle.

"Oh, I do," Marvin said, digging in his pocket. He pulled out a small red folding knife, which he promptly unfolded, handing it to Samuel who quickly cut the sturdy line, releasing the angry turtle. It lumbered off, sliding back into the swampy area where the bulrushes grew.

"Now it has that hook stuck in its mouth, Marvin," Samuel said.

"You shouldn't be fishing with such a big hook," Malinda told Marvin.

"I don't care if the turtle dies. I wish it would," Marvin defended himself with false bravado.

"Well, you sure scared everyone who was sitting around the kitchen table," Samuel said.

"Why?"

"Well, because. Lizzie, the poor thing, was all out of breath and terrified. We thought someone had drowned or something!"

"Aaah, it wasn't that bad. It was just an old snapping turtle. They don't even bite," Marvin said self-consciously, scratching his stomach with his pocketknife.

"Put a smaller hook on your line, Marvin. We're going to go up now," said Samuel, and he and Malinda walked off through the pasture. As soon as they were gone, Elsie told Marvin he was, too, scared of those horrible creatures.

"They don't bite!" Marvin insisted.

"Then why were you jumping around on the bank, yelling and screaming?" Elsie wanted to know.

"Well, you would, too."

"Let's drink tea and eat pretzels," Lizzie suggested, feeling thirsty after her run across the pasture.

"All right," everyone agreed.

So they sat on the old blanket, and Elsie passed cups of cold tea to everyone. They talked about snapping turtles, and Emma said that they could easily bite off a finger.

"How do you know?" Marvin asked, chomping on a pretzel, crumbs falling all over his legs.

"Swallow before you talk, Marvin," Elsie said.

So Marvin swallowed obediently and wiped his mouth on his shirtsleeve before taking huge gulps of cold tea.

"Hey! You know what?" he asked excitedly.

"What?" Lizzie asked.

"I just found out the other day that if you hold up a guinea pig by its tail, its eyes will fall out. That is true," he said.

"Really?" Emma asked.

"Mm-hmm. When we're done fishing, I'll show you all Samuel's guinea pigs, and I guarantee you if you try and hold it by its tail, the eyes fall right out of its head."

"Must be they have really weak eyes," Emma snorted.

"They do," Marvin assured her.

Lizzie thought about snapping turtles, snake doctors, and guinea pigs. She watched Marvin with narrowed eyes, wondering if he actually knew as much as he claimed. She wasn't too sure he hadn't been terribly afraid of that old snapping turtle, and she believed every word Emma said about them snapping off a finger. Also, she wasn't too sure about this snake doctor deal, either, because they were pretty insects; only now she would always eye them with suspicion, because Elsie said they were poisonous. She would ask Dat.

When they came to the barn that afternoon, the furry little guinea pigs were bustling around their pens, in clean sawdust, watching Lizzie with bright black eyes. They were so cute that she wanted to take one home in the buggy with them.

"Go ahead, pick one up by its tail," Marvin told Lizzie. "Here."

He caught one with a swift scoop of his hand, holding the little ball of fur out to her. Lizzie tried tentatively to find the tail, but no matter how hard she looked, there was none.

"This one doesn't have a tail," she said innocently.

Marvin and Elsie laughed and laughed. Marvin slapped his knee because he knew guinea pigs never have tails, so it was a joke.

Lizzie didn't think it was one bit funny, and she even told Emma on the way home that she didn't like Marvin nearly as much as she used to.

The Miller Relatives Visit

Mam could not hide the excitement in her eyes when she opened a letter from her brother's wife who lived in Jefferson County.

"Melvin! Guess what? Elis are coming for a visit! Next Saturday, she writes, and they're going to try and bring Junior's along! Oh, I haven't seen them for so long—this is just wonderful!" She smoothed back her hair, pulling her covering over her ears, and adjusted a pin in her dress. Mam always pulled her covering over her ears when she was excited or nervous, so Lizzie thought she must be very happy if she did all three things.

"Well, good!" Dat said.

"Oh my, what will I have for dinner? Mary wrote she'll bring a pan of dressing, and if Juniors come along, she'll bring a dessert. Let me see. I could have fried chicken. The butcher truck comes on Thursday, so I think my chicken would keep till Saturday. Mashed

potatoes, or should I have scalloped potatoes, or just
potatoes with a cheese sauce? What about a vegetable?
String beans? Or peas? I think maybe corn, but I don't
want to use all my corn too soon. I could make Jell-O
salad, or maybe macaroni salad would be easier."

Mam was known to be a good cook, and she knew it,
so when company came, it was her delight to impress
the visitors with her delicious meals. She would plan
and worry, fussing and stewing about what went well
together, and if it was all too fattening, too sweet, or too
heavy. Besides, she was on a budget and didn't have a
lot of money to spend on expensive things, so she would
need to plan carefully.

"We'll just set lawn chairs under the apple trees in the
yard," Dat said.

"Yes, you can, Melvin. Oh, I'm so anxious to see
them!" Mam was really quite beside herself, and Emma
was smiling happily. Lizzie was happy for Mam, too, of
course, but she was worrying about how many cousins
were coming along. She didn't know them very well, and
she felt uncomfortable and shy around them, especially
Elis' boys. They probably wouldn't come along, Lizzie
consoled herself, because they were older than she and
Emma were.

Lizzie loved when company came to their house, and
she especially liked to go away on Sunday to her friends'
houses. But when people came to visit who had children
their age, it usually made Lizzie feel awkward, because
she didn't know what to say. Emma didn't like to make
up with strangers, either, although it seemed to Lizzie

she was better at it.

So the whole week, while Mam cleaned the house and fussed about her two brothers and their wives coming for a visit, Lizzie worried. She had asked Mam how many children were coming along, and Mam said probably Elis' Edna, because Edna was almost exactly their age. That depressed Lizzie since she could not remember much about Edna, and what were they going to say? It was too hot to play in the playhouse, and besides, Edna might not want to play doll. They could swing, but that never lasted very long, and the bumblebees flew under the eaves of the kettle house by the swing set.

By Friday, Lizzie had worried herself into a state of despair. She flopped on a kitchen chair and sighed. She cleared her throat and made tapping noises with her fingernails on the plastic tablecloth. She got a drink out of the refrigerator, leaving the door open too long so Mam would notice her. But Mam was bent over the counter, squinting at a recipe card through her glasses, stirring something on the stove and muttering to herself.

"Mam," Lizzie ventured.

"Not now, Lizzie," Mam said, squinting and stirring.

Lizzie sighed and sat on the kitchen chair. She drank some water and wondered if the Jefferson County cousins were talkative, or if they would all stand around and look at each other.

When Emma bustled into the kitchen with Jason and Mandy, Lizzie looked at Emma, wondering why she wasn't worrying about the company. Emma went to the refrigerator and got a pitcher of juice, getting two plastic cups for Jason and Mandy.

Lizzie slid down in her chair and kicked the table leg. She told Mandy not to spill her juice. Mandy stood with her little hands on her hips and watched Lizzie kick the table leg. "How can I not spill it?" she asked.

"Why?"

"Because you're just kicking the table leg," Mandy replied, sliding over on the bench.

Lizzie stopped and watched Emma wiping up little drops of spilled juice. She wiped once with the wet soapy dishrag, then wiped it again to make sure it wasn't sticky, because she couldn't stand to rest her elbows on a sticky tabletop. Lizzie loved to put her mouth down to the spilled drops and make a slurping noise, because it cleaned up the juice and was a lot more fun.

"Emma."

"Hmm?"

"Do you think Elis' Edna will come along? And do they talk? Our cousins, I mean," Lizzie said, looking down at the tablecloth and pleating it with her fingers.

"I don't know, Lizzie. I guess they'll talk if we do," Emma said matter-of-factly.

"Oh." That was all Lizzie said, because there wasn't anything she could say. She sighed, noticing drops of juice on the kitchen linoleum and thinking that Emma would clean it up if she knew. Oh well, she would just have to wait and see about Saturday and the cousins.

· · · · · ·

When Saturday came, it seemed as if the whole house was bursting with cousins, aunts, and uncles. They were

all shapes, sorts, and sizes, and Lizzie thought they all
looked very strange. Some of the older boys had very
thick, curly hair, reminding Lizzie of a picture she had
seen in a history book of a pirate. She wondered if
Jason's hair would look like that when he was older,
pitying him with her whole heart.

The girls wore different coverings and did not comb
their hair back in sleek rolls like Emma and Lizzie. They
combed their hair straight back, loosely, and it was thick
and wavy and shiny. Lizzie was ashamed of her tight
rolls, wishing she could comb her hair like the Jefferson
County cousins.

Dat and Mam were both very happy, chattering and
laughing with Mam's brothers and their wives. Lizzie
liked Mary and Clara, who were both small with little
round eyes and noses. She thought they looked a lot
like Billy Beaver in her reading book. They both were
very kind, talking to Emma and Lizzie and
playing with Jason and exclaiming about
his curls.

"Edna, Fronie, come play with Lizzie
and Emma," Mary said.

"You'll have to get used to each
other sometime," said Mary with
a smile. She
pushed Edna
forward, and
she shrugged
her shoulders

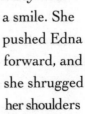

to get rid of her hand. She smiled shyly at Emma, and
Emma smiled back. Fronie stood behind Edna and
looked at both of them with a bored expression. Lizzie's
heart sank, because she just knew this wasn't going to
work. How could you become friends with someone you
didn't know?

Emma stepped forward and bravely asked Edna if
she wanted to swing, or look at Dolly, the pony. Edna
smiled and shrugged her shoulders, so Emma started
out the door with a nervous Lizzie and a bored Fronie in
tow.

"We have only one pony now, because Dat sold
Teeny and Tiny," Emma offered.

Edna snorted. "Who were Teeny and Tiny?"

Fronie snickered behind Lizzie.

Emma ventured on bravely, "Oh, they were little ponies. So small that Dat could bend over them and touch
the ground on the other side. That's why we called them
Teeny and Tiny."

"Why don't you have them anymore?" asked Edna.

"We sold them at an auction. Lizzie and I drove them
in the ring with a little spring wagon Dat made," Emma
said.

"Hah-ah!" Fronie said, wide-eyed.

"Did you really?" Edna asked, amazed.

Before Lizzie even thought, she blurted out, "And
when we drove around the ring, the people were clapping and standing up to see us better."

"Did they get sold that day?" Fronie asked.

"Mm-hmm. Oh yes, of course," Lizzie assured her.

They had reached the barn, and as Emma flung
open the door, Dolly nickered as she always did. Lizzie
smoothed back her forelocks, stroked her neck, and
murmured to her in pony language. Fronie and Edna
watched as Emma opened the gate. They scurried back
to the farthest wall as Dolly trotted to the water trough.

"She won't hurt you," Lizzie said.

"I'm not used to ponies, so they kind of scare me,"
Edna admitted.

"I'm not a bit scared. Watch!" And with that, Lizzie
jumped up on Dolly's back, or at least tried to, but Dolly
sidestepped, and Lizzie slid off, falling flat on her stomach in the loose straw and dirt on top of the concrete
floor.

"Oof!" Lizzie's breath was knocked out of her, causing her to grasp her stomach, making all kinds of strange
noises as she struggled to regain her breathing. She sat
on the concrete, gasping and holding her stomach, reel-
ing from the unexpected blow.

Emma bent over her. "Lizzie!"

"What? You know I can't answer you!" Lizzie was really upset, because how was she supposed to talk with no breath? She glanced at Fronie and Edna, whose faces were a mixture of concern and holding back their giggles. This really upset Lizzie, because how dare they laugh at her when she couldn't get her breath? She looked down at her legs, covered with dirt and straw, and her dress had slid up too far, too. She felt so utterly humiliated, so ashamed of herself, that she jumped up and slapped the straw off her legs, still gasping for breath.

"It isn't funny, either!" she yelled as loud as she could.

"Nobody's laughing," Edna assured her kindly.

"Yes, you are—you know you are!" Lizzie shouted, her face flaming with shame and embarrassment.

"Lizzie! I'm going to tell Mam," Emma said, struggling to keep her distress from showing.

"Go ahead! See if I care!" shouted Lizzie, flouncing out of the barn, tears threatening to completely upset any trace of pride she may have kept. She ran across the yard, yanked open the door of the playhouse, and flopped on the old couch. A spring that stuck up through the upholstery scraped her leg, and she winced as a deep scratch appeared.

She sat up, smoothed her hair, and picked a piece of straw off her head. She looked at it, and decided very firmly that she did not like company at her house, and she didn't like the Jefferson County cousins at all. She knew they were laughing at her, that was all there was to it. She wished they'd all go home so she would never have to see them again.

There was a slight sound on the creaky old boards of the playhouse porch. Lizzie lay as still as she possibly could, holding her breath, hoping no one would find her, because she didn't feel like trying to be nice all over again. She had really made a mess out of everything, so what was the use starting over? They already knew Lizzie was a show-off and a loser.

The door creaked slowly open, and a hesitant voice whispered, "Lizzie."

Lizzie kept her back turned, but was too polite not to answer. "Hmm?"

"Can I come in?"

Lizzie rolled over and sat up, pulling down her dress and smoothing her hair. She lifted humiliated eyes to find Edna standing shyly inside the door, her hands clasped properly in front of her. Her small brown eyes twinkled in her elfin brown face, as she calmly watched Lizzie desperately smoothing her dress.

"Lizzie, it's okay. Dolly stepped way over, and I guarantee if she wouldn't have done that, you would have been easily able to scramble up on her back." She came forward and sat on the corner of the couch, reaching out hesitantly to touch Lizzie's knee. "Don't feel bad, Lizzie, it was the pony's fault, not yours. I can see that you are used to being around ponies, and you aren't near as scared of them as I am. I wouldn't even lead Dolly out of her pen—not even near!"

Lizzie kept looking at the old rug at her feet, pushing her toes into the torn old rags. She turned her head slowly and met Edna's brown eyes that actually seemed to be smiling all the time, even if her mouth wasn't. They both started with just a slight, tentative turnup of the corners of their mouth, but it became steadily wider as their eyes picked up the feelings between them. Lizzie just kept smiling, all her teeth showing, and Edna smiled back.

"Do you really think it was Dolly's fault?" Lizzie asked.

"Of course."

Lizzie sat up straight, pulled in her stomach, and lined up her feet on the old rag rug. She sighed and told Edna she was so glad, because it really was the way ponies were. They were jumpy sometimes, and you could never tell what they would do next, even old Dolly. Edna nodded her head in agreement, because she believed every word.

"Edna, I really like you. I wish you wouldn't live quite so far away, because then we could go to school together. We'd be best friends, wouldn't we?"

"Of course!" Edna agreed, clasping Lizzie's hand firmly in her own. Lizzie was so consumed with grateful feelings to Edna that she knew without a doubt that she was one of the nicest girls she had ever met. She felt so proud that Edna was her real cousin.

"Lizzie! Edna!"

They looked together, and Lizzie ran to the door.

"What?"

"Mam said it's time for dinner. Hurry up! Nobody

knew where you were!" Emma shouted.

Edna and Lizzie dashed out the playhouse door, pounding up the steps to the kitchen. They were laughing and talking as they threw open the screen door.

"Mam, can I sit beside Edna?" Lizzie beamed.

Mam and Mary smiled at each other as their little girls sat close together on the bench, heads bent together, giggling, as Edna told Lizzie a story.

Mam bustled around the kitchen, filling water glasses and making sure everyone could reach every dish.

Lizzie clasped her hands between her knees and swung her feet, leaning her chest against the table. Everything looked so good that her mouth watered. Mam was a good cook, and Lizzie could hardly wait to taste everything. There were glass dishes of applesauce and little sweet pickles on tiny glass plates. Mounds of steaming mashed potatoes had a puddle of brown butter in the middle, like a little brown pond. Fried chicken was heaped on big blue trays, and gravy was put in glass gravy bowls. Mam never made greasy gravy—it was always light brown in color, not too thick and not too thin.

Mam had made macaroni salad, peas with a white sauce, and fresh, hot rolls with strawberry jelly and butter. Mam had bought real butter for company, which was really different, because they always used margarine. Mam said it was much cheaper and almost as good.

The grownups' chatter ceased, and Lizzie knew it was time to have a silent prayer, or "put patties down," as the children said. Amish people never prayed out loud as English people did, so Lizzie always felt ill at ease if she

heard someone praying out loud. Dat always told them
to thank the Lord for their food, and to look down at
their plates as they prayed. Lizzie often forgot to pray,
because she was peeping at someone and thinking other
thoughts. She didn't know why, but it seemed she could
never concentrate to pray a long prayer when everyone put patties down. She tried hard, though, because
Emma lowered her head very far and her lips moved
as she said her silent prayer. Lizzie often watched her
sideways, fascinated by her goodness.

When everyone's head was raised, Dat said, "Help
yourselves, and if you can't reach something, don't be
afraid to say so." Everyone smiled, acknowledging Dat's
welcome, as bowls of food were passed. The clatter of
silverware, and the grownups' laughter and conversation
were a bit overwhelming, so Edna and Lizzie just ate.

They smiled shyly at each other as they passed dish
after dish and ate hungrily. Edna was a bit heavy, too,
Lizzie could tell, because her plate was piled high with
lots of food.

Mam had made pecan pie, apple pie, and pumpkin
pie for dessert. She served it with vanilla ice cream and
frozen strawberries, drawing 'oohs' and 'aahs' from the
appreciative guests. Dat beamed as Mam's brothers and
their wives praised her cooking.

"Annie!" boomed Uncle Eli. "You are about the best
cook in all of Pennsylvania, maybe even Ohio!"

"Oh, now, stop it," Mam said, bowing her head in
humility. But her cheeks were flushed with pleasure,
and her eyes were shining as she spooned up her vanilla

ice cream and strawberries. Lizzie was so glad Mam was a good cook and felt very proud of her. Dat was telling Uncle Eli that was why he had to mow the yard in the evening, because he ate too well.

After dinner the men sat under the apple trees in the yard, and Lizzie, Edna, Emma, and Fronie played in the playhouse. Fronie was the mom, and Emma was the dad, so Edna and Lizzie were the children. They had so much fun that when it was time to start packing up to return to Jefferson County, Edna said she had a notion to stay in the playhouse, under the couch, so Uncle Eli couldn't find her.

Lizzie put her hand over her mouth and giggled. She was so glad Edna liked her, because Lizzie just loved Edna. She liked Fronie, too, of course, but Edna was just special.

When they all piled into the van, Lizzie stood with Edna and took her hand. "Will you write to me when Aunt Mary writes to Mam?" she asked.

"Oh, of course I will, if you write me back," Edna replied, squeezing Lizzie's hand.

"'Bye, Edna," Lizzie said soberly.

"'Bye, Lizzie," said Edna, as she stepped up and sat beside Fronie. Lizzie stepped back and waved as Mam and Dat said their good byes, closing the door and stepping back as the van moved slowly off.

Lizzie waved and waved, until they turned onto the road going past their house. She turned to Emma and they looked at each other. "Boy, Emma," Lizzie breathed, "making friends isn't even one bit hard."

They both agreed that they were their best cousins ever, and wished they could comb their hair like the Jefferson County cousins.

chapter 13

Potato Soup

After the Jefferson County cousins left, Lizzie was often feeling restless, which she didn't understand. She would soon be nine years old and school would be starting, but she felt bored, even with Dolly and the playhouse. Some days she even wished she did not have to go to school, because it was just the same as the year before.

Mam was busy sewing their new school clothes, even dresses and little black pinafore-style aprons for Mandy, because she would be in first grade this year. That was another reason Lizzie did not want to return to school in a few weeks. What if Mandy cried? What if she stood in singing class and burst into sobs like Lizzie had done? Mandy was so little, pale, and skinny that if she cried, there was just no way Lizzie could stand it. It just ruined Lizzie's whole summer, worrying about Mandy entering first grade.

Not just that; there was another thing that really worried Lizzie. Mam spent longer hours in the harness shop and snapped at Dat more often, leaving Dat sighing at the supper table.

It was still warm in the kitchen at supper, with a hot, dry breeze blowing through the window. Mam's face was flushed and perspiring, making her look more tired than ever. Lizzie figured their money from selling Teeny and Tiny was all gone, because they ate a lot of potato soup, and they got only one new school dress. The other dresses were old Sunday dresses that Mam lengthened.

She wished they could do something fun before school started. Her friend Betty's family had gone to the zoo, and Betty told Lizzie it was the most amazing thing she had ever seen. The elephants were as big as a house, and walked around grabbing people with their waving trunks. Lizzie asked Mam if that was true, and Mam said probably not the people, that Betty had meant they grabbed chunks of hay and put it in their mouth. Lizzie told Mam that Betty stretched the truth; anyhow she always did. Mam told Lizzie she shouldn't be jealous — that was from the devil. Lizzie wasn't jealous, really; she just wished with all her heart they could go to the zoo and see the elephants.

"Mam," Lizzie said, leaning on the harness shop counter.

Mam didn't answer, so Lizzie just watched them working for a while. It was almost time to close the shop after a long, hot day, and they were trying to finish an order of halters. Dat's shirt was wet across his back from perspiration, and he was bending over his sewing machine as he sewed.

Mam had her back turned, snipping threads and riveting the halters on a machine. Her face was red and flushed, her mouth drawn in a tight line, her dark hair escaping the confines of her covering. They weren't talking, bantering back and forth as they always did, and the shop seemed strangely quiet and hostile without Dat's happy whistling.

Lizzie rested her chin on her hands and wished Dat would whistle. Jason and Mandy came in through the back door, the screen door slamming as they entered. Mandy's dress had a huge rip in the hem, and her face was smeared with dirt. Jason was wearing a shirt that was much too small for him, and his diaper was loose and falling down. Lizzie knew he was soaking wet, as usual. His face was grimy and his nose was running, with his curls sticking out much worse than they should have if someone would have bothered combing them.

"Mam! Mam!" Jason slapped Mam's leg.

"What, Jase?" Mam snapped, barely noticing that he was there.

"Annie, I think he needs a clean diaper," Dat said, watching Jason after he turned from the sewing machine.

"Lizzie, go change Jason," Mam said.

Lizzie sighed and walked behind the counter, grabbing his hand. He looked startled, peered into Lizzie's face, and pulled away.

"No," he said, quite plainly.

Lizzie was not in the mood to run after him, because it was too warm in the shop and everybody was too grouchy. She grabbed his arm and pulled, causing him to sit down in the middle of the scattered leather and thread, and howl loudly.

"Come on, Jason!" Lizzie yelled.

Dat whirled around on his stool, glaring at her. "Stop that, Lizzie! Now go on and listen to your mother, or I'll have to make you," he growled. He ran a hand through his unkempt hair, turning back to his sewing.

Lizzie stooped and picked up a wailing Jason, wrapping her arms around his grimy little stomach. She shuffled around the counter with him as Mandy followed.

"Stop your yelling!" Lizzie said, between gritted teeth. "Or I'll smack you as hard as I can!" She tightened her hold on his stomach as he kicked and screamed in protest. His curls stuck against Lizzie's mouth, but she kept on struggling up the stairs, her head held high so she could breathe. As she entered the living room, she could hardly make her way to the bathroom because of toys, afghans, pillows, bottles, spilled juice, and clutter everywhere.

Emma stuck her head around the kitchen door. She watched as Lizzie entered the bathroom and smiled to herself. Must be Mam made Lizzie change Jason's diaper, and Emma thought that didn't hurt Lizzie one bit. She went back to folding laundry, carefully lining up the washcloths in neat little squares. She kept smiling as Jason's howls increased and Lizzie kept telling him to be quiet. After she was done changing him, she could help clean up the house, too.

Suddenly there was a sickening thump. A hard, solid sound that Emma knew instantly was serious. Jason's howls turned into a serious cry of pain, and Lizzie yelled for Emma, who dropped a washcloth and ran. Sure enough, he had fallen off the countertop, and already a big, purple bruise was forming on his cheek where he had hit the corner of the clothes hamper.

"Lizzie, you have to watch him," Emma scolded.

Lizzie's face was red with perspiration, and she was hopping mad. "Emma, why couldn't you change him? You know I'm too little to do this. I can hardly handle him, and you know it!" she wailed.

This was the scene Mam stepped into when she wended her tired way up the back stairs to make supper. Mandy sat on the recliner with large, scared eyes, while Jason cried in pain, Lizzie yelled, and Emma tried to fix everything, just like a little mother. Mam's tired eyes took in the trash and toys all over the living room and the half-folded laundry, wondering what she would make for supper in thirty minutes.

She took Jason from Emma, folding him in her arms, soothing his battered little cheek with tender fingers. "There, there, sweetie-pie. There, there," she crooned, as his crying changed to soft little sobs. She sat down wearily, cuddling Jason against her as Mandy came to lay her head on Mam's arm. She bent to plant a kiss on top of her head, one arm circling around her thin little body.

"What happened, Emma?" she asked.

Emma was back at the kitchen table, carefully folding the washcloths. She patted a neat square and turned to face her mother. "Oh, Lizzie was changing him and he didn't want her to. He was crying and screaming, and I guess she wasn't watching him right, because he fell off the countertop somehow." Emma spread her hands helplessly, shrugging her shoulders.

Mam sighed. She wiped her hand across her brow and closed her eyes for a moment. "Well, no doubt about it, I have to quit working in the shop so late in the evening. This just doesn't make any sense. I don't even have time to care for my little ones anymore," she said.

"Mam, I'm really hungry. Even our pretzels are all gone," Mandy whined.

"Yes, I know, Mandy. I used all my grocery money to cook for Elis' and Juniors'. I guess I shouldn't have, but . . ." Her voice trailed off wistfully. She got up and set Jason on the floor, where he promptly started crying again.

The kitchen door opened and Dat came in, looking as hot and tired as Mam. He looked at Jason, walked over, and scooped him up. "Hey, what's the matter here? Are you just as warm as the rest of us?" he asked, sitting at the kitchen table. "What's for supper?"

Mam smiled weakly. "I don't know."

"Well, we could have potato soup," Dat suggested.

Quite unexpectedly, Mam burst out laughing. She just sat at the kitchen table and kept laughing until tears rolled down her cheeks. Dat watched her, and soon he began to laugh too. "What's so funny, Annie?"

"Oh, I was just thinking about an old rhyme, which, if we're not careful, is going to be very true," she said. "Soup for dinner, soup for supper, soup, soup, soup!"

"Potato soup is good, Annie. If you make some, we could take the evening off and go for a drive with Red,"

Dat suggested.

"Yes! Yes!" Lizzie shouted. "Let's go for a picnic! Please! Let's go for a long drive and roast hot dogs in a woods with a creek!"

Dat looked at Mam and raised his eyebrows. Mandy hopped up and down, twirling around in the middle of the kitchen floor, while Jason clapped his hands and squealed, just because everyone else was excited.

Mam shook her head. "We have no food for a picnic, Lizzie. My groceries are all gone, and our money is all gone, too. So what would we do for a picnic?"

Emma was still folding clothes, but she stopped and looked at Mam. "We still have saltine crackers, Mam. We could put peanut butter and jelly between them. We still have some molasses cookies, too," she said, taking the planning of this picnic quite seriously.

Dat grinned. "I know. A pot of potato soup wrapped in an old quilt would be just fine. I'm hungry for potato soup!"

Mam laughed and got out of her chair. "Okay, potato soup it will be. Emma, you finish the laundry and I'll get the food ready. Lizzie, you make sure everyone has clean clothes and wash Mandy's face and hands. Jason's, too."

"I can wash my own face," Mandy said importantly.

Lizzie ran off with Mandy to change into clean everyday clothes. They pitched their soiled clothes into the hamper and dashed into the bathroom to wash their faces.

"Do we need to have our hair combed?" Lizzie yelled.

"No!" Mam shouted.

Mandy giggled as she splashed soapy water all over her face. "Lizzie, remember when you slopped all that water in the bathroom?" she asked, spluttering.

"Don't talk about that, Mandy," Lizzie said, still smarting about the incident.

When Dat led Red up to the house, everyone was ready to go. Emma carried the brown wicker picnic basket, and Lizzie brought a metal Thermos, ice jingling as it banged against her leg. Mandy brought an old quilt, as Dat opened the big door on the back of the buggy. They tucked everything inside, as Mam brought the soup wrapped in an old comforter. She dashed back up the stairs for a cardboard box containing soup plates, cups, and spoons, grabbing Jason on her way out the door.

The girls piled in the back, and Dat and Mam sat on the front seat, with Jason on Mam's lap. All the doors and windows were open, because it was a very sultry evening, the air heavy with late summer humidity. As they started off, Mam looked at the sky, her brow furrowed.

"Melvin, do you suppose we'll have a thunderstorm?" she asked.

"I guess if one comes up, we will," Dat teased, and Mam pushed him with her elbow. Dat smiled and waved to Aaron Beiler, who was sweeping his sidewalk.

Lizzie sighed. She was so glad everyone was happy this evening. Everything in the whole world was fine, as long as Mam and Dat were happy. She really didn't mind an awful lot that they had to eat potato soup in-

stead of roasted hot dogs on a roll with ketchup, even if
that was one of her favorite foods.

Whenever Lizzie did roast a hot dog, she always
burnt it until it was all black and wrinkled and greasy.
If you piled on a lot of ketchup, it was the best-tasting
thing, especially if the roll was nice and soft.

The breeze was warm, but the air felt so nice as it
blew through the buggy. Red's mane blew in the warm
air, but he was beginning to sweat. Dat was always careful to wash Red with the hose and a brush before they
went away in the summer. When Dat did that, Red just
became wet with sweat, but if Red was dirty, the clear
sweat turned to a white foam that blew back into the
buggy. Dat always told Lizzie he washed Red mostly
because he didn't like the white foam, because English
people always pitied a sweating horse; and it did look
cruel if a horse was covered with white foam on a warm
day.

Gravel crunched under the steel wheels as they
turned onto a dirt road. Red's feet threw little pieces of
it against the front of the buggy, making pinging noises.
They passed a tumbledown barbed wire fence, and posts
sagging and weeds growing almost waist high. There
were a few skinny cows inside the fence, and a barn
that had no paint on it, just black boards, and a reddish-
brown rusty roof. The house was under thick trees,
but there wasn't much left of it, except a few walls and
broken windows.

"Why is that farm so tumbledown?" asked Lizzie.

"Oh, that's old Clarence Heath's place," Dat said. "It's

just a shame. His wife left him years ago, they say, and it got the best of him. He hasn't been right ever since. His one boy joined the Army and was killed, and I think he still has a daughter somewhere. It's a pity. That used to be a nice place. They say he tried to burn the house down one night because he claimed it was haunted."

"What's 'haunted'?" Emma asked, absentmindedly digging her finger in one ear. She examined the tip of her finger, her head bent to the side to see better. Lizzie frowned at her.

"Haunted? That means people claim to hear ghosts, strange noises, and people walking, but they can't see anyone. That kind of thing," Dat said.

Lizzie sat straight up, her eyes opening wide. "You mean . . . You mean, they actually saw a ghost in that house?" she asked shrilly, her heart starting to beat faster. She strained to look out the back window for a look at this haunted house. She imagined long white ghosts hovering in the trees above it. There was no such thing as a ghost. There couldn't be real ones. What did Dat mean, it got the best of that man? Did he mean the ghost or his wife or his boy or the Army? A whirl of scary thoughts flew around Lizzie's head until she felt panicky.

"What do you mean, Dat? What got the best of that man?" Lizzie blurted out. "You mean the ghosts? Can ghosts get you?" She was hot all over, then shivered, because she felt cold.

Mam nudged Dat and gave him a warning look. *Time to stop talking about these things,* her eyes said. Dat acknowledged her look and nodded his head slightly. "Ach, Lizzie, it's just people talking. There is absolutely no such thing as a ghost. When we say something got the best of him, it means he was never quite the same after his wife left him."

"Why did she leave him?" Lizzie asked. She pitied Clarence Heath so much she could hardly stand the thought.

"I have no idea. Maybe they were fighting," Dat said.

"Why was his son killed in the Army?" Lizzie asked.

"Look! Here is a perfect spot," Mam said pointing.

"Dat! Why was his son killed?" Lizzie insisted.

"I don't know, Lizzie. Okay, this looks nice," Dat agreed, turning Red into a little lane that wound its way into a grassy woods. The trees weren't real thick, yet there was plenty of shade to spread their quilt. Dat pulled on the reins, stopping Red under a huge, spreading oak tree. Red threw his head up and down, because he wanted to be rid of the rein that held it up.

"Here we are!" Dat sang out, as he stepped down backwards. The first thing he always did when they stopped was unhook the rein. Red lowered his head gratefully, reaching out and stretching his neck. Then he lifted it as high as before, even if the rein wasn't attached, his ears pricked forward.

Mam spread the quilt, while the children scampered around the grass, dodging behind the heavy trunks of the old trees. Jason yelled as he fell down flat on his stomach, but he got up and toddled off again.

It was so nice and cool under the massive trees, with the

green grass soft and cool around the quilt. Mam was smiling as she unpacked the picnic basket, and Dat whistled softly as he tied Red to the branch of a maple tree.

They all sat around the quilt as Mam ladled the steaming soup into their plates. Dat passed saltine crackers, which they crumbled into the milky broth. Mam had packed a container of applesauce, so Lizzie crunched extra crackers into her bowl of soup until they were all soaked and her soup was like a stiff pudding. Then she put a big spoonful of applesauce beside it, and every time she took a bite of soup, she added a bit of applesauce. It was delicious, out in the open air, under the big green trees.

After they had eaten their soup, they ate crackers with peanut butter and jelly, washed down with frosty glasses of orange Tang. Mam passed a plastic container of molasses cookies, sugar crystals sprinkled on top, with wide cracks across the top. Lizzie loved molasses cookies, because they were both crispy and chewy. It was the only cookie that could be like that.

"Now, who missed hot dogs?" Dat asked.

"Not me," Lizzie answered.

Mam smiled and shook her head. "Who would ever go on a picnic with potato soup, except us?"

"It's much nicer here than at home," Dat answered.

"Yes, it is a welcome break from the heat. And we're so terribly busy, Melvin. If only the harness shop would pay better," she said, her voice trailing off quietly.

Dat covered Mam's hand with his own. He looked at her, saying, "Annie, it will be all right. You wait and see. Things will get better. When cooler weather comes, people will be buying more shoes and saddle blankets and things. I just know they will."

"I know," Mam said quietly.

Lizzie hated to have this perfect evening spoiled, so she jumped up and told Emma and Mandy she was going to explore. They ran under the trees, finding mushrooms that looked like toadstools, little blue flowers that hung from the stems like bells, and fistfuls of pretty white and blue stones. They did not notice the darkening evening sky, until a rumble of thunder sounded in the distance.

Dat called them back, as Mam hurried to pack the remains of the lunch. Emma hurried to help put everything in the buggy, as Lizzie found a container to put the beautiful stones in.

Red was restless and eager to get started. He pranced a bit, tossing his head, but held still long enough for Mam and the girls to climb in and settle themselves.

The woods seemed dark and sinister now, as lightning

flashed in the distance, casting an eerie glow across the waving leaves.

"I think we can beat the storm home," Dat said. He called to Red, and they lurched out of the woods, up the grassy lane to the gravel road. Red sensed the storm in the air, so his ears flicked back and then forward as his speed increased. Dat had to use both hands to hold him as they raced along, gravel spitting against the buggy.

Mam started singing softly. Emma hummed along. After a mile or so, Red settled down to a nice trot, so Dat joined in the singing. He started his favorite song, the one Lizzie loved because he sang it so fast, and often his eyes twinkled and he tapped his foot.

> *"There's a dark and troubled side of life,*
> *There's a bright and a sunny side, too;*
> *Though we meet with the darkness and strife,*
> *The sunny side we always may view."*

> *"Keep on the sunny side, always on the sunny side,*
> *Keep on the sunny side of life;*
> *It will help us every day, it will brighten all our way,*
> *If we keep on the sunny side of life."*

Lightning flashed and thunder growled as Red pulled the buggy steadily on the gravel road. The wind bent over the tall weeds that grew against the sagging fence, as they passed the old, unkempt farm. But Lizzie didn't mind thinking about ghosts, and the Army, or thunder, or anything. It was so cozy and safe in the buggy when Mam and Dat sang together that nothing really scared Lizzie.

She sang heartily, tapping her hand on her knee, and feeling so good and so safe that not even God or the end of the world gave her the blues. She guessed God must like when they sang, because Mam said He did. Lizzie hoped He liked this song.

chapter 14

A Lesson Learned

Lizzie arranged her skirt across her legs and wiggled into a better position. She was sitting in an old lawn chair under the apple tree, her nose in a book, and a little plastic bag of pretzels on her lap. There was a slight breeze stirring the leaves on the apple trees, and katydids and crickets were chirping and clicking away. Lizzie didn't really hear them, only in the background when she reached for another pretzel. She was getting awfully thirsty because of the salty pretzels, but the book was much too interesting to put down.

The book was called *Black Beauty*. Of all the wonderful books Lizzie had ever read, this one was the most interesting. She cried when Black Beauty was sold to the cruel owner who whipped him and laughed at the little pony named Merrylegs. With every chapter, her love of horses and ponies grew, thinking how she would never, ever, not once in her life, mistreat a horse or a pony.

Her thirst was getting really unbearable, so she peeped

around her book to see if Mandy was in the yard. She couldn't see her, and knew it was just as easy to get her own drink as it would be to start yelling for Mandy. She sighed, put her book down open-faced so she wouldn't lose her page, and heaved herself out of the old chair.

She thought of the red cooler filled with ice in the shop, wishing she would be allowed to have an ice-cold soda. She didn't know why Dat and Mam didn't let them have more soda. She wanted an orange one so badly, she decided to march right in and ask Dat for one. There was no sense in going up those stairs for a warm drink of ordinary water out of an ordinary spigot.

The bell above the door tinkled noisily, and she winced, hoping Dat wouldn't hear it. She wanted an orange soda, and she wanted it now. She would tell Dat later, so it really wouldn't be stealing.

The putt-putt of the diesel motor that provided power for the sewing machine was the only sound. Dat was nowhere around, although Lizzie looked very carefully, behind the counter, around the saddletree, even out the back door. She thought of calling for him, but decided it would be easier and she'd be more sure of getting a soda if she didn't.

Slowly she walked over to the red metal cooler, lifted the lid, and bent to peer into the dark recesses of black water. There was 7-Up, Coke, grape soda, and root beer, but no orange. Looking back over her shoulder quickly, she reached a hand into the icy water and moved the soda bottles. Sure enough, there was an orange one. She grabbed it, slammed the lid, and made a dash for the door. The bell jangled, setting Lizzie's teeth on edge, because she didn't want Dat to see her going out the door with a bottle of soda. It wasn't stealing, because she was going to tell Dat about it, after she had already drank it. If he saw her go out now, he would probably make her put it back, and she certainly did not want to do that.

She reached the old lawn chair safely, sat down, and unscrewed the lid of the bottle. It made a fizzy sound, and was so cold in her hand, it actually hurt, so she wrapped it in the hem of her skirt. First, though, she took a long, delicious swallow, found her pretzels, and ate a few. Mmm-mm!

She resumed her reading, eating pretzels and taking cold swallows of the sugary drink. She was reading about Black Beauty telling Merrylegs he missed his pretty mistress, when she heard pounding feet coming across the yard. It was Mandy and she was flying. She crashed into Lizzie's lawn chair and smiled at her.

"Hey, Lizzie! I couldn't find you. Do you want to play doll with me?" Her eyes opened wide, and her mouth dropped open as she said, "Liii-z-zz-ie!"

Lizzie covered the soda with her hand, glancing at Mandy, annoyance written all over her face.

"What?" she asked defensively.

"You aren't supposed to be drinking that!"

Mandy looked self-righteously toward the harness shop. "Did Dat say?"

"No. But I'm going to tell him as soon as I've drunk all of it."

"Lizzie, you stole it out of the cooler!"

"Hah-ah!"

"Mm-hmm! Yes, you did. I'm going to tell Dat."

"Do."

"Okay, here I go."

Mandy marched across the yard, her skinny little legs moving sturdily along, her mission to tattle on Lizzie foremost in her mind. That Lizzie. She had to pull hard, and could still barely budge the double door.

Lizzie guzzled her soda guiltily. For some reason, it didn't seem quite as wrong if the soda was all inside of her or something. Anyway, Dat wouldn't care; she guaranteed he wouldn't. Dat would have said yes, he just wasn't there to say yes, so Lizzie was going to ask him later if she was allowed to have it. That's how it was.

She returned to her reading, but she couldn't really concentrate, which was peculiar, she thought. She kept glancing nervously in the direction of the shop door, wondering if Dat was in good humor, whistling as he always did. It probably depended a lot on what kind of a mood he was in.

A fly sat on Lizzie's leg and bit her, hard. She reached down and slapped it swiftly, thinking how nasty ordinary houseflies could be. She forgot about Dat and Mandy for a second until she heard the shop bell tinkling. Her heart leaped to her throat as Dat came walking across the porch, his brows drawn low across his eyes.

Lizzie had a fleeting moment of panic. She thought about throwing her book, pretzels, and empty soda bottle and running as fast as she could. But she couldn't, be-cause Dat had already seen her, and besides, that would only make her look guilty. She hadn't stolen it, anyway.

"Lizzie."

Dat stood directly in front of her, looking down at the empty soda bottle.

"Hmm?"

Lizzie pretended to be calm and unconcerned, reading her book.

"Did you ask Mam for the soda?"

"Hmm-mm?"

"How did you get it?"

"I just reached in and got it."

Dat looked away across the yard, then up to the sky, and pulled his mouth into a sour expression. He turned his back and looked at the shop for awhile, his shoulders shaking. Lizzie couldn't see his shoulders shaking, because she was too afraid to even look at him. Mandy stood watching Lizzie, her mouth drawn into a severe line, her hands clasped behind her back, just waiting till Lizzie's punishment was announced.

"Well," Dat said, "you know you're not supposed to get

sodas whenever you want one. Certainly not without asking."

"I know."

"So, get your piggy bank and find a quarter, and put it in the cash box where the soda is kept. Then you come to the shop and sweep everything real good for me, and we'll talk about stealing things."

"I didn't *steal* it," Lizzie said.

"What else did you do?" Dat asked.

"I was going to ask you later. I just got it, not stole it."

"Alright, Lizzie. Whatever you want to call it. Just come to the shop with me now and help me clean up."

Dat stood towering over Lizzie, who was curled up in the old lawn chair quite miserably. She didn't want to look at Dat, because depending how fierce his expression was, she would be afraid to go help him. Sometimes Dat gave them a spanking when they really didn't think it was necessary. And sometimes, when Emma thought it was necessary, he didn't spank them at all. So Lizzie could never tell, which was almost worse than getting spanked every time. She always thought if you knew you were getting spanked, you could be given up to it for a while. If you didn't know, how were you supposed to handle it?

She sighed, smoothing back her stray hair and nervously adjusting a hairpin in her bob. Slowly, slowly, with her head bent wearily, she walked the long way to the shop. She wondered if this was how Daniel felt when they threw him into the lions' den. He didn't even do one thing wrong. She was pretty sure Daniel would never have taken the soda. But really, it was all in the family. Lizzie knew in her heart she would never take a soda from a grocery store or someone else's harness shop.

Mandy skipped up beside her and grabbed her hand, slowing to a walk. "Are you going to be spanked?" she asked, her huge green eyes filled with love and concern.

"Go away!"

"Well, Lizzie, maybe if I go along in, Dat won't spank you, because I didn't do anything."

"Go away, I said!"

Mandy went up the stairs, still watching Lizzie with worried eyes. Lizzie yanked open the shop door and flounced inside. *That Mandy*, she thought.

"Here's your broom, Lizzie." Dat handed her a large wooden push broom. Lizzie took it, averting her eyes. She started sweeping furiously, acting as if the leather scraps on the floor were the most important thing she had ever seen. She started in one corner, making fast, furious strokes with the large, clumsy broom. Thump! Crash! Thump! She repeatedly hit the door frame, counter, or some other solid object. Dat went back to his sewing machine, trying as hard as he could to keep a straight face. Thump! Whack!

The bell above the door tinkled and an English man walked in. He was wearing a dark navy suit, with a flashy red and yellow tie. His hair was smoothed back over his forehead and he wore a long, neatly groomed mustache.

Lizzie stopped her sweeping for only a second to stare at him. He was tall and smelled like perfume, so Lizzie thought he must be rich. He looked like the men in the Sears catalog that came in the mail.

"Hello, Melvin!" he boomed.

Dat smiled at the fancy gentleman, so Lizzie knew it was alright. When Dat came around the counter and they shook hands heartily, she pitied Dat. He looked so little and plain and different from the English man that Lizzie thought Dat looked poor. But they were talking, smiling, and laughing, so Lizzie knew Dat liked this man and felt comfortable around him. She was glad Dat could speak English so well, that was one thing. Lizzie understood everything in the English language now and could speak it quite well. But Pennsylvania Dutch was still her "normal" speech, because it was much easier.

She went back to work, her back bent while her arms pumped up and down furiously. Thump! Thump!

"Lizzie!" Dat was turned in her direction, a patient but polite expression on his face. The English man was watching her, too, but he wasn't smiling much. Lizzie's face turned red, so she looked at the floor.

"Would you wait to finish sweeping until this gentleman is finished?" Dat asked, more quietly than usual.

So Lizzie laid down the broom handle, and, without looking back once, she scuttled straight out of the shop. *Good*, she thought. If that man was there, Dat would forget all about spanking her, and maybe he would even forget to give her a talking to. She sat down on the concrete steps and put her chin in her cupped hands, which rested on her knees. She curled her toes around the concrete step and thought of orange soda, stealing, and whether or not it was actually stealing if your Dat owned the harness shop. She wondered what God thought. For one thing, she was absolutely sure God saw her reach into the cooler, because Emma said He always saw every little thing that you did. How could He keep track of every person in the whole world?

The shop door slammed, and Lizzie jumped, her heart leaping. Here he came! But it was only Emma, who was licking a big cherry lollipop, Lizzie's favorite. She plopped down beside Lizzie, took a long, extravagant slurp on her lollipop, and looked at her with narrowed eyes. Lizzie looked steadily back at Emma.

"Where did you get that?" she asked, pointing at it with her chin.

"Mam got a whole bagful when she got groceries. I bet you can't have one because Mandy said to me and Mam that you stole a bottle of orange soda," Emma said, lifting her chin an inch higher and sniffing self-righteously, followed by another lengthy slurp of her lollipop.

"Did you get a licking?" she asked, after she wiped her mouth carefully with her handkerchief.

Lizzie just looked at Emma. She knew one thing for sure—she was never as mad at Emma in her whole life, so she reached over and slapped her shoulder as hard as she could.

"Ow!" Emma howled. "What was that for?"

"You don't know if I stole it or not, Emma! You don't know how I feel, or you wouldn't act so . . . so . . . I don't know," Lizzie finished in despair.

"Well, you don't have to smack me. I'm going to tell

Dat." With that, Emma got up and was ready to walk
into the shop, when Lizzie stopped her with clinging
hands pulling her back toward the steps.

"Emma, please, please, please, don't. I'll never
smack you again, not ever, at least not for a long, long
time. Please, Emma, don't tell Dat I smacked you,
or . . . or . . ."

Emma looked at Lizzie's red face, her pleading expression, and the ring of orange around her mouth. Orange
soda was spilled on the front of her dress, so she knew it
must be true what Mandy had said.

They turned and sat down on the steps again. Emma
kind of pitied Lizzie, because she was always the one
to get into trouble. They sat quietly, side by side, while
Lizzie felt more and more miserable. She wondered if
Emma knew the difference between stealing and taking.
She sighed, looking sideways at Emma.

"Emma."

"Hmm?"

"If you were really, really thirsty, Emma, and you
were not one bit thirsty for ordinary spigot water, and all
you wanted was an i-i-c-y-cold bottle of soda, would you
think it was stealing if you took one out of the cooler,
but you were going to tell Dat about it later? For sure?"
Lizzie asked.

"Well, that all depends if you were truly going to tell
Dat. But were you?" Emma asked, looking long and
hard into Lizzie's face.

"Of course, Emma. After I had already drank all of
it—because, see, then I already had it, and even if he said

no, I at least had my orange soda. See?" Lizzie explained,
desperate to make Emma understand.

"Yes, but . . . Well, Lizzie, that's not quite right. You
shouldn't want something so bad that you just go get it."

"Give me a lick of your lollipop, Emma."

"Only one."

So Lizzie put the lollipop all the way into her mouth,
twirling the handle for a very long time. Emma watched
her, suspiciously, but allowed her quite a long time,
to think it was her lollipop. Lizzie handed it back and
sighed, looking off in the direction of Uncle James's
farm.

"Emma, I am kind of sorry. I mean, a little, anyhow.
It wasn't really stealing, but . . . still . . ." Lizzie's voice
trailed off dejectedly.

"Lizzie, I mean this very seriously. I don't know if it's
really truly stealing if you take something from your Dat
or Mam. I mean, stealing like a thief, where the policeman comes out and puts you in jail. But you still dis-
obeyed Dat and Mam, which isn't right. Would you do it
again?" Emma asked.

Lizzie looked over the fields and thought very hard.
She watched an orange and black woolly worm inch its
way across the concrete sidewalk before she shrugged
her shoulders. She said nothing, because she felt so confused. If only she hadn't been so thirsty for it, she probably would have just been happy with an ordinary drink
of water. Plus, she was so afraid Dat was still going to
spank her.

"Emma, I probably wouldn't."

"Well, if you're so afraid of a licking, why don't you just go tell Dat you're sorry, and that you won't do it again?"

"E-mmm-a!" Lizzie wailed. It was the last thing she wanted to do, because she wasn't sure if she had done anything wrong or not, for sure.

"Well then, you just have to take your punishment," Emma said, getting up to walk away.

"No! No, Emma, alright, but you have to come with me."

They walked into the shop together and Emma gave Lizzie a small shove. Dat was looking at a catalog and stopped to smile at them. "Are you two looking for work?" he asked.

Lizzie took a deep breath. She crossed her arms on her chest and kicked at some scraps of leather. She held up her head bravely and looked directly into Dat's blue eyes. "Dat, I am sorry I took the soda. I won't do it again," she said, in a loud, clear voice.

Dat's eyes crinkled at the sides, and a slow smile spread across his face. He bent to take Lizzie's hand and pulled her into the circle of his arms.

"Lizzie, that was very nice. I'm glad you apologized to me, and I'm glad you won't do it again. I forgive you, Lizzie, I really do."

Lizzie looked into Dat's eyes, and her small, hesitant smile turned into a wide one, and it made her steadily happier the longer her smile stayed. "So . . . so that means I don't get spanked?" she asked.

"Ach, Lizzie, I guess not this time. But don't do it

again, okay?" Dat said very, very seriously.

"I won't," she said solemnly.

Dat pulled her close, his beard tickling her forehead. "You didn't finish sweeping, Lizzie."

"I know," Lizzie said happily. "Me and Emma will do it." Together they swept as fast as they could, and Lizzie thought her heart was so light, she doubted if it weighed as much as a feather. She knew one thing for sure: she would never, ever take another orange soda without asking Dat.

Washing

Emma and Lizzie were in the washhouse, sorting loads of laundry. A big plastic hamper was between them, still packed full of dirty clothes, even if it seemed they already had big piles. The hose hung in the white Maytag wringer washer, with steaming hot water pouring out of it. The granite rinse tub was pushed up against it, ready to be filled with rinse water.

The washing machine was powered by a small gas engine, which Dat would start for them, because they were too small to fill it with gasoline or try to start it. Lizzie always made sure she was close when Dat poured gasoline into the engine, because she loved the smell of it.

The morning sun shone through the old glass-paned windows, warming up the washhouse in a short time. Emma stopped to wipe a hand across her forehead. "Lizzie, open the door. It's getting warm in here," she said.

Lizzie was not in a good mood, so she just went on sorting laundry. Besides washing dishes, this was her least favorite job, and she felt irked because Mam made them do the laundry this morning.

"Lizzie."

Lizzie didn't answer. Emma could open the door herself, she thought. She couldn't see why she had to do it. She picked up a dirty little shirt of Jason's and flung it on the white pile.

"Lizzie! Answer me!"

"What?"

"Go open the door."

"You can."

"Lizzie, I'm going to tell Dat."

Lizzie looked at the washing machine. The water was almost to the top, but she didn't say anything. That was Emma's job, and she wanted to see what would happen if the water ran over. So she straightened her back and walked slowly over to the old wooden door, giving the loose porcelain knob a yank. Morning sunshine flooded the old oak floor, just as the water started running over the sides of the wringer washer. Lizzie was rewarded with an exasperated sound from Emma as she dashed over to put the hose in the rinse water.

Lizzie stood at the torn wooden screen door, looking out over the yard and garden. She stretched and scratched her stomach, feeling tired and irritable. Probably the reason she felt so tired and grouchy was because she had lain awake last evening, hearing Mam and Dat talking until way into the night.

She yawned, and tears formed in her eyes after the yawn. She wiped them away, stretched, and leaned against the door frame. She had felt so sick to her stomach last night, so horribly afraid, that her heart whacked against her ribs, pushing up a lump in her throat. She had rolled over from side to side, trying to shut out her parents' voices with the palm of her hand, even grabbing the pillow and molding it over her whole head, her face smashed against the sheet until she couldn't breathe. She had longed for a quiet, restful sleep, like Emma, who lay beside her, breathing evenly and deeply.

But Dat's voice would rise, followed by a soft murmur from Mam, until her voice would yank Lizzie to reality again, talking fast and loud, almost as if she could cry any moment. It had been quite an ordeal, listening to their conversation. Lizzie even blamed herself in a way, because maybe if she wouldn't have taken that orange soda out of the cooler, Dat might not have been in the shop when that fancy, smooth-talking salesman had walked in. Because there lay the trouble, Lizzie could easily tell. Evidently Dat had bought an expensive piece of equipment from the salesman, which Mam felt they could not afford. Dat had pleaded with Mam, saying it was a great new invention to fix the soles of the heaviest shoes, farmers' boots, and carpenter and road crew boots, and it would boost their profit easily to help pay for the machine.

Mam had reminded him about the new sewing machine, the saddletree, and other numerous items, and that the shop still was not making enough money for a decent living. Dat had agreed, and for a while, Lizzie was so glad they were talking sensibly. She knew they were poor, because they took potato soup on a picnic, but she didn't know it was as bad as Mam said. The

thing that struck terror in Lizzie's heart, that caused
her to lie awake deep into the warm night, was when
Mam said she just couldn't see how they could hang on
any longer. Dat had answered Mam in the most awful,
loud voice, stomped across the living room, and went
out on the porch, the door slamming behind him. Lizzie
thought she would surely die of feeling dreadful when
she heard Mam crying softly, sighing, and blowing her
nose. She even thought of crawling out of bed to get
on her knees to ask God to please come help them all,
because Dat and Mam didn't know what to do because
they had so many bills and no money.

But that would make her feel too dumb, so she didn't.
But she did turn on her back and clasp her hands over
her chest and thought a loud thought to God, asking
Him to help Dat and Mam. Later, she thought, maybe
Jesus would hear her better, because He was much
smaller and not near as fierce-looking. Mam had shown
her a picture once of Jesus sitting on a little boy's bed
when there was a thunderstorm outside, and He didn't
look one bit scary, except He wore a long, white dress,
which was very strange. So Lizzie thought the same
thought, except she said it to Jesus.

She felt strangely quiet and not so scared after that.
Maybe it was because the light went out in the living room and Dat and Mam went to bed, or maybe it
was really that God had heard her, or Jesus. Her last
thought had been, that they probably had, because she
felt so much better.

Now, leaning against the door frame, Lizzie thought

she bet when you were almost ten years old, your
prayers amounted to something. She didn't know for
sure, so she'd have to ask Emma about that.

The rinse tubs were full, and Emma closed both
spigots. She added a cup of Tide to the wash water, and
some kind of blue stuff to the rinse water.

"Lizzie, go ask Dat to come start the motor," she said
over her shoulder.

So Lizzie walked to the shop, where Dat was riveting
halters. The machine came down on the leather, going
'thump, thump' with a powerful, satisfying clunk. Lizzie
loved to hear the riveter.

"Dat!"

"What?" he asked, stopping the machine.

"You have to come start the washing machine motor."

"Alright-y, Lizzie." He slid off his stool and followed
her into the washhouse, grabbing the gasoline can and
turning the cap from the tank on the motor. Lizzie bent
over close to smell the wonderful scent as the gasoline
trickled into the tank. Dat smiled at her, turned the
lid tight, and stood up. He set the gasoline can away
carefully, giving the rope on the motor a hard tug. The
motor popped right off, settling down to a quiet, steady
'putta-putta-putt.'

Emma pulled a lever, and the agitator in the washing
machine spun back and forth, back and forth. She bent
to put the first load of diapers into the machine, which
Mam had prewashed with a stronger detergent.

"There you go, girls. Be careful," Dat said, walking
out the door. Emma and Lizzie sat on the wooden porch

steps, closing the washhouse door behind them.

"We have to let the diapers wash a while," Emma said matter-of-factly.

"I know."

Emma looked at Lizzie. "Why didn't you comb your hair, Lizzie?"

Lizzie shrugged. "Too tired."

"Why?"

"I don't know." Lizzie dug a finger into her ear, turning her head toward Emma. "Emma, did you go to sleep early last night? I mean, as soon as we went to bed?" she asked hesitantly.

"Why?"

"Did you hear Mam and Dat argue last night?"

"Were they?"

"Well, yes, Emma. Really bad. Mam was crying. Emma, we're so poor that we can barely hang on here, whatever that means. Emma, do you think that it could be my fault? I mean, you know I took that orange soda from the cooler? Do you think that salesman would not have come into the shop if I wouldn't have had to sweep the floor?"

"Ach, Lizzie, that's dumb."

"I know."

They sat in silence as Emma brushed a finger across her teeth. "I forgot to brush my teeth."

"Do you brush them every morning, plus every night?" Lizzie asked, incredulous at the thought that Emma actually did.

"Of course."

Lizzie thought about that for awhile. She would probably never do that, because brushing your teeth was
almost as bad as washing dishes or washing clothes, like
this morning.

"Emma, who hears prayers the best, God or Jesus?"
Lizzie asked, very suddenly.

"They both do the same," Emma said firmly.

"How do you know?"

"Oh, I just know."

"Does God hear it better if you go on your knees or
not?"

"You have to ask Mam that. You should go on your
knees, though. I mean, everyone does in church. Two
times."

"Mm-hmm. Emma, I wish we had chips," Lizzie said.

"Why?"

"'Cause we haven't had chips for so long, and I'm
hungry for some. All we ever have is stale pretzels or
popcorn," Lizzie wailed.

"That's 'cause we're poor."

"I hate being poor."

Emma got up, turning to go into the washhouse.
"C'mon, we have to get these diapers out."

Lizzie got up to follow Emma, yawning again. She
was so tired that it didn't seem fair that she had to help
Emma wash. She was jerked out of her sleepiness when
Emma howled in despair. She reached into the fast-
moving water and grabbed a big blob of tightly knotted diapers. Water sloshed over the side of the washing
machine when she put it back in.

"Lizzie!" Emma yelled at the top of her voice, so her sister could hear her over the sound of the 'putta-putta-putt' of the engine. "Go get Mam!"

Lizzie cast one wild-eyed look at the water slopping out of the washer, and dashed madly out the door and up the steps to the kitchen. She burst into the house, shouting, "Mam!"

Mam looked up from the stovetop she was cleaning, an alarmed expression on her face. "Lizzie, whatever is wrong with you?" she asked, her face turning pale.

"Come quick! Water is slopping over the washing machine and the diapers are all wrapped up in each other so tight it feels as hard as a stick," Lizzie panted.

Mam followed her down the stairs, scolding as she went. "Lizzie, you have to stop leaving the diapers in so long. I have often told Emma. What were you doing?"

They came to the washhouse, where Emma stood wringing her hands, an expression of despair on her face. She looked relieved to see Mam and burst out, "Mam, the diapers are knotted so tight it isn't even funny!"

Mam's mouth was pinched in a firm line, and she pulled up her sleeve with one hand as she plunged the other into the washer. She came up with a mass of very white, very knotted diapers, which she proceeded to yank apart with strong hands, scolding as she did so.

"Emma, where were you and Lizzie? You know you can't let these diapers wash for so long! Ach, I should just wash by myself, I guess. You girls just aren't old enough yet." Mam twisted and pulled on the hard knot of diapers, dropping them back into the swirling, sudsy water as she loosened each one. Emma stood beside her, watching with a bewildered expression.

"Well, Mam, I can't understand why they knotted like that. Me and Lizzie were just sitting on the steps talking for a little while."

"Just be careful. You have to mind your business when you wash." Mam wiped her hands on her apron, watching as Emma put the diapers through the wringer, which pressed out the water from the diapers, depositing them into the blue rinse water.

Mam turned to go, but watched Emma rinsing them. "Be sure and rinse them thoroughly. The last time you washed, the diapers were as stiff as a board."

That did it. Lizzie decided she didn't like Mam this morning. That was the thing, if your parents disagreed, it was hard to know whose side you were on. First Lizzie pitied Dat, then she pitied Mam, then she pitied them both. It just made life hard and much more complicated, she decided. Who felt like washing now? She knew the diapers may have been stiff and not rinsed very well, but they weren't as stiff as a board. Mam stretched her stuff, so Lizzie supposed that's where she got it, 'cause Emma claimed Lizzie did, too—stretch the truth, that is, not rinse the diapers.

Lizzie followed Emma to the washline, as she lugged the wicker clothes basket filled with wet diapers. She handed the wooden clothespins to her, as she hung up the snowy white, sweet-smelling diapers. They blew away from them, on the soft summer breeze, flapping quietly as each one was hung up.

Lizzie was feeling sleepy again, standing in the warm sun. She yawned, clapping one hand over her mouth, as she handed Emma another clothespin. Suddenly, without warning, there was a horrible buzz in Lizzie's ear, followed by a soft, fuzzy feeling and a frightful, searing pain on her cheek. She dropped a clothespin, screaming and batting at the bee on her face. She danced around the soft grass, screaming and screaming, as Emma dropped the diaper she was holding, hovering over her protectively.

"Shh! Shh! Lizzie, you were stung! By a bee! Oh, oh!" She started screaming herself, as she found the bee, writhing in the grass.

"Get it, Lizzie, get it!"

"Ow! Ow!" was Lizzie's only response.

"Lizzie, go up to the kitchen and get Mam to help you put something on your sting. I'm going to get Dat to stomp on this bee."

As Lizzie wailed and howled her way to the kitchen, Emma found Dat in the shop, who promptly came to their rescue. He stood looking at the angry bee and told Emma there was no use killing the poor thing, because after they stung someone, they naturally died by themselves. Emma stood solemnly beside Dat as the bee died, then remembered her wash swirling in the washer. She told Dat she had to go get her wash, striding across the lawn with the empty wicker clothes basket like a girl much older.

Dat watched her go, thinking how much responsibil-

ity Emma took naturally on her capable little shoulders.
He felt a terrible pang of guilt for making Annie work
long hours with him in the harness shop. If he was very
honest with himself, he knew they couldn't go on very
much longer, unless things changed. Annie did what
she could, and his heart swelled with love for his wife.
He just didn't know what else he would do, because he
loved the harness shop and enjoyed the feel and smell of
the leather beneath his fingers.

He turned to go, running a hand through his hair.
He would leave it to the Lord, he thought, and if they
weren't meant to stay here, something would come up.
A small smile appeared on his face as she stepped up
on the porch, listening to Lizzie's alarming yells of pain
and rage. If ever anyone could make a fuss about pain,
Lizzie could.

He found Mam bent over Lizzie, who was lying on
the couch, yelling at the top of her voice. Mam applied a
soft cloth that had been soaked with apple cider vinegar,
a cooling, soothing remedy for stings.

Lizzie's yelling ceased almost instantly, and her
nose wrinkled as she sat up, saying quite loudly, "That
stinks!"

Mam was very patient with Lizzie's yelling, but she
decided it wasn't that bad if all she thought about was
the smell of the vinegar.

"You hold it, Lizzie. It will make it feel much better,"
Mam said.

"No, I don't want it on my face. It stinks!"

So Mam got up and marched into the kitchen with the

cloth. *Well then, let her yell,* she decided. That Lizzie tried her to the absolute limit when something painful happened. It was always much worse than the other children, so if she minded the smell of vinegar more than the pain of the sting, so be it.

Lizzie lay back down, her cheek hurting cruelly. She touched it tentatively with her fingertips. It felt so hot, and she wondered if you could die from a bee sting. Probably not. She remembered Marvin saying you could die if a copperhead snake or a rattlesnake bit you, though.

Dat rolled his eyes in Lizzie's direction, and Mam rolled her eyes back at him. Dat smiled and Mam smiled back. As Dat went back to the harness shop, his heart was light again, because his beloved Annie had forgiven him for buying that expensive piece of equipment.

Emma worked all by herself, whistling under her breath, putting load after load of laundry through the wringer. She loved her work, taking immense pleasure in hanging out the clean laundry and watching it flap in the breeze.

Her thoughts wandered, thinking how strange Lizzie was, lying awake listening to Mam and Dat. She would never worry about such things. She'd much rather daydream, thinking about her own house someday, with her own husband to care for, cooking, baking, washing dishes, and sweeping the floor of her kitchen.

That Lizzie sure was strange, no doubt about it.

A Visit to Jefferson County

Lizzie wriggled into a more comfortable position on the slippery plastic seat. She tugged at her black apron to fold it properly under her knees, along with her purple skirt.

She glanced at Emma, who was looking straight ahead, past Dat's head and out the window of the old station wagon. Emma was always neat, because she held herself still, Mam said. Lizzie looked down at her skirt, then over at Emma's skirt, and decided she was just as neat as Emma. Mandy sat on Lizzie's other side, but Lizzie never worried if Mandy was neater than she was, because she was such a skinny little girl who still wore a black pinafore-style apron.

Lizzie wished Dat would remove his hat. She would have been able to see much more, but she was afraid to say anything, because the driver might think she was complaining. So she didn't say anything. Besides, she could look out the side window, but the only trouble with that was, if she saw something interesting, they were past before she could really see it as well as she wanted to.

She could hardly believe they were actually on their way to Jefferson County to her Uncle Elis. Lizzie could only remember a little of ever having been there before, so she was excited beyond words.

The evening before, Emma and Lizzie had hung their purple dresses on a special hook, laid out their best school aprons, and cleaned their black and white sneakers vigorously. Emma gave Lizzie one of her best handkerchiefs to use. It had blue and yellow roses all along the edge, and at one corner there was a huge cluster of roses. Lizzie told Emma that she could have it, but she really hoped Emma wouldn't take it back. She didn't, because Emma was not selfish at all.

Cars whizzed past them on a big four-lane highway. Sometimes the driver turned his steering wheel and passed other cars. Lizzie was always glad when he did, because it was a good feeling to know they were going faster than the others. Lizzie wondered where all these people were going and where they lived. She sure hoped they were not all going to Jefferson County. She doubted it, but still, why were they all on this road going in the same direction?

After a while, the driver slowed down, and they coasted off the big highway onto a smaller road. It was more bumpy and they couldn't go as fast, but there were more houses, farms, and people to look at now.

"There's the mountain!" Dat said excitedly. Lizzie

scooted forward, straining to see. To the left was a long, low line of purplish hills, and Lizzie couldn't see what was so exciting about mountains. But the farther they drove, the bigger they became, until Lizzie's nose was pressed against the glass of the car window, absolutely speechless at the size of the towering mountain.

"That's the Tillebet Mountain! The river runs right along the bottom of it, and the train track runs between the river and the mountain. Oh, it sounds so pretty when the train blows its whistle there—just beautiful!" Dat said.

Lizzie glanced at Mam, who was smiling, just beaming with delight. Mam loved Jefferson County; she had told Emma and Lizzie this. So when Dat exclaimed about the mountain, it pleased Mam very much, because her relatives lived here.

They turned onto another road and wound their way slowly along, because they were getting closer to Uncle Elis. Straight ahead were a few scattered houses and another mountain, except it was only a small one. Dat said it was a ridge. At the foot of this pine-covered ridge was a stone house, and a barn that had no paint on it. The boards were black and weatherbeaten, but the roof was shiny with silver paint. Behind the barn, up a steep hill, was a long, low building that Dat said was Uncle Eli's sawmill.

They turned in the drive, and Lizzie could see the house better. The stones were not gray like the stone houses where Lizzie lived, but a sandy color. The roof was green, and there were lots of doors and windows.

The yard and flower beds were all kept very neat, with a concrete sidewalk leading up to the entrance of the sandy-colored stone house.

They stopped, and as Dat opened the door of the station wagon, Uncle Eli's smiling face appeared at the front door. Dat got out and Uncle Eli opened the door, saying, "Looks like you made it alright." They shook hands warmly, Dat's face wreathed in smiles.

"Yes, we did. We had a nice trip down this morning — not too much traffic," Dat said.

Aunt Mary bustled out, looking smaller than ever. She smiled and shook hands with Mam, her eyes twinkling behind her gold-framed glasses. Her eyes looked like a bird's, Lizzie decided, and her nose and mouth were small and round. She talked quietly, but must have had a great sense of humor, because Mam often laughed genuinely when she was with Mary.

Emma and Lizzie hung back shyly, but when the door opened and Edna came flying out, chattering excitedly before she even reached them, Lizzie did not feel one bit shy at all. She loved Edna so much! Edna tucked one hand under Emma's arm, and her other one under Lizzie's.

"Oh, I was so excited for today!" she said.

"We were, too," Emma said. "We could hardly sleep last night."

"Me, either."

"What are we going to do today?" Lizzie asked eagerly.

There were so many things she wanted to see — she

couldn't imagine exploring everything in only one day. For one thing, Lizzie had never seen a sawmill, and she was wondering what that big pipe was that hung over the embankment in front of it.

"Probably we'll go meet Atlee Yoders' children, because they're coming for dinner, too," Edna said.

"Who are they?" Emma asked.

"Our cousins who live down the road."

"Oh."

"Mom said we have to tell them when you get here. So do you want to walk along down?"

Uncle Elis' children didn't say 'Mam' and 'Dat.' They called their mother 'Mom' and their father 'Daddy.' They kind of made the 'a' sound flat, so that it sounded different. When they spoke Pennsylvania Dutch, the words were pronounced differently, like their Ohio cousins, because Uncle Elis was originally from Holmes County, Ohio. Mam talked like that, too, but not as much, because Dat and all the Amish people where they lived spoke their Dutch differently. When Mam was with her relatives, her accent became much thicker, and she rolled her 'r's, using the same descriptive words they did.

"Mom, we're going to get Atlees' kids," Edna said.

Emma and Lizzie looked at each other. They never called children 'kids,' because Dat said only baby goats are kids, and Amish people don't say that. Edna said it more like 'kits,' so Lizzie guessed it was a usual way of saying 'children.'

They walked only a short distance, past a few English people's homes, until they came to a short gravel drive. Lizzie was amazed when she saw the house. It looked like a house, in a way, because it had a porch with windows and doors opening to this porch. But it had no roof, or so it seemed. The roof itself was flat, and the yard went up a steep hill on each side so that there really was no house in the back, just a yard with a big, flat black roof. There was a small barn beside this very strange house, and a white board fence surrounded the pasture.

"Atlees live in a cellar house," Edna explained.

"Is that what you call a house that is halfway under the ground," Lizzie asked.

"Well, in English, you say 'basement home,'" Edna assured her.

"Is it nice?"

"Oh, yeah, it's nice." Edna knocked on the screen door, and a friendly voice hollered out, "C'mon in!"

Edna opened the screen door, and Emma and Lizzie

followed shyly. Lizzie could soon tell there was nothing
to be shy about, because a plump lady hurried into the
kitchen, drying her hands on her apron.

"Oh my, did Melvins get here? Are these Annie's
girls? Don't you look pretty in those purple dresses?
How do you roll your hair like that? I declare," she
laughed, touching Lizzie's hair, turning them around to
look at how their dresses were made.

Lizzie loved her on sight. She exuded kindliness,
warmth, curiosity, and a great sense of happiness. Her
hair was dark brown, with a creamy complexion and
bright twinkling eyes. When she talked, which was almost continuously, she had a lisp in her words when she
pronounced certain letters. Lizzie would have listened to
her for hours without tiring of it.

Two girls about Emma and Lizzie's age came and
joined them. They were not shy, just walking easily into
the kitchen with a friendly expression, quite unselfconscious.

Lizzie had never seen anyone look like those two girls.
She didn't mean to stare, because Mam said that was
rude, but she just looked at them for a long time without thinking. Their hair was bouncy and wavy, combed
back loosely. The most astounding thing was the color
of it. It was bright orange-red, like the sun shining on
a new copper penny. Lizzie thought it was the prettiest
thing she had ever seen. Their eyes were round and light
blue, almost sky blue, and their faces were covered with
hundreds of freckles that matched their red hair exactly.

Mrs. Yoder pushed her daughters forward. "Girls,

this is Nancy and Mollie! Say hello to these girls!"

Both girls smiled widely, their small white teeth flashing, and said, "Hi!"

Emma said "Hello," but Lizzie just smiled, because she felt so shy of these red-haired girls.

The door was flung open, and three boys charged into the room. "Hey, Mom, those people are at Elis!" They stopped when they saw Emma and Lizzie. They just stood there and stared at them, and Emma and Lizzie stared back. They looked like Nancy and Mollie, with the same red hair and freckles, except they were boys.

"Two of them are twins," Edna said.

Emma was too dumbfounded to answer, and Lizzie was too busy just looking at them. They were covered all over with freckles and looked as if they laughed most of the time.

One of the twins came over to Lizzie and said, "What's your name?"

"L-Lizzie," she stammered quietly.

"Oh, Lizzie. I guess you must be a busy Lizzie!"

The other boys laughed loudly, but not in a nasty or mocking manner. Lizzie felt a giggle start at the bottom of her throat, mostly because when those red-haired boys laughed, it just became infectious and you had to laugh, too, whether you felt like it or not. She covered her mouth with one hand, her eyes crinkled, and she giggled. The boys looked at each other, pleased that they could make this new girl giggle.

"Hey, Mom. We're going!" And like split lightning, they were all out the door, slamming it loudly behind them.

Lizzie thought that here in Jefferson County, the parents must be easy to get along with. The children just said where they were going and left. Maybe that was why everybody was so happy and unselfconscious. They didn't worry very much about small matters, like running down the road to their uncle's place.

Nancy and Mollie joined the others, and they all walked back to Uncle Elis, where Mam and Mary were hurrying around in the kitchen, getting the plates on the table and preparing the huge company dinner. Edna had two older sisters, named Esther and Lavina. They were folding silverware in napkins, but stopped to tug at Emma's skirt as the girls passed.

"Hello, Emma."

Emma stopped to say hello, and they picked at the material of her dress.

"That's a pretty purple color."

Emma smiled, and they moved through the kitchen, up the stairs to Edna's room. The girls fussed over her pretty treasures on her dresser, but Lizzie sat on the bed and kicked at the braided rug beside it. She was insulted because Esther and Lavina had noticed Emma's dress and not hers. Lizzie's was just as pretty as Emma's — in fact, it was the exact same thing. Why did they just notice Emma?

The other girls were chattering and laughing, and Lizzie felt more and more left out and alone. They didn't even notice she was quiet, because they were all crowded around Edna's dresser, admiring a small vase.

Lizzie flopped back on the pillow, but her stomach

looked too big when she did that, and her knees came
out from beneath her apron. She didn't want the other
girls to see her knees, because they were soft and round,
too, so she sat up. She felt her hair to see if it was
messed up, and wondered again what the difference was
between her and Emma. Why did they notice just her
dress? She felt steadily more miserable, so she got up
and wandered into another room across the hall.

It was full of rocks, pheasant feathers, squirrel tails,
and deer antlers, so she guessed it must be the boys'
room. She walked over to the windowsill, wondering
why they were so wide. You could easily sit on them,
like a small seat that was up too high.

There were pencil drawings on the wall of bears,
deer, and pheasants. Lizzie walked over to examine
them more closely. Someone could really draw, because
it looked exactly right, except there was no color, only
pencil. She wished she could draw like that.

Heavy feet pounded up the stairs and two boys came
into the room before Lizzie had a chance of getting to
Edna's room. She turned around in front of the pencil
drawings, her eyes wide. They were Edna's two brothers, Ivan and Ray, who were older than Lizzie.

"What are you doing in here, Lizzie?" Ray asked
kindly. Ivan just looked at Lizzie and didn't say anything.

"I . . . I just walked in here to . . . to . . . see who draws
these pictures," Lizzie said nervously.

"I bet," Ray said, his eyes twinkling at her.

"Well, kind of," Lizzie said bravely.

"Just don't touch any of these eggs or feathers," Ivan said.

"What eggs?"

"These." Ivan showed her an old plastic container, the bottom covered with tiny, fragile birds' eggs. There were aqua-colored ones, spotted brown ones, and sky blue ones. Lizzie bent her head to peer at them and a soft exclamation of wonder escaped, in spite of her shyness.

"Wow."

"Hey, if we get done cleaning up the sawmill this afternoon, I'll show you a real nest of these," Ivan offered.

Lizzie looked up and smiled. "Okay!"

"D-i-nnn-er!" Uncle Eli's voice boomed up the stairway, and Lizzie came out of Ray and Ivan's room with them at the same time the girls ran out of Edna's room. Emma looked aghast, pulling on Lizzie's sleeve as they went down the stairs.

"Lizzie, what were you doing in the boys' room?"

"Nothing." Lizzie pinched her mouth shut tightly, offering no more information. If Lavina and Esther noticed her dress, and not Lizzie's, then Emma didn't have to go along to see the bird's nest, either. That was just the way it was.

. . . . . .

Aunt Mary did not set the table the way everyone did where Lizzie lived. She piled all the plates on one end of the table, with the silverware and drinks in one big group. Then big stainless steel kettles, roasters, and casseroles were lined up along one side of the kitchen table. The other side held pies, cakes, fruit desserts, and puddings, until the table fairly groaned—it held so many good dishes.

Uncle Eli told everyone to bow their heads in silent prayer, as their driver was asked to come in to dinner. Because he was English, maybe he didn't know what a silent prayer was, so that's why Uncle Eli said that. Lizzie bowed her head, clasping her hands in front of her, and peeped at everyone else. Emma's eyes were closed and she was saying her prayer, so Lizzie remembered to pray quickly. She forgot and opened her eyes, peeping at the driver, who also had his eyes closed, his lips moving in silent prayer. So English drivers had dinner prayers, too.

Of course, the men and boys were allowed to go first, and to Lizzie it seemed as if the row was endless. She sincerely hoped Aunt Mary had made enough to eat, because probably the little girls would be last, at the very end of the line. Her mouth watered and she swallowed. One of the boys scraped the spoon on the bottom of the kettle and looked at Aunt Mary, who was watching carefully. "Is it empty?" she asked, moving forward to peer into the kettle. Lizzie's heart sank. Sure enough, it was the macaroni and cheese, too. But Aunt Mary whisked it away, returning with another container filled to the brim with golden, bubbly macaroni. Lizzie was greatly relieved, because that was a good sign. If she had plenty of one dish, she probably had enough for everyone.

Finally it was Lizzie's turn. She tried not to be too eager, but she grabbed a clean plate, heaping mashed potatoes and gravy, macaroni, filling, and fried chicken, corn, and green bean casserole on her plate. It smelled so good, and she felt weak with hunger. Balancing her plate carefully, she carried it out to the yard where Emma, Edna, and the little red-haired girls had formed a circle, sitting cross-legged on the grass, balancing their plates on one knee.

First, Lizzie tasted the macaroni and cheese. Mmmm! It was absolutely delicious. Next, the crispy fried chicken melted in her mouth, followed by big spoonfuls of mashed potatoes and gravy. While she was eating, she watched Nancy and Mollie pick at their food, taking delicate little nibbles, before they decided they didn't like certain dishes.

Lizzie thought everything was good—in fact, everything was just wonderful. She could hardly wait to see what was for dessert. She was so busy eating that she really didn't worry much about being heavier than Nancy and Mollie. She was just too hungry.

They returned to fill their plates with dessert. Because Lizzie was not as hungry anymore, she took her time selecting dishes she thought looked best. There was a chocolate cake, but it wasn't a layer cake like Mam made, and it didn't really have enough frosting. But the nut cake, oh, what an astounding thing! It was cut in big, triangular wedges, covered with thick, creamy caramel frosting. The whole top of it was covered with finely ground walnuts. Lizzie slid her knife under a piece, and pulled gently, balancing it carefully with her other hand. She sighed in relief when it landed in the middle of her plate, in all its perfect goodness.

Lizzie moved on down the line of desserts, passing up the fruit salad. There was just one thing wrong with fruit salad. It tasted so sour if you ate it with cake, especially if the frosting was sweet.

She discovered a bowl of creamy vanilla pudding that had layers of whipped cream and bananas. Mmmm. That was the perfect thing to go with the nut cake. She took two big spoonfuls and plopped it carefully beside the cake, following Edna out the door and back to her perch in the grass.

She cut a piece of cake and arranged a bit of pudding on top, tasting it. It was so good that Lizzie decided it was probably the best thing she had ever eaten in her whole life. It was even a lot better than hot chocolate and shoofly. She wasn't too sure if it was better than french fries, though.

A Wonderful Afternoon

The girls did not need to help with the dishes, because they were too small. The older girls helped, and Mam and Aunt Mary, plus the friendly Mrs. Yoder.

Lizzie asked Edna if they could see the sawmill first. Lizzie had never seen one, so she was curious what Uncle Eli did with those large piles of logs. She definitely wanted to know what that huge pipe that stuck way out over the steep embankment in front of the sawmill was for.

"Why do you have to know all that stuff about a sawmill?" asked Emma. "You're not a boy."

"I know," Lizzie huffed.

"Well, then."

"I just want to see what they do. You can stay at the house."

But Emma trudged along as they walked up the hill behind the weatherbeaten barn. There was lots of sawdust mixed into the black earth and weeds grew around the piles of logs. Edna said they absolutely were not allowed to go close to the logs, because they could start to roll and crush someone. Lizzie was so amazed that logs were trees that were cut down. She wondered what happened to the branches and all the pretty green leaves.

Edna showed them the huge, round sawblade that cut the logs into lumber. She explained that the pieces of lumber that had bark on one side were called 'slabs,' and showed them the cutoff saw that sawed the long slabs into small pieces of firewood. Most wonderful of all, the long pipe was where the sawdust was blown out over the bank, where it lay in a huge pile below.

Lizzie stood at the top, craning her neck to see below. There was a sea of tiny little wood particles in a huge, soft pile. She couldn't imagine what Uncle Eli would do with all that sawdust.

"Jump down!" Edna said, smiling.

Lizzie looked at her with narrowed eyes. "No!"

"Yes! Do. You may!"

"Well . . . no, I'd hurt myself," Lizzie said skeptically.

"No, you won't. Go ahead. Step back, run, and jump out as far as you can."

"Did you ask Uncle Eli?"

"No, but he doesn't care. He lets us jump in the sawdust pile."

Emma stepped forward. "Lizzie, don't. You have your good dress and apron on. You'll ruin it."

Lizzie's heart beat rapidly and her face flushed with excitement. "No, Emma, these are not our Sunday dresses. They're our school dresses; you know that."

"Lizzie, if you jump down there, I'm going in right now and telling Mam. You aren't allowed."

"She won't care."

Edna sat down in the weeds, pulling one and chewing on the end.

"Your mom won't mind if you just jump once," Edna offered.

"My mom doesn't care." said Nancy. With that, Nancy stepped back a few paces, and took off running. Her skirts billowed out as she made a flying leap, landing far below in the soft sawdust. She called up, "You won't get hurt, but you have to get out soon, because the sawdust is hot underneath."

Lizzie stepped back and propelled herself forward as fast as she could. Her feet pummeled the ground before she launched herself into the sawdust pile below. She felt her skirts flying out the back, but only for a moment, before her feet were firmly embedded in warm sawdust. She opened her mouth and laughed with the joy of jumping so high and not getting hurt one little bit.

Edna and Mollie stood on top of the bank, bent over laughing, slapping their knees. Emma was marching off down the hill, her mouth in a straight, tight line, to tell Mam what Lizzie had done.

Edna gasped, and between giggles she called to Lizzie, "If you come up here in a hurry, you can do it again, before your mom comes!"

So Lizzie floundered out of the sawdust, scrambling her way to the top as fast as she could. She was breathing hard, and sawdust was stuck in every pleat of her dress and apron. She stepped back again, repeating the process of running and jumping. This time she jumped a big farther, almost tumbling head over heels, because she jumped too far. It wasn't quite as funny this time, because she almost got a mouthful of sawdust.

She scrambled out and was hurrying to the top when she caught sight of Emma coming out of the house with Mam behind her. Emma was talking rapidly, waving her hands, and Mam was walking fast.

They reached the top at about the same time, and Mam said loudly, "Lizzie, look at you!"

"What?" Lizzie looked down at her dress, smoothing her apron. Sawdust fell out of her hair, and she was beginning to feel itchy. Mam looked at Lizzie, then at Edna. She peered down over the edge of the bank, looking at the sawdust pile below.

"Does your dad let you jump down there?" she asked.

"Oh, yeah, we're allowed to."

"I wish you wouldn't because Lizzie and Emma have their school dresses on. Could you find something else to do, do you think?"

Lizzie faced her mother eagerly. "Mam, Mam, please, please, may we jump?"

"No, Lizzie, because how will you get all that sawdust out of your hair, and stay clean enough to go home?"

Lizzie was horribly disappointed, because she knew Mam did not want her to jump. Emma was always the troublemaker.

"We can go find something else to do," Mollie volunteered.

"Let's go to the river!" Edna said.

Emma said she was not going to the river, not ever, unless Mam or Dat went along. It was too far, and they had to cross a busy highway.

"Well, you girls decide," Mam said, and walked off down the hill to the sand-colored stone house.

The girls all sat down in a circle in the weeds, chewing at the ends of the fat, juicy ones. Lizzie's hair was disheveled, and the itchy feeling was getting worse. She scratched her back, then pulled at the neckline of her dress.

"Why don't you want to go to the river?" Edna asked.

"It's too far."

"I know what. I'll ask Esther to go along," Edna said. Emma looked at her doubtfully, but she jumped up with everyone else and ran down the hill.

.   .   .   .   .   .

The river was the most amazing thing Lizzie had ever seen. It was dark green, but sometimes when you looked at it slanted, it was blue or purple. It ran on and on, silently, without even one tiny sound, wide and deep and so scary that Lizzie shivered. She had never seen a river, and it made her feel afraid, but she was thrilled by the power of its relentless flow.

There was a grassy bank which was mowed, with trees along the banks. Edna said the Fish Commission kept the yard looking so nice. There were a few men fishing where a small stream ran into the river. Edna said they had to stay away from the fishermen, because sometimes if you were noisy, the men became angry.

A car rumbled past with a boat on a trailer. A man in the car backed the trailer carefully down a steep incline until it disappeared into the dark water. Lizzie held her breath as the men stopped the vehicle and scrambled out. One of them got into the boat, while the other unhitched some straps, pulling some levers, and the boat drifted slowly away on the current.

Lizzie could hardly stand the suspense. The man in the boat made his way to the back, flipped a few switches, and started pulling on a rope to start the motor. He pulled and pulled, as blue smoke rolled along the top of the water. Lizzie was almost panicking, because the current was carrying him farther and farther away. The man seemed quite unperturbed about this, steadily yanking on the rope. His partner was whistling quite merrily as he started the car and eased the trailer out of the river. Lizzie thought he was terribly mean to the other man, who was still patiently trying to start the motor. By now, he was actually really far away.

"Doesn't he know how far away he's going?" Lizzie asked, when she could stand it no longer. She imagined the poor man being swept helplessly out to the wide open sea, where waves would toss him unmercifully for days and days. She had seen a picture of a small boat with a strong wind blowing huge waves in a book once, and she had never forgotten the despair that picture evoked. It would be just awful to be at sea in a storm.

Esther looked at Lizzie and smiled. "Oh, he'll get it started."

Sure enough, there was a welcoming cough and a
sputter, and the man sat down, steering the boat from
the back, as he made his way back up to the launchpad
to pick up his whistling friend. Lizzie was greatly relieved when both men were safely seated in the boat, the
motor chugging purposefully, on their way upstream.

The girls sat in the grass, talking and laughing, but
Lizzie was not joining in the conversation. She was looking at the huge, towering mountain, wondering what
would happen if you had to sleep there because you
were lost. It was so big that Lizzie decided she would
never, ever cross this river and climb that mountain.

She watched as small, dark-colored birds swooped
down so close to the running water, she thought they
were diving in. But always they swooped back up again.
Lots of insects skimmed across the top of the water,
even dragonflies. There was an insect that looked like a
long-legged spider that walked on top of the water. Or
rather, it scooted along in short jerks, which looked really funny.

Lizzie heard a distant rumble, a steady sound that
reminded her of a summer thunderstorm. She glanced
anxiously at the sky, but it was calm and blue, with
puffy white clouds scattered like huge cotton balls. The
rumble became louder, and Lizzie cleared her throat
nervously.

"What is that?" she asked, biting her fingernails.

Esther sounded bored. "The train."

Edna, Mollie, and Nancy went right on talking as if

nothing was wrong. Emma glanced nervously at Lizzie, and Lizzie knew she thought it was terribly noisy to think it was only a train.

Lizzie jumped fitfully when the low, mournful sound of the whistle reverberated through the air. It seemed as if the sound was flung against the mountain, and the mountain threw it back at Lizzie. It was very loud, but in a way it was a pleasant, lonely sound. It was also a sad sound, which gave her goosebumps when it wailed again. As the train clickety-clacked along, it reminded her of Doddy Millers and going to Ohio. She missed them and wished they could go for another visit on the train.

Lizzie sat and watched the water gliding along. She wondered where it was going, and why it was blue and green and purple.

"Let's go sit on the dock," Edna suggested. So they found the wooden dock, plopping down on the wooden boards, and hung their bare feet in the cool water. It was the most delicious feeling, the water rushing over Lizzie's bare legs, never stopping, almost like a faucet that never shut off.

"Do you go swimming here?" Lizzie asked.

"Oh, yes," Edna yawned. "A lot."

Lizzie couldn't believe her ears. Edna could actually swim! How Lizzie longed to be able to learn how to swim, but Mam always told her Amish girls don't learn to swim. She looked at Edna with wide eyes.

"You don't," she stated.

"What do you mean, we don't? Of course, we do,"

Edna said.

"You mean you go in deep water and swim? In water that's so deep you can't touch the bottom?"

"No, we stay in water that's safe, and just doggie paddle, but it's still swimming."

"What's doggie paddling?"

"Just paddling along under the water, kicking your arms and legs, and you stay afloat. It's really easy. I'll show you how sometime."

"Could we go swimming now?" Lizzie asked.

"Of course not. We don't have our swimwear, and, besides, it's almost time for us to go back."

"I wish I could learn," Lizzie said.

"Someday, maybe you will," Edna assured her.

"But how could I? We don't have a river. We don't have anything except small creeks, and we're not allowed to swim in English people's swimming pools. Are you?"

"No."

"So, see, I'll never learn," Lizzie said, sighing.

. . . . .

When they got back to the house, Ivan asked Lizzie if she still wanted to see a real bird's nest with speckled brown eggs in it. Lizzie followed him eagerly to a huge tree with strange-looking white and beige-colored bark on it. The branches hung low to the ground, but Ivan climbed up about as high as the shop roof.

Lizzie heard the small branches cracking as he came back down, cradling a perfectly formed bird's nest in one hand.

"Now, look!"

Lizzie bent her head and was amazed at the perfectly soft lining of the nest. There were four beautiful speckled eggs nestled in perfect harmony, with one egg having as much space as all the rest.

"See this? The bird uses the softest material to line the inside, so the eggs don't break. This bird has pieces of string and horse hair woven in, along with different grasses and pieces of hay and straw."

"Can I touch them?" Lizzie asked.

"Oh, no! Huh-uh! Never touch eggs in a bird's nest, because you might hurt them."

"They're so pretty. I never saw a bird's nest before."

"Now you did."

And with that, he scrambed up the tree, returning the nest in the exact same position.

"What kind of bird lays those speckled eggs?" Lizzie asked.

"These are cardinal eggs," Ivan replied.

"What's a cardinal?"

"You know, those bright red birds with a crest on top of their heads."

"Oh, yes, I know."

"I hope they all hatch. I'm going to watch them every day until I know what happens to them."

Lizzie looked over at Ivan. He really meant it, she could tell. He must really be a nature lover, caring so much about these birds.

"I wish we lived here," she blurted out suddenly.

Ivan looked at Lizzie, and he could tell she really

meant it.

"Why?"

"Because."

"No, really—why?"

"Well, there's so much more to do and see here. We don't have any mountains or rivers or ridges or sawdust piles or birds' nests or . . . or anything." Suddenly Lizzie felt shy, because she hadn't meant to say all that to Ivan. But after this wonderful afternoon, Lizzie's world was not so small anymore. There were lots of things in Jefferson County—almost too many to imagine. Even swimming. In her greatest dreams, she had never thought it was possible to learn to swim. And now . . . you could never tell.

The First Day of School

"O come, angel band,
Come and around me stand;
O, bear me away on your snowy wings,
To my immortal home:
O, bear me away on your snowy wings
To my immortal home."

Waves of song rolled across the classroom on the first day of school. Emma sang heartily along with everyone else, her voice lowering and rising in perfect unison. Lizzie tried hard, and for awhile she could sing well, except she kept glancing down at the top of Mandy's head, wishing so much she could have stayed at home with Mam. She just knew Mandy was going to cry like she herself had on her first day.

Lizzie pulled a pin from her apron, and pushed it back in. She swiped nervously at a stray hair that hung down the back of her neck. She adjusted a hairpin in the bob at the back of her head and tried to look at Mandy's face by leaning to the side. She helped sing awhile, until she couldn't stand the suspense of wondering when Mandy would burst into tears and start chewing her thumbnail.

Lizzie wished with all her heart they wouldn't be singing this song. It was almost as bad as "When the Stars Begin to Fall." Every time they sang this song, she could only think of the little blue book Dat read on Sundays. It was written in German, so Lizzie couldn't read it, but the old-fashioned pictures always made her feel sad and fearful, because someone was dying and the angels hovered around his bed. The angels weren't very pretty, and neither was the man lying in the bed, because it was always so black and white. If the angels looked more beautiful and the man on the bed a bit less fierce, Lizzie would not have minded this song as much.

Lizzie had asked Dat what the book was about, and he told her somberly it was the "*Hots-bichly*," a booklet about the "Heart of Man." It was no comfort to Lizzie to know that if you died, that's what it looked like.

The song ended, just as Lizzie tore a hole in the cuticle of her thumb. She had chewed it down until it hurt so bad that she caught her breath and wrapped her other hand tightly around her thumb.

"Someone else may pick a song," Teacher Katie said brightly. Lizzie thought she said it too cheerfully, as if she was trying to convince herself that she was happy on the first day of school. She couldn't have been too happy, or else she wouldn't have picked that mournful song. It irked Lizzie.

"Two-eighty-four."

Lizzie quickly thumbed the pages till she found the right one. She sighed with relief when she found the title, "Life's Railway to Heaven." That was good.

"Can you start it?" asked Teacher Katie.

Abner shook his head, grinning sheepishly. So Teacher Katie started the song on a high, clear note, with the pupils following, singing along lustily, because this was an old favorite that everyone knew well. She leaned sideways and peered as close to Mandy as she could without getting too far out of line.

She could not believe her eyes. Mandy's eyes were shining, and her voice rang out as she sang the chorus, smiling at the little girl beside her, who was also singing along. Mandy actually looked happy! Lizzie was so relieved that her knees even felt weak after the song ended. Her love for Mandy swelled in her heart, because she was actually not going to cry.

After singing class, it took a while until everyone found their seats, because it was so different from the

year before. Either that, or usually Lizzie forgot lots of
things over the summer, especially where she was sitting
the year before.

Mandy hesitated, lifting her big green eyes question-
ingly at Teacher Katie, as she stood quietly by a small
desk. Lizzie could tell that Mandy was uncertain what
to do, or where she should be seated. Lizzie wished
Teacher Katie would hurry up and tell Mandy where
to sit. She knew Mandy felt like crying being so unsure
of herself. Mandy's hand stroked the top of the desk
self-consciously, but she just remained calmly standing
beside one desk, her thin little body pressed against the
side, as if it made her look smaller.

"Now, first grade!" Teacher Katie called loudly.

Lizzie relaxed, relieved to know that she had noticed
her first graders.

"Can you find your name on a desk?"

The first grade watched Teacher Katie shyly, before
they looked at each desktop for their name tag. Lizzie
could have cried with relief to see Mandy point triumphantly at a name tag, quickly scooting into a seat and
folding her hands on the desktop. She looked at the little
girl beside her and smiled timidly.

"Good! Good!" Teacher Katie stood by the first graders' desks, pushing up her sleeves and smiling. Mandy
smiled up at her teacher, her huge green eyes crinkling
at the corners.

"Can you all write your names?" the teacher asked.

"I can," Mandy said clearly.

Lizzie cringed in her seat, because Mandy was not

supposed to speak without raising her hand first. But
how was she supposed to know? Lizzie thought it wasn't
fair, asking new pupils a question without telling them
they needed to raise their hands first.

Teacher Katie didn't say anything about raising
hands. She just smiled at Mandy and said, "Very good,
Amanda. You may write your name on the blackboard
to show your friends. Do you want to?"

Lizzie was horrified. She could not believe Teacher
Katie was going to make Mandy go up to the blackboard
and write her name the very first morning she ever went
to school. But Mandy slid quietly out of her desk and
walked softly to the blackboard. Bending, she carefully
selected a nice piece of chalk.

Lizzie's breath came rapidly, and her heart thudded
in her chest. Mandy had never written on a blackboard
before, and she didn't know how, not even one tiny bit.

But Mandy held the chalk carefully, and slowly wrote
"Amanda" in nice, straight letters, a bit crookedly, but in
good writing across the blackboard. She laid the chalk
carefully in the tray, turned, and walked daintily back to
her seat, her big green eyes sparkling.

Teacher Katie was very pleased, Lizzie could tell.
"Why, thank you, Amanda. That was very good. Does
anyone else want to show me how you can write your
name?"

Two more pupils in first grade shyly wrote their
names on the blackboard. Teacher Katie praised them
as well, but Lizzie couldn't help but notice that Mandy's
name was written the best.

After that, the first grade was given a picture to color. Lizzie watched carefully as Teacher Katie passed out clean white sheets of paper and new yellow boxes of crayons. Mandy sat up straight in her seat, wiggling a bit more than necessary, because she was happy to be able to color a brand new picture. Lizzie knew how much Mandy loved to draw and color with crayons, so she relaxed and started to put away her own things.

She had a new pencil box this year, one that she really loved. It was blue, long and narrow, with a white plastic top that you pushed back like a rolltop desk. Lizzie could never quite figure out what happened to the rippled white plastic, because when you pushed it back, it just disappeared. Emma had told her it curled down under the layers of blue plastic on the bottom, but that's how Emma was. She didn't know for sure, she just thought she did and acted as if she knew. Lizzie figured the top rolled up like aluminum foil or bathroom tissue, but Emma said it couldn't, there was no room for a roll like that at the back of the pencil box. Lizzie didn't care what Emma said; the back of the pencil box was a little bigger than the front, if you looked at a certain angle.

Lizzie also had two new pens. One was clear, so you could see through it to the tube of blue ink in the middle. The other pen was sparkling silver and purple, with a purple cap on the top. It was the prettiest pen Lizzie had ever owned, so she snapped the top of it with her thumb, clicking it noisily, until her friend Betty looked over at her pen. Lizzie smiled at Betty with a pleased expression, holding up her pen.

Betty looked away and didn't smile, so Lizzie knew she was jealous. She laid the shining pen in the wooden groove of her desktop and swung her feet, pretending to look in the other direction. If she looked sideways, she could see Betty looking at her pen, but only for a very short time before she looked away again. Lizzie was happy with her silver pen, because she almost never had anything nicer than Betty. It was kind of a good feeling, so she rolled the pen with her fingers.

At recess, Lizzie asked Betty if she had a new pen. Betty turned her back to Lizzie and started talking to Susie, as if she hadn't heard her at all. That hurt Lizzie terribly. She just couldn't understand what was wrong with Betty.

She found Emma at the water pump, talking to Abner and Elam about picking baseball teams. Emma was often the boss at school, as much as she was at home. That was just how Emma was.

"Emma!" Lizzie tugged at her sleeve.

"What?"

"Emma, you know what? Betty won't talk to me. She's ignoring me," she whispered.

"Why?"

"I don't know. I have no idea what I did wrong."

"Well, don't worry about her. Just be nice."

"I'm not going to be, if she's not nice to me."

"Just forget about it, Lizzie. Maybe you hurt her feelings or something."

Lizzie walked away. She couldn't help it if Betty was jealous about her pen. She wasn't showing off, she was

just clicking the top of it so she'd notice it. She wished
Betty would have noticed her new pen more. That was
the trouble with friends—you could never tell when they
would decide not to like you.

Lizzie was relieved when the bell rang, because she
had nobody to talk to, and it felt so different. After she
resumed her studies, Lizzie forgot all about Betty. She
was doing vocabulary, which she just loved to do, and it
seemed as if her new book was going to be a lot harder
than last year. She bent over her work, wondering if
she could do all these words without using her diction-
ary. Without thinking, she reached up for her shiny new
purple and silver pen, and pressed her thumb on the top,
making a clicking noise. She was looking for the cor-
rect definition for the word "wonder," clicking her pen
repeatedly.

Unexpectedly, she felt a sharp nudge in the side of
her leg. She looked over at Betty, a smile on her face,
because she was so happy that Betty liked her again.
Betty's eyebrows were drawn down and she mouthed
the words, "You think you're smart, don't you?"

Lizzie was shocked. The smile disappeared from her
face, and she lowered her head, her face flaming with
shame and embarrassment. If Betty had slapped her,
it probably wouldn't have hurt any worse. Slowly, she
put the pen in the groove and picked up her pencil. She
pressed her lips tightly together to keep from crying, trying to think of funny things before tears spilled over her
eyelashes. She was too big to cry, but Betty was her best
friend, and Lizzie could not remember her being unkind

like this—not even once.

Lizzie felt awful. She was ashamed, but also fighting mad. That Betty was just jealous of her new pen, because she didn't have one nearly as pretty. Lizzie peeped at Betty, who was writing with an ordinary blue and white pen, one that didn't even have a clicker on top. Well, good for her, then. Lizzie sincerely hoped Betty would never get a pen even half as nice as hers.

At lunchtime, the upper graders were allowed to go home, because in the fall the farmers were still busy harvesting crops in the field. The big girls were allowed to go home to help their mothers with canning. Tomatoes, pears, and apples were all ready to be put into jars. Lizzie knew, because Mam was canning things every day.

Teacher Katie dismissed the seventh and eighth grade, while the rest of the pupils took turns washing their hands in a basin of water, drying them on the sweet-smelling green roller towel in the back of the room. They were called out by rows, so only six or seven pupils went back at one time. Lizzie was so glad Betty wasn't in the same row as she was, because that Betty was going to find out, there was no doubt about it. Mam had often told Lizzie that it was the devil who made you jealous, and it was not a good thing to do. Betty had better watch out.

Lizzie splashed her hands a lot more vigorously than usual, until Teacher Katie told her to be careful, she was splashing too much. Lizzie didn't even look at her; she was too busy thinking about how Betty was going to catch it, and how much fun it was going to be to tell her exactly what Mam had said about jealousy. She marched back to her desk and thumped her lunchbox on the top of her desk, looking straight ahead so she wouldn't have to look at Betty.

After everyone had washed their hands, Teacher Katie washed hers, got her lunchbox, and sat down at her desk. She explained to the first grade about saying the lunch prayer, because little Amish children are used to silent prayer at mealtime in their homes. Then they all bowed their heads and said the prayer softly.

"Can we eat outside, Teacher?"

The heads were barely lifted before Emma asked this question.

"Yes, you may. Just be careful, and put your trash back into your lunchboxes or into the waste can," Teacher Katie said.

Lizzie loved to eat outside. She dashed out with the others, finding a soft grassy spot on the playground. She plopped down beside Susie, hoping Betty would sit beside them, too, because she was going to tell her what Mam said. Emma and her friends joined the circle, talking and laughing about things in their lunchbox.

Sure enough, Betty walked over slowly and sat beside Susie, so she wouldn't have to sit beside Lizzie. Rachel told her to sit on the other side; there was more room for her there. "You're making it too tight!" she said.

Before Betty could protest, Lizzie looked at Betty and said evenly, "She won't sit beside me, because she's jealous of my pen."

Betty's face turned red, and she looked straight at Lizzie. "I am not!"

"Yes, you are!"

"No, I'm not!"

"Mm-hmm."

Emma was mortified. Lizzie had never acted like this in school. She was always the friendly one who loved everyone and everyone loved her. This was just awful. Emma was horribly embarrassed.

"Lizzie!"

Lizzie looked straight at Emma without blinking, and just gave her a long, level look, not even flinching.

Lizzie turned to Betty, and with the same level stare, she told Betty that if she didn't stop being jealous of her pen, the devil was going to get her. Betty was so surprised at Lizzie, her mouth formed a perfect 'O' of astonishment. There was absolute silence after that. All the lunchboxes remained closed, because no one really felt like eating. The wind stirred the tall grass by the fence, and a grasshopper whirred into the center of their circle. The schoolhouse door slammed as a little boy dashed back inside for a forgotten item.

Finally, Lizzie opened her lunchbox and examined the contents. The others did the same. Rachel began munching soberly on her sandwich, and Lizzie took a long drink from her Thermos bottle. Susie started eating cornstarch pudding from a small plastic container, but a bit self-consciously, not with the usual ease and happy chatter that accompanied their lunch hour.

"The devil can't get you, Lizzie!" Betty burst forth, unexpectedly.

"Mm-hmm. By making you jealous," Lizzie said.

"Who said?"

"My mom."

"Oh."

Lizzie bit into her cheese sandwich, which was so dry it stuck to the roof of her mouth. She scraped it off with one finger and chewed methodically. She wished Mam would let them put bologna and cheese on their sandwich, but there was no use asking. Mam never did, because it was too expensive. They were only allowed two pieces of bologna and no cheese. Or just cheese and no bologna. Mayonnaise helped to make cheese sandwiches less dry, but they weren't very good.

Betty watched Lizzie eat her sandwich. She leaned over to her and said quietly, "Does your mom know stuff like that about the devil, or did she make it up?"

Lizzie chewed her bite of sandwich, swallowed, and said, "Oh, she knows, Betty. She reads her Bible a lot."

Betty looked very seriously at Lizzie. "I'm sorry, then."

"You're welcome," Lizzie replied.

Rachel, Susie, and Emma burst out laughing. They choked on their food, rocked back and forth, slapped their knees, and kept on laughing. Lizzie and Betty looked at each other and smiled, but couldn't really laugh, because neither of them knew what was so funny.

Finally, Rachel gasped, and Emma spluttered, "Lizzie, you don't say 'you're welcome' when someone says they're sorry!"

"What then?" Lizzie asked.

"It doesn't matter," Betty said.

The other girls started laughing again, so Betty and Lizzie got up and walked to the porch. Betty turned to Lizzie and asked her if she was still mad.

"No, I'm not. But, Betty, you should never act jealous, because you are my very best friend. And besides, I never have nicer things than you do. You know that."

"I wasn't really, really mad or jealous. You were just kind of clicking it too much."

"You mean, I was showing off?" Lizzie asked.

"You were kind of, yes."

"Well then, I won't."

"Good."

"Betty?" Lizzie asked.

"Hmm?"

"Do you want my new pen? Just to use next period?"

"May I?"

"Sure you may!" Lizzie said generously.

"Oh, goody, Lizzie!" Betty said.

They hurried inside to find the pen, which Lizzie handed to Betty, her head held high, and her face wreathed in smiles. Betty examined it carefully.

"Where did you get a pen like this?" she asked.

"My aunt Fannie gave me and Emma each one for . . . actually, I don't even know what for. But you may use it for a long time, Betty."

Betty looked at Lizzie, and Lizzie looked back at Betty. They shared a smile of pure delight, because they were back to being the best of friends.

"I'm going to ask my mom if you may come home with me overnight! Do you want to, Lizzie?" Betty beamed.

"Of course!"

"We would have so-o-o much fun. You could help me feed my calves and look at all my pretty things I got for Christmas!"

Arm in arm, they left the classroom, and Teacher Katie wondered vaguely what that was all about. That was the thing about girls—they were a lot harder to figure out than boys. Teacher Katie smiled to herself and shook her head a few times, before folding her waxed paper neatly, closing her lunchbox, and proceeding to check second grade papers.

Grandma Miller Is Sick

Lizzie, Emma, and Mandy burst through the kitchen door, their bonnets dangling and their sweaters hanging open or buttoned crookedly. The crisp fall air swirled around their feet as they banged the door shut behind them. Their tin lunchboxes made a clattering sound when they threw them facedown on the oilcloth-covered table. The kitchen seemed strangely quiet without Mam, but they thought nothing of it, because Mam wasn't always in the kitchen when they returned home from school.

"I'm hungry!" Lizzie said loudly, going into the pantry. She rummaged in the plastic containers, looking for molasses cookies. They were her favorite when she came home, especially if Mam made hot chocolate.

"Where's Mam?" asked Mandy, opening her lunchbox and finding a yellow apple she hadn't eaten at school. She rubbed it across her apron and took a huge, crisp bite.

"Mmm!" she said.

Lizzie watched her eat the apple, wondering why Mandy always ate things like oranges and apples. She even liked Jell-O better than chocolate whoopie pies, which was unthinkable to Lizzie, because Jell-O tasted sour, same as most fruit. Mam said that was why Mandy was so thin—she ate good, healthy things that weren't so fattening. Lizzie didn't worry whether something was fattening or not, she just ate whatever tasted good. All she knew was that a whoopie pie tasted a whole lot better than an apple, especially a green one.

There were footsteps coming up the stairs, and the girls heard Mam and Dat talking as they appeared in the living room doorway. Mam's nose was red and her eyes looked swollen, her lips quivering with emotion. Dat had his arm across Mam's shoulder, as if trying to comfort her.

Lizzie looked carefully at Mam, her heart sinking. *Now what is wrong?* she thought. She could easily tell that Mam had been crying, and Lizzie felt very distressed.

Dat looked at Emma and said soberly, "Emma."

"What?" Emma had been reading quietly, kneeling on a kitchen chair, bent over the table with the paper spread on top. She looked up, quite unaware that anything was wrong.

"Do you think you three girls could stay here with a 'maud' if we decide to go to Ohio?" Dat watched Emma's face carefully as he spoke.

"Why would you go to Ohio? Where are you going?" Lizzie blurted out before Emma had a chance to answer.

Mam sat down wearily, putting her arm around

Mandy's thin shoulders. Mandy snuggled against Mam, her eyes carefully searching Mam's swollen face. Mam reached over and brushed a few stray hairs out of Mandy's eyes, smiling at her in reassurance.

Dat broke off a piece of molasses cookie and took a bite. He chewed thoughtfully as Mam answered Lizzie's questions.

"We got a letter from Aunt Vera, and she says Grandma Miller is not well. She's weak and sick and often has to lie down and rest, because she just doesn't have her strength." Mam's voice rose at the end because she felt so helpless, and Lizzie knew she didn't like to be so far away when her mother was sick. She pitied Mam, but Dat looked so miserable that she almost pitied him more.

Mam sighed and wiped her eyes and nose with a crumpled handkerchief. She adjusted a loose pin on the front of her old brown dress, smoothing her covering in one swift movement. Mam was very upset, and Lizzie felt like burying her face in Mam's soft stomach, the way she used to do when she was younger.

"If we go," she continued, glancing at Dat's worried face, "we'll go tomorrow on the train. It doesn't suit Rachel to stay with you, because Elam Kings just had a baby boy and she's helping there. So if it suits Malinda Zook, would you stay with her for a few days?"

Emma sat down in a chair and asked, "Why her?"

"Who is Malinda Zook?" Lizzie asked nervously.

"She has helped me already, with canning and housecleaning. Don't you remember Abner Zook's Malinda?" Mam asked.

"Who?"

"Lizzie, you know who Mam means. That girl that made you put your books on the toy shelf, and you were so provoked," Emma said.

"Oh, her," Lizzie said.

"We'd take Jason along, then Malinda can go to her job till the evening. You girls can go to Lavina Lapp's house till Malinda picks you up," Dat said.

"Lavina is out of school. We can't go to her house," Lizzie said crossly. This whole thing was just not something Lizzie wanted to do. Why did Mam and Dat have to go to Ohio in the first place? "Mam, Mommy Miller will probably be better soon. Do you have to go to Ohio?" she wailed.

"Lizzie!" Emma said. "Of course they want to go. How would you feel if it were Mam?"

Lizzie shot Emma an angry look without answering. Emma was always good, that's just how it was. Lizzie did not want to stay at Lavina Lapp's house, and she did not want to be in the house alone at night without Dat. Besides, she was sure Malinda Zook would play her harmonica, then Lizzie would get the blues and have to go into her dark bedroom all alone.

"Why can't we go along?" Lizzie asked.

"Lizzie, you have to go to school. You can't go along this time," Dat said firmly.

Lizzie turned and walked slowly into the living room. Her eyes blurred with tears, but she would not cry. She sat on the blue platform rocker, smoothing her hands along the swans' heads on the arms. She rocked back and forth, thinking about Malinda Zook. She was a good *maud* when she helped Mam work, but for some reason, Lizzie thought she was bossy. She had told Lizzie that little girls should always put their toys away after they were done playing with them, and Lizzie could see absolutely no sense in that. If you got out a book, looked at it, and put it away, then got another one and soon put that one away, there was no use even reading. It was the same way with her dolls, puzzles, or whatever. She solemnly vowed to herself that if she was ever a *maud*, she would never tell someone else's children to put their toys away.

"What is wrong with Mommy Miller?" Lizzie heard Emma ask Mam.

"The doctors don't really know yet. They want to take some tests at the hospital in Baxter, but Mommy won't. You know how she is, Emma—she's probably afraid it would cost too much."

"Is she coughing, or does her stomach hurt, or what?" Emma asked.

"I really don't know, Emma. I'm just so anxious to go and be with her, and find out more about the reason for losing her strength like this." Mam put away the empty lunchboxes while Emma set the table for the evening meal. Mam started peeling potatoes, glancing out the kitchen window repeatedly. Dat had gone to ask Malinda to stay with the girls, so she was anxiously awaiting his return.

Supper was much more quiet than usual, spoons and forks scraping loudly against their dinner plates. Dat kept glancing anxiously at Mam, who was barely eating, her head bent, trying to keep her emotions in check for the girls' sake. Malinda had given her consent, so Mam had to pack their suitcase that evening, because they had to catch the train very early the next morning.

Lizzie tried hard to be a good girl. She knew it was selfish to complain, so she ate her supper in silence. At least the food on her plate was comforting. The mashed potatoes had brown butter floating across the top, and the ground beef gravy was a bit too salty—exactly the way Lizzie liked it. Mam had put a few slices of Velveeta cheese on top of the green beans, which made them easier to eat. Green beans were so flat tasting, unless you dipped them in ketchup.

So Lizzie scooped up a forkful of mashed potatoes and gravy, enjoying the taste of the salty, greasy meat. She felt grateful for the good food on her plate, even if Dat and Mam had to go to Ohio.

That evening when Mam tucked them in, her eyes were bright with tears. She told the girls if they were good for Malinda, she would bring them something nice when they came home. Mam was like that, Lizzie thought. She could hardly bear to leave them, and always brought them a small gift. Lizzie put her arms around Mam's neck and held her more closely than usual, because she would be gone in the morning.

"Can Malinda Zook comb our hair?" she asked worriedly.

"Oh, yes. She can good enough for a few days, Lizzie," Mam assured her. When she closed the door softly behind her, Lizzie had never quite felt so alone. She lay for a long time, staring at the square of light on the ceiling, wishing with all her heart Mommy Miller did not have to be sick.

. . . . .

In the morning, Lizzie stretched lazily, quite happy and relaxed, until she remembered that Dat and Mam were gone. Then she snapped her body rigidly, and pulled herself into a tight curl, pulling the covers over her head. She lay there in the soft darkness, not wanting to come out from under those covers, ever. Emma awoke and slapped the top of the covers.

"Lizzie! Where are you?" she whispered.

Lizzie peeped out and said, "Emma, I guarantee Malinda Zook does not know how to roll our hair right."

Emma giggled. "Lizzie, you don't know," she said.

Lizzie threw back the covers. "You can laugh, Emma, but it's not funny."

"Girls!"

They held perfectly still at the sound of a strange voice calling them. Lizzie whispered to Emma, "Answer!"

Emma whispered back, "You do!"

"Girls! It's time to get up!"

Emma cleared her throat. "Alright."

Steps receded across the living room and Lizzie looked sourly at Emma. "Why did you say 'alright?' That was dumb. We always just say, 'Hmm.'"

"Well, you could have answered."

"No, you're the oldest."

"Lizzie, if you act this way when Mam and Dat are in Ohio, I'm going to tell them when they come home. I mean it."

Lizzie yanked at her purple dress. The metal coat hanger clattered to the floor and Emma told her to pick it up. Lizzie didn't pick it up, because Emma was being too bossy. She did help her make their bed, knowing if she didn't at least try to behave, Emma most certainly would tell their parents about her behavior. Lizzie knew that between Malinda Zook and Emma, it was going to seem like a long time until Dat and Mam returned.

Malinda was short, with wavy brown hair and a crisp, clean white covering. She had on a light blue dress with a gray apron, and was bustling around the kitchen, packing their lunchboxes. There was a delicious smell coming from the frying pan on the stove, and Lizzie watched as she turned bacon with a fork.

Bacon! Lizzie's mouth watered, because bacon was a treat for them. Mam almost never bought bacon from the meat man, because it was too expensive. Lizzie loved bacon, so without thinking, she walked over to Malinda and asked, "Where did you get bacon?"

Malinda put her hands on her hips and said, "Don't I even get a 'good morning' or a 'hello' or anything?"

Lizzie looked up shyly and giggled. "Hello!"

"That's better. Good morning, Emma. Mandy is still sleeping in your parents' room. Should I wake her?" she asked.

Emma looked seriously at Malinda and said quietly, "Probably. She goes to school now, too."

"Oh, Lizzie, we just butchered two hogs, so I brought some fresh sausage and bacon for you. Do you like it?" Malinda asked.

"Oh, yes! I love bacon!"

"Good, because we'll have it as soon as breakfast is ready. Can you see what else should be put in your lunchboxes?"

Emma peered into her lunchbox as Lizzie opened the lid of hers. Malinda had put in sandwiches, a yellow apple, a bag of pretzels, and a small container of peaches. Lizzie looked over at Emma and wrinkled her nose as she pointed to the peaches. Emma lowered her brows and held up a finger to her lips, so Lizzie knew she should not say anything because it wasn't polite. But they never put peaches in their lunch. Never. They were too sticky and hard to eat.

It was almost more than Lizzie could bear. Mam and Dat in Ohio, and peaches in her lunch.

Malinda made different eggs. She mixed them all together, adding milk, salt, and pepper. When they were almost done, she mixed some cheese in with them. She served them on a small plate, with three pieces of crunchy bacon and buttery toast with jelly. The eggs

were so light and fluffy and cheesy that Lizzie thought
they seemed more like pudding than eggs.

"Mmm!" she said.

"Mmm!" Emma answered.

Mandy giggled and Malinda smiled as they all ate
that delicious breakfast together. Lizzie wasn't even
very sad, thinking of Dat and Mam in Ohio. But when
Malinda combed her hair, she pulled so horribly on the
snarls that tears sprang to Lizzie's eyes. Malinda rolled
her hair so tightly that Lizzie could hardly close her eyes
without stretching her forehead. And when she bent her
head, so Malinda could put up her bob, she cringed with
every hairpin being jabbed firmly in place. Mam was not
nearly as rough, and Lizzie was glad they had only one
more morning to go.

On the way to school, Emma told Lizzie her hair
looked really flat. "It makes you look homely, the way
she combed your hair," Emma told
her matter-of-factly.

"Yours looks the same," Lizzie
said.

"No, Lizzie, Emma is
combed much nicer than
you are," Mandy said.
Lizzie reached up to touch
her hair, which did seem as if it
was rolled a bit more flat than
usual. She grimaced as she
pulled it forward from under the tightly applied

hairpins.

"She rolled it so tightly I can hardly close my eyes," Lizzie muttered.

Mandy laughed. "You won't fall asleep at your desk, then."

Lizzie didn't answer. There was nothing to say. If your parents were in Ohio and you had peaches in your lunch and your hair combed too tightly, there was nothing to be happy about, either. She kicked viciously at a sharp stone, sending it skittering across the road.

"Stop that!" Emma barked.

"I can kick stones if I want to!"

"Lizzie, you know what I said," Emma replied, her voice rising on the last words in that threatening way of hers.

Lizzie didn't say anything to that, either.

. . . . . .

That evening, after the sun had gone down and twilight crept into the living room, Emma, Mandy, and Lizzie all had the blues. It was alright if Dat and Mam were in Ohio, as long as the sun was shining, but when the shadows fell after the sun slid behind the houses, it was hard to be brave.

Malinda was writing letters at the kitchen table. She had been doing that for a very long time, Lizzie thought. She hoped Mam wouldn't pay her too much, because she wasn't a very good babysitter. She could at least read to Mandy.

Lizzie wandered over to the bookcase. She had read every book that was in the house, almost, except the

Bible. Sometimes she read parts of it, but it was too hard to understand. It was fun to memorize verses at school, though. She wished Mam would buy more books for her, but she guessed if they couldn't afford bacon, they couldn't buy more books.

Suddenly, there was a loud knock on the door. Actually, it was more like a banging on the screen door, which rattled horribly. Malinda jumped, and her eyes grew very large and afraid. She looked at the girls, but they just stared back at Malinda. She swallowed and rose hesitantly from her chair, keeping her hand on the back, as if for protection.

There was another bang on the screen door.

"Do your parents often have evening visitors?" Malinda asked.

"Sometimes," Emma said.

Slowly, Malinda walked to the door and turned the knob. She bent to peer into the darkness on the porch.

"Anybody home?" boomed a very loud voice.

"Y-yes."

"Where's the man of the house? Don't you know there is a pony running down the middle of the street? Only people I know who have one is you guys!" he shouted.

Malinda explained that Mr. Glick was away, but she'd be right out.

"Lizzie, get your sweater! Hurry up!" Malinda called.

Lizzie's heart raced as she grabbed her sweater and hurried down the stairs after Malinda and the big neighbor man. *It must be Dolly*, she thought wildly. *Oh, I hope*

Dolly doesn't get hit by a car!

They hurried across the yard, while the large man tried to tell them where the pony had been. Malinda said she had no idea where this pony would go, and the man told her someone had better, because that pony was going to be killed, running around the streets in the dark.

Lizzie was so scared that her mouth was dry and her tongue felt thick and choking. *Oh, please, please don't let Dolly be killed*, she thought over and over. She stopped, and the rustling of leaves left an eerie quiet. Lizzie strained to see in the darkness, but she could see nothing. And then she seemed to hear a steady, clipping sound, but she figured it was only her imagination.

Her breath came in little puffs of fear, and she strained to hear, to see, just anything to know if it was Dolly.

Clippity! Clippity! There! Now she knew it was Dolly. "Please, Dolly, come here," she breathed.

Clippity! Clippity! Clop! Clop! Clop!

Lizzie ran, unafraid, toward the sound, knowing in her heart it was truly Dolly. A shadowy, white figure broke through the darkness as Dolly trotted in the drive. Lizzie ran as fast as she could, blindly, stumbling across the gravel, with Malinda and the neighbor man.

"Whoa, Dolly! Whoa," she soothed, as the pony stood shaking at the barn door. "How did you get out? What happened, Dolly? Whoa, girl!" Lizzie reached out for her halter, but there was none. So she gripped her mane hairs in one hand, cupping her hand under Dolly's chin as Malinda opened the door.

"This door isn't latched, Lizzie," she said.

"Well, I guess not! How else would the stupid animal have gotten out, unless he's a ghost!" yelled the big man.

Lizzie was almost crying with relief and excitement, so she didn't trust her voice to say anything. Dolly was not a stupid animal—she was a smart pony, and someone had left the door open or she would never have run away.

Malinda thanked the man for telling them about Dolly, and he walked out the gravel driveway, muttering under his breath.

Malinda helped Lizzie find Dolly's stable with the aid of a flashlight, where they secured the gate tightly. As they shut the barn door and shuffled through piles of leaves, Lizzie looked up to Malinda and said, "Thank you, Malinda."

"For what?" she asked.

"For helping me catch Dolly."

"Well, you did, Lizzie."

"I did, didn't I?"

"You sure did," Malinda replied.

Lizzie's heart swelled with pride and happiness. She decided then and there that she liked

Malinda as well as Rachel, even if she put peaches in
their lunch and combed their hair too flat. Malinda was
really nice.

chapter 20

Another Trip to Ohio

After Mam and Dat returned, Lizzie's life settled into the normal routine. School days followed in quick succession, with Lizzie learning more every week. Mandy was a good pupil in first grade, so Lizzie was no longer nervous about that.

The air turned colder again, with leaves swirling at their feet when they walked past the woods on their way to school. Mam had to make Emma and Lizzie new coats for winter, but she handed down Lizzie's coat for Mandy. She had to open some seams and make the coat smaller, because Mandy was so thin.

The coats were slippery on the inside, because the coat lining was a heavy material. Lizzie loved the feeling of wearing a new coat with a slippery inside, because if she held out her arms and turned first one way, then quickly in the opposite direction, her coat swished around her, making her feel like she was being twirled. Emma told her to stop that, because it looked as if she was dancing. Lizzie couldn't see anything wrong with holding out her arms and twirling around, so she didn't stop. Emma walked ahead, but Mandy stayed with Lizzie and giggled.

More and more, Mandy was Lizzie's playmate at home. Emma was ten years old now, and loved to sweep the floor, bake cookies all by herself, and watch Mam at the sewing machine. Sometimes Mam even let Emma sew all by herself, and Emma could make little homemade handkerchiefs that were hemmed well for a ten-year-old.

Lizzie did not enjoy housework at all. She didn't care if the toys were scattered all over the living room, or if the dishes went unwashed, as long as she didn't need to do it. So Lizzie and Mandy played in the yard or playhouse. They picked up the bruised or partly rotten apples from beneath the apple tree, put them on the wagon, and threw them to the neighbor's hogs, whose pasture was across the alley. Lizzie loved to watch the hogs eat. She often wished she was one, being allowed to slurp all you wanted, because it was the proper pig thing to do.

Sometimes they watched Evelyn's husband, Jim, feed the hogs. There was a long, narrow iron trough on the ground, and he flung a big bucket of finely ground grain along the trough. Then he filled it with water. The hogs chomped, slurped, and slopped their way along the trough. Sometimes when they were greedy, they even put in their two front feet. Lizzie and Mandy squealed with excitement when they did that.

There were lots of other interesting things to do in the
fall. They picked up hickory nuts, breaking off the heavy
outer shell, which was divided into four pieces. These
pieces looked exactly like little slices of a cantaloupe, except they were brown and a cantaloupe was orange. But
they played with them, putting them carefully on their
dolls' plates as cantaloupe.

One evening Lizzie and Mandy got too cold, playing
in the yard, so they went through Dat's harness shop to
go upstairs and warm themselves. They ran through the
entrance, laughing and talking, but stopped instantly
when Dat said, "Lizzie!" His face looked so sad and so
terrible that Lizzie knew something was very seriously
wrong.

"What?" She turned toward Dat, rubbing her hands
together to warm them. Dat got down on one knee, taking Mandy's hand, and told them quietly that Mommy
Miller had died that afternoon. They had just received
the message, and now they must go to Ohio in a few
hours. Dat's eyes were very blue and filled with tears, so
Lizzie knew he was awfully sad about Mommy Miller.

"Go upstairs to Mam, Lizzie. You need to have a bath
and help her," Dat said.

"But . . . but . . . how soon are we going? Right now?
On the train?" Lizzie was a bit confused, because everything was happening so fast.

"No, with a driver. It's faster. Now go."

They hurried up the steps to the kitchen, without finding Mam or Emma. The water was running in the bathroom, so they hurried in to find Mam leaning over the tub, bathing Jason. She turned as the girls entered, and with a small cry she gathered Mandy and Lizzie in her arms. The back of Lizzie's dress was wet from Mam's soapy arms, as she held them against her. Lizzie cried because Mam was crying, and also because she did not want to have Mommy Miller die. She was a kind, sweet, quiet Mommy, who made mush and milk and custard pie. But Lizzie understood death now, because Susie had died, so it was not as confusing anymore.

Mam sighed and shuddered, wiping her eyes with the corner of her apron. "Now come, Mandy. Your turn to bathe now. Lizzie, you go help Emma pack your things in your little suitcase, then you can have your bath."

Lizzie blew her nose on some bathroom tissue and went to find Emma. She was bent over their bed, arranging nightgowns, socks, and a comb and brush neatly in a small blue suitcase. She looked up as Lizzie entered and said, "Lizzie, it's just awful; Mommy Miller died."

"I know," Lizzie nodded.

"I pity Doddy," Emma said wisely.

Lizzie bit her lip, nodding her head up and down in acknowledgment. "One thing for sure, Mommy Miller probably went straight to Heaven because she was so good and quiet and kind."

"I know."

Mam bustled in, putting their navy blue dresses and

black capes and aprons carefully on top before closing the suitcase. As was the custom, Mam would wear her black dress for a long time, and the girls would wear black capes and aprons to go to church, instead of the usual crisp white organdy. That was a symbol of mourning, to show grief and respect to the memory of the deceased.

.   .   .   .   .

After riding in a vehicle most of the night, the whole Glick family was very rumpled and tired when they reached Uncle Homers' house, where they would sleep. Dat and Mam went to be with Doddy Miller for a short time during the night, so the girls had to stay with Aunt Vera.

She was bustling about, as usual, clucking over the girls, helping them into their nightgowns, lighting lamps, and asking if they were hungry or thirsty. Lizzie was so tired, but it seemed like a long time since she had her sandwich for supper. She whispered to Emma, "Are you hungry?"

"Kind of," Emma whispered back.

Aunt Vera was knocking on MaryAnn's bedroom door. MaryAnn was their only daughter, and Leroy was their only son. They had just two children. MaryAnn was older than Emma and Lizzie, but she was always friendly. She had been chubby like Lizzie, but when she became older, she didn't eat very much anymore. Mostly apples and things Lizzie didn't like, so now she was thin. Her waist was so small, Lizzie was amazed, wishing her waist was so little. But it was too hard eating only apples, so she didn't worry about it very much.

MaryAnn came out of her bedroom, pulling on a soft lavender housecoat. Her hair was not combed, but she was pretty anyway. She smiled at the girls and told them to come with her. Aunt Vera was tying on a head scarf on her way out the door to go down the hill to Doddy Miller, Mam, and Dat.

"Do you want some hot cocoa?" MaryAnn asked.

"You don't have to make cocoa," Emma answered.

Lizzie wished Emma would not have said that. She should have said yes, because that would be good. But, of course, MaryAnn didn't make any, and Lizzie was disappointed.

"Well, here. You can have some cookies, and we have leftover date pudding. You're probably hungry, aren't you?" MaryAnn asked.

Before Emma had a chance to say, "No," Lizzie said quite clearly, "Yes."

MaryAnn smiled again, getting down three dishes from the kitchen cupboard. She filled them with spoonfuls of moist date and nut cake, mixed with sweet whipped cream, and carried them to the table. It was delicious, and Lizzie would have eaten more, but she was ashamed to ask. Mandy did not finish hers completely, so Lizzie ate that, too.

After a cold drink, MaryAnn led them to the spare bedroom, where the blankets and sheets were turned down, so inviting and clean. Lizzie yawned as she crawled into that smooth bed and could barely remember if she was asleep before or after her head touched the cool, sweet-smelling pillowcase.

. . . . .

That was a long, sad day. Lizzie did not like sad funerals, because there were so many people and everyone cried. Well, not quite everyone. Lots and lots of people shook her hand, asking her name and who her parents were. Doddy Miller's house was packed with people wearing black, crying and blowing their noses, and talking and talking.

Lizzie and Emma had to sit on a bench for a very long time, until they became too restless, then Mam let them go outside for a while.

Doddy Miller was so sorrowful that he didn't put his cane around their necks or say, "Goobity, goobity." It seemed so strange to be at Doddy's house and nothing was the same.

When it was their turn to see Mommy Miller in her coffin, Lizzie felt awful. She did not want to go into that room, but knew there was nothing else to do, so she followed Emma. Everyone looked so sad and weary, standing in that bare room, looking at poor Mommy. They spoke in hushed tones, of how young she looked, what an exceptional lady she had been, and how she no longer needed to suffer here on earth. Lizzie just looked from the farthest corner and was relieved when they were allowed to go back out to the living room.

They found their cousin Hannah with Leroy and MaryAnn, so they all walked up to Uncle Homers' house for a while. They talked about school, and things that had happened since the last visit. Emma told them about Dolly running away when Mam and Dat were in Ohio, and how Lizzie had caught her. MaryAnn thought Lizzie was very brave, catching a pony in the dark.

After that, the Jefferson County cousins arrived, so Lizzie was happy to be with Edna. They had lots to talk about, until they all had to go sit on a bench at Doddy Miller's house.

After spending the night at Uncle Homers' again, they all got up very early, eating a quick breakfast, and hurrying around the house, getting dressed, washing dishes, and preparing for the funeral service. It was held at a neighbor's barn, swept clean and prepared. Long rows of benches were set on the wooden plank floor, which were soon filled with hundreds of people, the men on one side of the room, the women on the other.

Lizzie sat close to Emma, and listened carefully to what the minister was saying. She loved to hear the Ohio people talk, because they had such a different accent. This preacher's hair was cut differently, too. His bangs were shorter and cut around his head, like a bowl, which looked different than the ministers at home.

Lizzie could understand almost everything he said, because he talked loudly and clearly, pausing after an especially informative lesson. She liked his eyes, because even when he spoke of serious matters, they twinkled at the corners. Lizzie guessed he must be a kind man, like Jesus was.

The congregation filed past Mommy Miller's coffin at the end of the service, viewing her for one final time. The family was heartbroken, sobbing out their grief at the loss of a very dear mother. Lizzie cried, too, but not too long, because she was watching other people cry. She wondered why some of them didn't cry, and others cried a lot. She guessed some people became sadder when someone died, and others didn't care as much. She had heard Dat tell Mam once that an English lady had to go to a hospital because she couldn't cry. She kept all her sorrows bottled up inside, and she became sick. Lizzie hoped everyone would be alright after the funeral, because some of those boys were not crying at all.

The funeral procession wound slowly along the gentle hills, along dirt roads, and past fields of brown corn and green hay. The Glick family rode in someone else's surrey. That was what two-seated buggies were called in Ohio. They had very narrow bottoms, built out farther to accommodate wider seating space. Lizzie always felt as if she would fall out on the road if she didn't sit in the middle.

Dat drove this borrowed team, with Mam sitting beside him. They didn't talk much, and sat quietly as the horse followed the team ahead of them.

"Why do they call these buggies 'surreys'?" asked Lizzie.

"I don't really know," Dat answered. "Maybe that's just what they were always called, ever since they started to build them."

"Ours at home are called a *"dach-veggly,"* right?" she asked.

"Yes," answered Dat. "Do you know what that means in English?"

"Roof wagon."

"Yep."

"A wagon with a roof on it."

"Mm-hmm."

"Look!" Mam pointed across the field. "That's where I grew up. The old home farm."

The girls strained forward, peering between their parents' shoulders, to see a white barn and a two-story white house nestled in a grove of trees. It looked quiet and peaceful, an unhurried simple farm, where Doddy Miller had milked cows and kept a few pigs and chickens. There was a small grade where the lawn sloped down beside the house, and Mam told them it was the little hill that Mommy had told them she would throw them down if they misbehaved. Mommy was only teasing, of course, Mam said, but it still brought back warm memories.

There were huge pine trees surrounding the graveyard, and they bent and sighed in the autumn breeze. As they buried Mommy Miller, the minister's voice rose and fell, while the pine trees swayed, almost as if the trees were part of the group of mourners.

Lizzie shivered under her wool shawl as she watched the men shovel the cold, wet earth into the deep grave. She could not bear to look at Doddy Miller, bent over his cane, his white beard and hair blowing in the wind. His white handkerchief was held to his nose while tears coursed freely down his weathered face.

All his life he had lived here, and now he was alone, which was so unbearable to Lizzie. She pitied Doddy Miller so achingly that she felt almost weak with emotion. She wanted to go stand beside him and touch him, but it was not proper, so she stayed. But for her, a love that was strong for her beloved Doddy only deepened as she watched him mourn his departed wife. Lizzie wished she could stay in Ohio with Doddy, eating Swiss cheese and Trail bologna, but she knew she had to go home with Dat and Mam and go to school.

After the graveside services, they were served a meal at the same farm where the funeral service had been held in the barn. Lizzie was so hungry and cold that she thought the food was the most comforting, delicious thing in the world.

Hannah, Edna, and Lizzie stood together afterward, talking quietly. Edna told Lizzie that Dat had told Uncle Eli that they were thinking of moving to Jefferson County.

"Move?" Lizzie was astounded. "You mean our whole family? To live there? But where would we live?"

Edna giggled. "I don't know for sure, Lizzie. Maybe

they're just thinking about it, and it isn't even serious. But you could." Her eyes twinkled at Lizzie, but Lizzie did not smile back. She was too busy wondering why nobody had ever said anything to her. They shouldn't plan these things without telling her and Emma.

"We'd have so much fun, Lizzie!" Edna was saying.

"Mm-hmm," Lizzie answered absentmindedly.

But on the way home from Mommy Miller's funeral, Lizzie told Emma that it wasn't right if parents planned to move without telling their children. Emma said that was the parents' business, not Lizzie's. And Lizzie firmly resolved to run away and live with Doddy Miller if Emma was going to stick up for Dat and Mam and want to move to Jefferson County.

chapter 21

Thinking of Moving

Two trips to Ohio had been very expensive for Dat and Mam, and times were hard for them because of the harness shop not having as much business over the years as they had hoped for. Mam worked hard alongside Dat, sewing halters, blacking harnesses, and waiting on shoe customers. Dat remained hopeful, until the day when they could no longer pay their bills. There was hardly anything in the pantry to put in their lunchboxes in the morning, and when Mam baked, it was always shoofly pie or sugar cookies, because those ingredients didn't cost as much as cocoa powder or chocolate chips.

Emma and Lizzie sat on their bed one Saturday afternoon, sorting their stickers and erasers from school. Emma had more stickers, because she saved hers, storing them in a small greeting card box on her side of the bed. The sun streamed through the sheer pink curtains at their window, making their room seem sunny and cozy. They never thought much about being poor,

because it was just a way of life. As long as Mam was
happy and Dat did not become too worried, their life
took on its normal contentment.

Mam had started making hand-tooled leather wallets. She started with a rectangular piece of soft leather,
imprinting it with a plastic pattern of deer, pheasants,
horses, or birds. She could add initials of a person's
name, so that it became personalized.

Lizzie loved to drape herself over the oilcloth-covered
kitchen table as Mam bent over her work. She had different steel tools that gouged or shaded patterns into the
leather. A flat deer became one that stood out from the
leather, with realistic muscles and a background that
actually seemed real. With a little twist of a certain tool,
the deer's antlers stood out, looking so genuine that it
never ceased to amaze Lizzie.

Mam had started this wallet making to acquire some
extra money to buy Christmas gifts and necessities she
would otherwise have gone without. She enjoyed her
work, often working late in the evening after the girls
and Jason were sound asleep in their beds.

Emma was humming softly, while Lizzie paged
through her old coloring book. Their quiet was interrupted by the steady tap-tap of Mam's rubber mallet as
she started hand tooling more wallets.

Emma sighed. "I wish she'd stop pounding if Jason
is asleep," she said, putting three apple stickers on a
separate pile."

"Give me one of your apple stickers, Emma. I don't
have one," Lizzie said.

"Alright." Emma handed her a green one.

"Not a green one!"

"Which one do you want?" asked Emma.

"That one." Lizzie pointed to a shiny red one.

"No, Lizzie. Teacher Katie gave me that one for 100% in arithmetic two mornings in a row."

"You probably cheated, Emma. How could you have 100% two times in a row?"

Tap, tap, tap, tap. The pounding increased, until Emma jumped up, scattering her stickers.

"She's going to wake Jason; I just know it."

"Emma, let her go. She makes lots of money with those wallets. We're going to be rich, then we won't have to move to Jefferson County," Lizzie said.

Emma bounced back on the bed. "I want to move to Jefferson County."

Lizzie stared at Emma. "Do you?" she breathed.

"Sure. It would be more fun than spending another summer in this hot house on top of the harness shop."

"But . . . Emma! We'd have to have a new school, new friends, and a new teacher. And their dresses are so long and they wear black coverings and . . . and Emma, I'll never be able to wear high heels as long as I live."

"Lizzie," Emma said, shaking her head, "you don't have to wear high heels. You are almost ten years old, and you still think you have to wear high heels."

"Not English ones—just Amish black ones."

"I know how you are, Lizzie. You'd clack your heels down as hard as you could, so people would look at your shoes."

Lizzie watched Emma sorting sitckers and didn't say anything. She knew she would not clack her heels hard—just enough so that they sounded a wee bit fancy. Not much.

"But Emma, in Jefferson County we couldn't even have a refrigerator."

"So? I'd rather have a big cooler like Uncle Elis have in their pantry."

"You mean their *'butry'*?" Emma looked at Lizzie, and they burst out laughing.

"They do say *'butry,'* don't they?" Lizzie gasped.

"They do. But, did you ever notice how cold their drinks are? A lot colder than ours."

"Well, if you had a *butry* with a cooler in it, I guess we could learn to like it. But Emma, their long dresses and stuff!" Lizzie wailed.

"Well, Lizzie Glick, you just have to stop being so fancy sometime, anyway," Emma said flatly.

Tap, tap, tap, tap.

There was nothing much to say, so Lizzie got down her book, flipped on her back, and started reading. Her book was not very interesting, so she was just about to put it away and go find Mandy, when she heard the kitchen door swing open and Mam exclaim loudly in an enthusiastic voice. They heard a man's low voice and then the unrestrained laugh of their Uncle Eli.

They turned to look at each other and said at the same time, "Uncle Eli!" Quickly, they jumped off their bed, Emma stashing her stickers in the sliding door of their bookcase bed. Lizzie stuffed her coloring book in her drawer, and they yanked open their bedroom door, hurrying to the kitchen to see Uncle Eli.

He was delighted to see the girls, shaking their hands, while Mam beamed, her hands folded across her stomach. Dat came pounding up the steps from the harness shop, his face alight with welcome. Everyone loved Uncle Eli, because he was a large, friendly man, who laughed so easily that it seemed to roll from his stomach with no effort at all. He never seemed to have any worries, and his smile was always there for everyone, his eyes crinkling at the sides more readily as he grew older.

He shook hands with Dat, laughing easily as he told him how good it was to see them all. Dat laughed too, just because that's what everyone did with Uncle Eli. Mam hurried to put on the coffeepot, and set out sugar cookies and some cheese for an afternoon snack.

Lizzie and Emma scooted back on the bench along the wall, eager to hear the conversation, because Eli always knew lots of things, making Dat laugh as easily as he did.

"Yessir, Melvin, I had to stop in for a minute. I can't stay long—my driver has his wife to worry about, can't stay out ten minutes longer than he promised her, or he's in trouble, mind you." His eyes crinkled almost completely shut, and his stomach shook as his laugh rolled out over the table. Lizzie smiled, then she laughed out loud, just because his laugh made everything so funny.

They talked of everyday things, Mam's voice chiming in, quite unashamedly, because Eli was, after all, her brother. They teased each other about their weight, and

Dat smiled, seeing how happy Mam was.

After a while, Uncle Eli said soberly, "Now, Melvin, I want to tell you the real reason I stopped in. Now, this is not to tell you what to do or anything." He stopped, shaking his head from side to side for emphasis. "But Atlee Yoders are moving back to Ohio. They have homesickness for the old hometown, I guess," he said, chuckling. "But . . . here's what. That basement house will be sold over public auction, and you have a chance to buy it as well as everyone else. It'll go cheap, Melvin, mark my words, because not many English people want a basement house."

Lizzie glanced at Mam, who was chewing on the side of her fingernail, her eyes shining with eagerness. Dat sat up straighter, his hands clasped on his knees.

"Now, I don't want to tell you what to do, Melvin. But you did say you would consider moving over our way if the opportunity came up," Uncle Eli continued.

"Oh, yes," Dat nodded his head. "I sure would. We're really losing hope here, trying to make ends meet."

"Well, my sawmill is going pretty good. We're not rich, mind you, but it's going pretty good, and if you want to, Melvin . . ." he paused as Mam served the coffee, leaning back to allow her more room.

"Mmm . . . boy!" He sniffed his steaming cup, and set it aside to let it cool for a minute before he tasted it.

"Now, here's what I have in mind. The lumber I cut mostly goes for pallet lumber, and if you want to start up a pallet shop, I'll supply the lumber. I'll let you have it at a very reasonable price, and the pallet shop part of the deal is yours. Pallets are a real good thing to get into right now, and I already have a broker willing to give you work."

Dat wiped his hands on his knees and shook his head. "Oh my, Eli. This is going kind of fast. Do you think I could even get a loan to go into something like that?"

Lizzie pitied Dat. He looked so scared and uncertain; actually, he looked all shook up. He didn't really know what to say. Emma was watching Dat, and Lizzie thought Emma looked as if she hoped with all her heart Dat would say yes.

"When is the sale for Atlee Yoders' house?" he asked finally.

Uncle Eli glanced around the kitchen, looking for a calendar. "Mmm, see here, next Saturday, the twenty-fifth."

"Oh, I don't think so. We'd have to sell all this, the harness shop and all the inventory. It's just impossible,"

Dat said.

"Well, if you really want to make pallets, and you do actually want to move over our way, Melvin, I can help you out till you have this place sold," Uncle Eli said, tasting his coffee and reaching for a sugar cookie.

Dat sighed. "It does seem like a golden opportunity. We just have a hard time paying the bills here. It seems as if saddles and harnesses are more of a hobby than a necessity for a lot of people. Even the Amish aren't farming the way they used to."

Uncle Eli's laugh rolled out. "Tell me about it, Melvin! We farmed down on the Rowe place all those years, and if my cows didn't die, my horses tried to!"

Dat laughed along with Uncle Eli, and Mam beamed. They talked about more serious things, punctuated by Eli's laughs, until he stood up, saying his hour was up, the driver had to leave.

After Uncle Eli left, the sun was low in the sky when Mam remembered to make supper. They talked for a very long time, but Lizzie did not listen to everything, because she really didn't care to know whether they were moving for certain. It did sound exciting when she heard Uncle Eli talk about an auction. That was the funny house with a flat roof, and they would live in it.

Lizzie thought of the huge mountain and the river. That was something she liked about Jefferson County. Here, they had no mountains—well, not very big ones, and they were all far away, so it really didn't seem as if there were mountains nearby.

But Teacher Katie, Betty, Susie, Rachel, and all her

friends at school! How could they leave Grandpa Glicks
and Marvin and Elsie? It was too much to think about,
and it gave Lizzie a headache. Besides, if she thought
about things like that, she started chewing her fingernails again, and there was hardly anything to chew. So
she went to find Emma.

She was in the kitchen, helping Mam make supper. Mam was making potato cakes, which Lizzie did
not care for. Potato cakes were hard, leftover mashed
potatoes with raw eggs beaten into them, splatted by the
spoonful in a skillet with grease. Sometimes Mam added
eggs to cold, congealed leftover noodles and fried them,
too, which Lizzie didn't like, either. Emma often put
ketchup on leftover noodles and eggs, which only made
them worse.

Lizzie was feeling confused and miserable, because
she didn't know what was going to happen. It seemed
as if she were trying to put a puzzle together and some
of the pieces were missing. She liked living here above
the harness shop, with the apple trees in the yard, and
the neighbors, back alleys, and hogs to watch. They had
Red and Dolly, the bread man and the meat man, shop
customers, and everything always happened the same
way—or almost. There was nothing to be afraid of or to
worry about—not too seriously, anyway. She worried a
little bit about the end of the world coming soon, but not
as much as she did in first grade.

Where would they buy their groceries in Jefferson
County? And what were pallets? The whole thing just
irritated her. She leaned over the stove, watching the

potato cakes sizzle in the hot grease.

"What else do we have?" she asked grumpily.

"Oh, some warmed-up hamburger gravy," Mam said absentmindedly.

"What else?"

"Peas."

"Ewww!"

"Step back, Lizzie, so I can flip these potato cakes. You'll be splattered with hot grease," Mam said.

"Why can't we have a good supper for once?" Lizzie asked.

"This is a good supper," Mam replied.

"I hate potato cakes."

"Then you can eat gravy bread," Mam said, her mouth in a firm line. "Now go help Emma set the table."

"I hate gravy bread, too."

Mam put her hands on her hips and glared at Lizzie. "Now stop that, Lizzie. If you don't like what I'm making for supper, you just won't have anything to eat then, will you?"

Lizzie looked at Mam defiantly. "Then I won't eat," she said and turned to go down the steps to the harness shop. She sat down hard on the oiled wooden steps, alone in the darkening stairway, and let the tears of frustration well over. And that is how Dat found her on his way up to the kitchen.

"Ach, Lizzie, what's wrong? Why are you sitting here on the stairway?" he asked.

Lizzie was not going to let Dat see her tears, so she wiped her eyes fiercely, swiping her sleeves across them. "N-n-nothing is wrong," she said. And then, because the stairway was dark, and because Dat was so kind, she wailed out her misery to him. She told him all about how hard it was to leave Teacher Katie, her friends, and Red and Dolly.

Dat sat and listened, looking down at his shoes, his hands propped on his knees. He listened as Lizzie told him all her fears, and wondered if he didn't have a lot of those same fears himself. When Lizzie stopped talking, she sniffed, swiped at her eyes with her sleeves, and started chewing her fingernails. Dat took hold of Lizzie's hand and pulled it away from her mouth gently.

"Don't, Lizzie." He sighed. Then he said, "You want to know something?"

"What?" Lizzie looked at Dat.

"I feel exactly the same."

"You do?" Lizzie could not believe it. Dat was so old and big and brave, and she didn't think anyone ever felt the same way that she did.

"Yep." Dat sighed again. "But you know, Lizzie, sometimes we have to give up and accept different, strange things. I would like to go right on living here, making harnesses, but we can't anymore. We simply can't go on. And I have to think of Mam, too. She would love to live in Jefferson County, where her three brothers and their families live. You know Doddy Millers live three hundred miles away and Mam often gets homesick. Then if we can't afford to go to Ohio very often, Mam isn't always happy."

"It's only Doddy Miller in Ohio now, not Mommy." Lizzie said.

"You're right," Dat said.

There was silence on the darkening stairway as Dat and Lizzie sat together in companionable quietness.

"It's hard for you to think of moving, Lizzie. But think of Abraham in the Old Testament. God told him to go into a strange country that he had never even heard of. At least we know where Jefferson County is and what it looks like."

"How could God talk to him, anyhow? He doesn't talk to people now, does He?" Lizzie asked.

"Maybe not as clearly, but if we pray, and we feel led to do something, it's like a still, small voice guiding us," Dat said, very seriously.

Lizzie almost told Dat how she felt when she prayed, but she was afraid there was something wrong with her, so she didn't say anything.

"Do you feel better about moving?"

"Mm-hmm."

"Alright, then let's go eat supper."

"I'm not going to eat any."

"Why?"

"Mam said I can't."

"Ach, Lizzie, come on."

So they turned, walking into the kitchen together. Mandy and Jason were seated on the bench, the food was steaming on the table, and Emma was pouring water.

"Melvin, it's so late that these children are going to fall asleep at the table," Mam said smiling.

"That's alright, Annie. We had an unexpected visitor, and we have more important things to talk about later. Making decisions is a lot of hard work, isn't it?" he said with a smile.

Mam beamed. She absolutely shone; she was so happy. Dat told her he would make a phone call to Uncle Eli and they would be going to the public auction at Atlee Yoders' on the twenty-fifth of September.

When they folded their hands in their laps, bowing their heads for silent prayer, Lizzie peeped at Dat. His head was bowed extra low, and his lips were moving, his eyes shut tightly as he prayed. Lizzie decided then and there, if Dat could feel like she did and be so brave, then she could be brave, too. Besides, Mam was so happy, and that made Lizzie happy, too. So she prayed, asking God to help her be brave, and that she would someday like potato cakes, as well.

It almost seemed as if God heard her, because when she lifted her head, everyone was smiling, even Jason, and the potato cakes shone with the golden light of the setting sun.

Dat looked at Lizzie. "Didn't you say it would be hard to leave Red and Dolly? Well, we don't have to. When we move, they'll be going along in a horse trailer — Dolly on one side and Red on the other."

"Really?" Lizzie asked.

"Oh, yes. We need Red to pull us over those Jefferson County hills. They have some huge hills to cross, because the country has so many ridges," Dat said.

"Widge! Widge!" Jason yelled.

Everyone looked at each other, laughing. Happiness made potato cakes taste almost like mashed potatoes.

Saying Good-bye

"Lizzie, I simply don't believe it."
Lizzie nodded her head up and
down as hard as she could. Betty, Susie,
Rachel, and all their friends sat in a circle, eating their
lunches on the playground. Betty always smashed her
sandwich flat with her thumb and forefinger when she
became nervous, so she was squeezing her poor sandwich until there was nothing left of it.

"You're moving to where?" Betty was incredulous,
because she could not imagine school without Lizzie.

"To Jefferson County."

"Why do you have to?"

"I don't know. I guess because we're poor," Lizzie
said bluntly. There was a long, awkward silence. Emma's face turned red, because it embarrassed her to hear
Lizzie tell all her school friends that they were poor.
They weren't *so* poor that they had nothing to eat.

"I hate to think of coming to school and you not being
here," Betty said.

"We won't move for a while yet. At least a month,"
Emma said.

"Oh."

There was silence in the circle of friends as they all
thought about it. The cool breeze sent shivers up Lizzie's
spine, in spite of the sweater she was wearing. She
pulled it around her back, hunching her shoulders and
crossing her arms around herself to keep warm.

"We have to wear coverings to go to school in Jefferson County. And much longer dresses. When I'm in
eighth grade I'll wear a cape, too," Emma said.

Lizzie was the one to be embarrassed now. Why did
Emma have to say that? She felt like her friends did not
need to know that they would be dressing differently.

"A cape!"

"To school?"

Their friends were laughing at them now, Lizzie could
tell. She wished they could move tomorrow, so no one
could make fun of them. She got up, saying she was
putting her lunchbox away, so she didn't need to hear
the remaining conversation. She dreaded the thought of
changing their dress, and she certainly didn't want Betty
to know. So she put away her lunchbox, slid into her
desk, got out her library book, and started reading. The
clock ticked loudly on the wall, but Lizzie didn't notice;
she was too engrossed in her own thoughts. The book
she held contained nothing as far as she was concerned.
It was just to hide behind, so Teacher Katie would not
notice her expression. Lizzie sat there for a very long
time, until Teacher Katie rolled back her chair and
stopped to look at her.

"Have you been sitting there during the entire recess?" she asked, peering closely at Lizzie.

"Just about," Lizzie said dourly.

"Why?"

"I don't know."

"There must be a reason."

"There isn't."

So Teacher Katie shrugged her shoulders and forgot about Lizzie. She had a headache, because it was one of those days when nothing went smoothly, so she put her lunchbox away, folded her arms, laid her head on top of them, and closed her eyes. The clock ticked steadily. The pupils on the playground shouted or talked loudly, running past the windows playing "Piggy Wants a Motion." Lizzie shuffled her feet, wriggling in her seat to change positions as the silence continued.

The front door opened very softly as Betty slipped in, quietly putting away her lunchbox. She hesitated before she walked over to Lizzie's desk, where she placed both hands on the back seat, leaned over, and asked, "What are you reading, Lizzie?"

"This."

"Oh. Mmm . . . Lizzie, I don't care if you have to wear a covering to go to school. I just wish you wouldn't have to move. And, Lizzie, you're not poor. We are. You have chips in your lunch much more often than we do," Betty said, raising her eyebrows as she looked straight at Lizzie.

Lizzie looked sideways at Betty, her mouth a thin, straight line. Betty blinked. Lizzie kept looking, until Betty giggled, her eyes shining, because she thought Lizzie looked funny, so strict and stern.

"It's not funny," Lizzie said. She swiveled in her seat, putting both feet in the aisle, and faced Betty squarely. "You know you are my best friend, and now I probably won't see you again as long as I live. I don't know why you think you have to laugh about it."

"I'm not laughing about you moving away. You just looked so funny because you . . . well, you act like an old mommy," Betty said.

Lizzie put her hand up to her mouth and laughed with Betty. She slid over in her seat, patting the seat beside her so Betty could sit there. They sat together, side by side, discussing every aspect of letter writing if you lived far away. Together they decided each one would write faithfully every Friday evening after a whole week of school was over, so they could write their arithmetic scores and whether they had received 100% on their spelling test.

.   .   .   .   .   .

Things weren't much better when they drove Red to Grandpa Glicks for the last time before they moved. Marvin and Elsie were a bit subdued, thinking of them moving so far away. They sat on the wooden porch swing that hung from a heavy wooden pole down by the garden, while leaves swirled around them. The garden was almost all cleared out, except for a few late tomato plants. Lizzie thought the garden looked old and tired, making her feel more solemn than ever.

Marvin was taking a bright yellow leaf apart in layers, ripping it along the seams. He threw the pieces away, picked up another one, and proceeded to do the same.

Elsie, Emma, and Lizzie rocked slowly back and forth, the rusty chain squeaking with every move.

"What I can't see," Marvin began, "is why your Dat is going to make pilots."

"Not pilots," Lizzie corrected him. "Pallets."

"Whatever," Marvin said glumly.

"What are they?" Elsie asked.

"Wooden flat things that you put a pile of boxes on at a warehouse or factory. It's so a forklift can slide under them to lift a whole stack at a time," Emma explained.

"How do you know that?" Marvin asked.

"Uncle Elis children told us," she answered.

Marvin thought about this for a while. He kept ripping maple leaves apart, and the girls continued their swinging. Uncle Samuel's dog came running through the leaves and plopped down beside Marvin, his tongue lolling, watching them with bright, inquisitive eyes. Marvin reached down to scratch his ears before he asked who drove the forklift at Dat's "pilot" shop.

"Not 'pilot'," Lizzie corrected him.

"I bet it is 'pilot'. You know how flat those Ohio people talk that moved to Jefferson County. They probably just pronounce it 'pallet' because for '*gleich*' they say '*glach*'," Marvin said.

"Not if they talk English—just Dutch," Lizzie said.

"I bet not."

"You don't know."

"I bet you won't live there very long until you talk exactly like they do—so flat, and rolling your 'r's the way they do," Marvin said, laughing.

"Marvin!" Elsie huffed.

"That's not nice," Emma chimed in.

There was silence again as they listened to a wedge of geese flying overhead. They honked together, flapping their long, heavy wings to stay in flight.

"Well, at least you're not going as far as those geese are flying. They're going the whole way to Canada," Marvin said.

"I guess," the girls answered.

"And another thing. We're getting older, so we couldn't always play together the way we do now. I'm a boy, you know, and it looks childish if I'm always with three girls when we're all together," Marvin said.

"But you're our uncle!" Lizzie wailed. She couldn't bear the thought of being too old to play with Marvin. He was the best, most interesting uncle anyone could ever have. If you had to give up your uncle just because you were getting older, then Lizzie never wanted to grow up.

Marvin knew lots of things. He told Lizzie if you ate a puffball mushroom you could die from the poison. That was a big help to her, because they looked delicious. Lots of other things, like salty pretzels and ice water, were interesting bits of knowlege that fascinated Lizzie. If you ate a salty pretzel, chewed a while, then took a cold drink of ice water, it tasted so good you could hardly believe it. He also taught the girls to pull a wide, flat blade of grass, grasp it between the fleshy part of your thumb and forefinger, put your mouth against it, and blow as hard as you could. If you did it exactly

right, it made a shrill, whistling sound. No one could
do it as well as Marvin, but he taught them how to try,
which Lizzie did for hours before she tired of it.

"Well," Elsie said, "what spites me the most is that you
can't come to our Easter program in the spring. We're
going to have the best program in the whole county. Did
you know that the Mennonite teacher we have has such
good Christmas programs, that some years the people
don't all fit in the schoolhouse?"

"Really?" Lizzie breathed.

"Yes, and this year instead of a Christmas one, we're
having an Easter program. And you'll live far away in
Jefferson County," Elsie said.

Lizzie and Emma tried hard all evening to be their
usual happy selves, but they were actually glad when it
was time to go. Grandpa Glicks sincerely wished them
the best, moving to Jefferson County, and promised
to come help them load their belongings when the time
came.

They were quiet on the way home, wrapped in their
woolen buggy blanket, rocking together companionably
as Red pulled the buggy over the bumps. There was
not much to say, and besides, it only made the lump in
Lizzie's throat bigger when she tried to say something to
Emma.

. . . . . .

Mam was busy packing their belongings in boxes,
singing as she worked. Dat was sorting things in the
harness shop, preparing everything for his sale. The girls
went to school every day, until the day of Atlee Yoders'

sale in Jefferson County. Dat told them to go along, so
they could see where they were moving to because they
were big girls now.

The mountains never ceased to amaze Lizzie. The
mountain closest to their Uncle Elis was the biggest one
of all. It loomed over the countryside, large and deep
blue or black. When the sun shone on the face of it, the
ridges and hollows were easily visible. Lizzie was awed
by this huge mountain, and yet, it thrilled her to live so
close to it—almost like Heidi and the Alm Uncle.

When they arrived at Atlee Yoders' place, there were
cars parked along the road, and a crowd of people were
milling around in the yard. The driver couldn't find a
parking space, so they had to drive past the house, walking back a short distance. Lizzie felt a bit shy, because
of all the Amish people she did not know, but Emma
reassured her, telling her everyone was very friendly in
Jefferson County. They stood with Mam, quietly watching the crowd. There were lots of men, because this was
a public sale, and Mam said they all wanted to see what
the home sold for.

When Uncle Eli saw them, a broad grin spread across
his face, accompanied by his unreserved laugh. Dat
talked with him for a while, but Lizzie could tell that he
was nervous, because his face was so pale.

Other men came to talk to Dat whom Lizzie didn't
recognize, except for one small, thin man who had twinkling brown eyes. She supposed he was the father of all
the red-haired children, and she was right, because two
of the boys walked over and started pulling on his sleeve.

Lizzie and Emma decided to explore, because they were curious what this home was like. They asked Mam's permission, and walked slowly around to the back of the house. There was a garden in the back yard, but it had numerous round stones and big pieces of rock in it. Lizzie told Emma she couldn't imagine growing anything in those stones.

There was a row of trees in the side yard that went all the way along the back of the garden. There were some blackberry bushes and weeds, along with a field lane, as if a neighboring farmer used that lane with his tractor. A white fence enclosed a small pasture behind the barn. The barn was almost new, with a rounded roof and white siding. It was much nicer than their old barn at home. There was even a stairway that went up under this rounded roof, and Lizzie became very excited, telling Emma to imagine how much fun they could have, playing in that hay with their dolls.

Emma didn't say much, because she never played with dolls anymore. She was too old, Lizzie thought sadly.

The white board fence went the whole way around the barn and down the gravel driveway. The pasture on that side of the drive was big—much bigger than Red and Dolly's pasture at home.

The lawn in front of the house was flat, with an embankment at the end beside the road. The porch went out flat, same as the lawn, and it all seemed so low and even, because they were accustomed to stairs and steps going every which way where they lived now.

Inside the low, flat basement house was a nice kitchen that opened into a large living room with shiny hardwood floors. The kitchen cupboards were much nicer than theirs, being varnished to a glossy sheen on a light-colored wood. There were plenty of windows along the front, so it really didn't seem like a basement at all.

Emma pushed open a swinging door along the back wall of the kitchen and found a kettle house. Mrs. Yoder did her laundry in this room, with the washer and rinse tubs along one wall and shelves along another where hats and boots were kept. It was painted in a nice cheery yellow color, with a bright rug spread in front of the door that opened to the side of the basement house.

There were three bedrooms, but Lizzie didn't like them very much when she looked in, because they had only one window up high. Emma said that was because the ground floor was right outside, so they had to put the windows up that high. Lizzie shivered, because the bedrooms were dark and a bit damp. The bathroom was the same way. It had only a small window up high, but that room was pink, with pink rugs and a nice bathtub, and cupboard space for lots of things like towels and washcloths. Emma loved that pink bathroom.

Lizzie loved the whole place. She desperately hoped Dat would be able to buy it, because it really was a lot nicer than where they lived now. For some reason, it almost felt like home. The houses across the road were very nice, new homes with their lawns well kept, and Uncle Elis lived just a hop and a skip away.

"Listen!" Emma said.

The bidding had started. Lizzie's heart leaped to her throat, and without thinking, she clutched it with both hands. Her eyes grew as big as saucers as she opened her mouth to say something to Emma, but only a hoarse squeak came out.

"Let's go listen to him!" Emma said.

"N . . . No! No!"

"Lizzie, come on. We don't know if Dat's going to buy it. Come on!"

"No. I . . . I'll just stay here. You go." Lizzie sat down weakly, slumping down on a lawn chair on the front porch. Emma left and Lizzie stayed there, trying to calm herself, thinking about her friends at school and Marvin and Elsie, so she wouldn't mind so much if Dat would not be able to buy this home. It made her feel a bit confused, because at first she really hadn't wanted to move to Jefferson County, but now things were different, because she dearly loved this funny house, the mountain beside it, and the neat homes across the road. Everyone was so friendly, even if their clothes looked a bit different. She didn't care much about things like that—she wanted to live here so badly.

She sat for a very long time, or so it seemed, before she heard a breathless, "Oh, my!"

It was Mam, with Atlee Yoder's wife, and Mam had her hands crossed over her chest, just saying, "Oh, my! Oh, my!" over and over. Mrs. Yoder was half laughing and half crying, patting Mam's shoulder as they walked. They spied Lizzie, and Mam cried out, "It's ours, Lizzie — Dat bought this home!"

Lizzie flew out of her chair and ran over to Mam, who promptly hugged her shoulders with one arm, holding Jason with the other. Lizzie absolutely could not hold still, so she hopped up and down, squealing and putting her hands over her mouth. Emma came dashing across the lawn, caught Lizzie's hands, and twirled her around the porch.

"Goody! Oh, GOODY!" was all they could say.

Mrs. Yoder and Mam laughed to see the girls become so excited, then Mam's face became serious.

"Where's Mandy?"

"Mandy?" Lizzie looked up. "I don't know, Mam. Emma and I were walking around looking at everything. I thought she was with you or Dat."

Mam told them to go look for her, as she sat weakly on a porch chair, still holding Jason. She looked drained and tired after all the excitement. Emma and Lizzie pushed through the crowd of men, looking into the big open doorway of the barn. They ran back to the house, looking in every room, calling her name, becoming more frantic by the minute.

"Mand-dee! Mand-dee!"

They burst through the screen door, telling Mam they had looked everywhere. Lizzie was trying hard not to panic, because kidnappers were one of her worst fears. And in a crowd this size, and with Mandy being so little and skinny, Lizzie could not bear to think about it.

Emma was standing against a porch post, looking out across the lawn. Mam got up from her chair, her voice sounding hysterical, saying, "Lizzie, we have to find her! Please go get Dat!"

Mrs. Yoder looked very alarmed, wringing her hands and turning to go back into the house to be certain Mandy was nowhere around.

"I think I see her," Emma said, still looking across the lawn. Lizzie looked, and, sure enough, a small brown head was barely visible out at the end of the lawn. It might be Mandy! They both hurried out across the flat yard, and there she was, her thin little arms wrapped around her knees. Her rounded shoulders were sloped downward, the buttons pulled tight across her back. She was sitting perfectly still, as far to the end of the yard as she could go without touching the road.

"Mandy!" Lizzie said breathlessly.

"She's here!" Emma called to Mam.

"What?" Mandy turned her big green eyes in their direction, quite unaware of all the distress she had caused.

"Where were you, Mandy? We couldn't find you," Lizzie scolded.

"Lizzie, look!" she said, pointing to the yard across the road. Two pure white cats emerged from beneath a

flowering bush. They were long-haired, with their thick
coats floating around them, seemingly unreal. Even their
tails were long, thick, and glossy, every strand combed
and flowing with the delicate movement of the cats'
dainty feet. Emma and Lizzie had never seen anything
like it in all of their lives. They stood in awed silence,
watching the cats glide across the green lawn.

A man opened the door beside the garage and called
to the cats. They ran slowly and
gracefully when he called,
then he closed the door behind them, going inside.

"Do you think they're real?"
Mandy breathed.

"Of course!" said Emma.

"What kind of cat are they?" asked Mandy.

"I don't know. All I ever saw were ordinary barn cats
and Snowball. But Snowball looks common compared
to those cats," Lizzie said.

On the way home, Mandy would talk of nothing
else. Mrs. Yoder had told them they were Persian cats,
and the man's name was Jim Zeigler, and his wife was
named Janet. They had six of those cats, and no children, so they loved those cats dearly. They were very
nice neighbors, but you had to like their cats, mind you.

Everyone was a bit quiet, because the day had been
hard on their nerves, Mam said. But Dat was smiling and Mam was beaming with genuine happiness, so
Lizzie was content to sit back and watch the mountains
slip away as they sped toward home.

Settling In

The following weeks seemed like one big blur, almost like Doddy Glick's windmill on a windy day. It just kept going and going, sometimes faster than other times, but constantly going around and around. There was no rest for anyone; even Emma and Lizzie got along amazingly well, because they had no time to push duties on each other. Lizzie even discovered that if you washed dishes as fast as you could, then wiped the counter clean, moving things and cleaning under them, it was not even half as depressing as sitting at the table thinking about washing them.

Emma told her very seriously that she was growing up. She could work as hard—if not harder—than any ten-year-old girl she knew. That's all it took. Lizzie pitched in and helped with the packing, cleaning, and running errands for Mam without complaining. Not quite always, but there was a decided change in Lizzie, Mam and Dat both agreed.

Emma was always the dependable one—in fact, she had been for years, at a very young age, but now it seemed as if Lizzie could work alongside Emma. Dat was pleased, Lizzie could tell, so she worked harder than ever.

The day dawned bright and clear when the moving truck rolled into the gravel drive. Grandpa Glicks came without Marvin and Elsie, because they were not allowed to come help move. They had to go to school. Lizzie thought it was just as well, because they would be too sad, leaving them behind when they pulled out of the drive to their new life in Jefferson County.

Uncle James and Aunt Becca were there bright and early, because they were always finished with their morning chores in good time. Dat always said Uncle James had good management, and Lizzie wondered if that meant he managed to finish his chores long before lazy farmers.

All the rest of the aunts and uncles were there to help load boxes, furniture, and even their buggy and pony cart. Harnesses, halters, brushes, and combs were packed in huge saddle boxes and carried on the truck by strong men.

It was a windy day, so the men had to smash their straw hats down hard on their heads, because the wind just picked them off and flung them away. The women's skirts flapped in the stiff breeze, and they clutched their sweaters around their shoulders if they had to carry something down the steps.

When they took a break for coffee and cookies, the men's hair was in complete disarray, and they laughed and teased each other about it. Uncle Alvin looked the worst. He had lots of curly hair, and they stuck straight up and out the sides, as if someone had blown them up from beneath. Dat told him he never was very good-looking, and now he just looked worse. Alvin punched Dat in his upper arm with his fist, telling him if he was no taller than that, he wouldn't say too much.

Grandpa Glick sat on a crate, dipping a huge oatmeal cookie into his coffee. He was smiling, his eyes crinkled along the sides and his hair disheveled wildly. He started chuckling after he had finished his cookie, and said, "Alvin, maybe it's a good thing Melvin was short and thin when he tried to fly!"

Alvin was taking a sip of coffee. His eyes flew open, and he choked and sputtered, spewing coffee over his shirt. He coughed and coughed, clutching his throat, while Dat threw back his head and whooped. Uncle James laughed and slapped his knee with his work-worn hands, until Alvin quit coughing.

Lizzie and Emma looked at each other and smiled. They knew exactly what the men were talking about. When Dat and Alvin were younger, at home on the farm, they designed huge wings made of cardboard, wire, and other materials. Alvin persuaded Dat to climb up on the shed roof and jump off the roof to try out his wings. He told Dat he was positively sure it would work, but of course, it didn't.

As soon as Dat jumped, his arms were pulled straight up by the huge wings. That is how the wings stayed, as Dat plunged to the ground below. Alvin laughed and laughed after he knew Dat was unhurt, and they often told this story to appreciative audiences. Dat must have been very afraid, but he would do anything to impress

Alvin, Grandpa Glick always added. That was because Alvin was bigger—actually, a lot bigger—than Dat.

Grandma Glick was already washing cups and sorting cookies, but she stopped to listen, shaking her head and chuckling to herself. That was Mommy's way, Lizzie thought, because she never made much of a fuss. She must not have been able to watch everyone all the time if she had fourteen children. That was a lot of children.

After the truck was completely packed, everything loaded and tied down, and old blankets carefully folded between the furniture, Mam, Emma, Lizzie, Jason, and Mandy got into a car with a driver. Grandma Glick and all the aunts told them good-bye, shaking their hands, while Mam thanked them for helping. She asked them to come visit as often as they could, because it wasn't *that* far way, and they all promised they would.

Lizzie solemnly shook Doddy Glick's hand, then Uncle James's, Alvin's, and all the rest. She felt a bit sad, but it was mixed with excitement, because she was so eager to live in the funny basement house.

When they passed the schoolhouse, Lizzie felt strange. It seemed as if a part of her was sitting in her wooden desk, doing her arithmetic with Betty, Susie, Rachel, and all the rest of her good friends. She would miss them terribly, but the lump in her throat did not stay there very long. She supposed it was because she actually wanted to live in Jefferson County now, since that is where her thoughts were since they bought the home there.

The car was too warm. Lizzie just hated to ride in

a vehicle if the driver turned the heater on full blast, then sat there talking and waving his one hand, his face bright red from the heat, quite unaware of how stifling the air was becoming. That was the thing about being Amish, Lizzie thought. They hired a driver, because they weren't allowed to have their own car. But when it got too warm in the car, no one had enough nerve to ask the driver to turn down the heat, because it seemed as if they were complaining.

So Lizzie and Emma became steadily more uncomfortable. The driver kept up a lively conversation and Mam talked and smiled politely, but her face was so red, Lizzie had never seen anything like it. Even Mam's ears were red.

"Emma," Lizzie said, sticking her elbow in Emma's side.

"What?" Emma jumped, looking irritated. After a careful look at Emma's face, Lizzie decided Emma was almost as red as Mam. She put up her hands, touching her own cheeks which felt warm to the touch.

Mandy and Jason were sound asleep, but they looked flushed, too.

"Are you too warm?" Lizzie asked.

"Yes!" whispered Emma, rolling her eyes in the driver's direction. "Ask Mam to ask him to turn the heater down."

"No, you do."

"No, Emma. I don't want to."

So Emma leaned forward and tapped Mam's shoulder. Mam looked back at the girls and asked what they

wanted. Emma put up a hand and whispered softly to
Mam. After that she sat back against the seat, waiting to
see what Mam would do.

The driver launched into another extended story, so
Mam didn't say anything. She just smiled and nodded
politely.

Lizzie could not take it one moment longer. She was
getting a terrible headache, so she decided to open a
window. She looked at the handle on the door for a long
time, hoping if she turned it, she would not open the
door. Slowly she reached over and gave the handle with
a little knob on the end a firm yank. Cool air rushed in
as the window was lowered a few inches. Emma looked
alarmed when she realized what Lizzie had done, but
before Lizzie had a chance to open her mouth, the driver
dipped his head to look at them in his rearview mirror
and yelled, "You too warm?"

"Yes," Emma said clearly.

"Ya shoulda said something. Better close the window.
The little boy will get sick. Close it. There you go! Now,
I'll turn the heat down and we'll all be more comfortable.
That better?" he shouted, dipping his head sideways to
look at them in his mirror again.

"Yes," Emma said again.

Lizzie didn't say anything. She decided she did not
like this driver—the fat, noisy man. How could he stand
to have it so warm in the car if he was so fat? It just
irked Lizzie. Besides, if you paid a driver, you should
be allowed to open the window one tiny little crack. But
she kept this all to herself, because Emma looked red-

faced and unhappy. Lizzie figured if she'd try and talk about this driver, Emma would tell her it wasn't nice. Besides, Mam always said drivers put up with a lot, waiting outside a store while the women went shopping.

Lizzie was very glad to see the mountains, because she knew it would not be long until they were at their new home. Just when she thought they must soon be there, the driver told Mam he needed to pull into this gas station for some gas, because it was the cheapest he'd seen in a long time.

As soon as he stopped the car, heaving himself out the door to go inside, Emma and Lizzie started complaining to Mam. She told them to be quiet; they were almost there.

"Hush," she said, "you'll wake Jason."

When they pulled up the short driveway to the new basement house, Lizzie was in no mood to work hard unloading things and putting them away. For one thing, she was terribly hungry, and her head hurt and her apron pins were pricking her back.

The moving truck had not arrived yet; neither had the horse trailer with Red and Dolly. But the door of the basement home was flung open as soon as the car rolled to a stop, with Aunt Mary walking out across the porch in her short, rolling gait. She reached for Jason, who was just waking up, his curls stuck to his head because of the excessive heat.

"So you made it okay, Annie?" she asked, her little brown eyes beaming at Mam.

"Oh, yes!" Mam smiled at Aunt Mary. "We're here!"

Lizzie could not stay unhappy very long, because Mam and Aunt Mary were so happy. Mam's voice contained a giggle, even if she wasn't laughing at all. When her brother Eli came walking down the road, Mam's happy laugh just bubbled over in spite of herself. She was so glad to be with her relatives. They all went inside the house after Mam had paid the driver.

Aunt Mary had been cleaning, because a bucket of soapy water stood beside the kitchen cupboards. The whole house was completely empty. There was no washing machine in the kettle house, no beds or couches or chairs anywhere. The house echoed when Emma and Lizzie walked through it.

"No," Aunt Mary was saying, "the children had to go to school. Edna wanted to help us today, and be with Emma and Lizzie, but I told her they can all stop here on their way home this afternoon."

Emma and Lizzie looked at each other. They could hardly wait to see all their cousins. Ivan and Ray were older boys who were in sixth and seventh grade. Edna was exactly Emma and Lizzie's age, and Danny was in first grade. They would be walking to school every day with their cousins.

They had never seen the school in Jefferson County, but on Monday morning they had to go. They had brought along their pencil boxes, notebooks, pens, erasers, and even the workbooks they did not finish. But for now, Lizzie did not need to think about going to school. Not till Monday.

Lizzie was so hungry, she told Mam she had to have

something to eat or she just couldn't make it anymore.
Mam told her to be quiet, that Aunt Mary was providing
dinner, and it was impolite to say too much now.

There was a funny-looking stove standing beside the
kitchen cupboards. It had an iron top, but the burners
were down a lot farther, and they looked like individual
fat kerosene lamps with different wicks. The oven door
was on top, with more of those burners underneath.

When Lizzie asked Mam what it was, she said it was a
kerosene stove. Here in Jefferson County, they did not
have propane gas for stoves and refrigerators. They had
ice boxes with blocks of real ice in the top and kerosene
stoves. That was the *"ordnung"*.

"Oh," was all Lizzie said.

Then the moving truck came, followed shortly by
the horse trailer. Lizzie forgot all about being hungry,
because the truck backed slowly up the drive, with
Dat jumping down the minute it rolled to a stop. Uncle
Eli's laugh rang out as he shook hands with Dat. Uncle
Junior and Aunt Clara arrived to help unload. Uncle
Andy and Aunt Ida also came. They lived about four
miles away. There were three of Mam's brothers living
in Jefferson County, and they all had big families, with
children older than Emma and Lizzie.

Aunt Ida carried a blue and white granite roaster,
which she held with red potholders. Her face was
wreathed in smiles as she set it on the kitchen counter
and shook hands warmly with Mam. Aunt Clara was
a sister to Mary, so those two looked very much alike,
except one was heavier than the other. Aunt Ida was

also small in stature, with small blue eyes and teeth that
protruded in front, like Lizzie's.

Uncle Andy had white hair that stuck out in every
direction. Lizzie was afraid of him. He never said hello
to them, and didn't say much at all, especially not to
children. But the main reason Lizzie was afraid of him
was his piercing blue eyes. They never missed anything,
so Lizzie imagined he was stricter than God or Moses.
Even the men who threw Joseph in the pit in the Bible
story didn't look as fierce as Uncle Andy. Although
Mam often assured the girls he was a nice brother, and
actually quite friendly, Lizzie always stayed out of his
way as much as she could.

Uncle Junior was thin and quiet. He had wavy brown
hair, very blue eyes, and a soft smile. He smiled often,
but did not say as much as Uncle Eli. All three of Mam's
brothers liked Dat, because Dat would talk and fuss,
singing and whistling, making them laugh. He was much
shorter than Mam's brothers, but he had a quick wit,
and they loved to be around Dat.

Delicious smells came from the funny stove, so Lizzie
followed the aroma to the kitchen. The women had
set up a line of food on the kitchen counter, and some
folding chairs and cardboard boxes to set their plates
on. Everyone stood, bowing their heads in silent prayer
before filling their plates.

When Lizzie's turn finally came, she was almost weak
with hunger. Her stomach felt so flat she doubted if she
was one bit chubby anymore. Certainly not fat, that was
one thing sure. So she took a huge spoonful of cheesy

noodles and ground beef, one of baked beans with large
chunks of bacon and onion floating in a pungent red
sauce, a thick slice of ham, and a crusty piece of whole
wheat bread spread with raspberry jam. She balanced
her plate carefully, setting it on a cardboard box, then
returned for her drink and utensils. Emma joined her on
one side and Mandy sat on the other.

They ate in silence, because they were too hungry to
say anything. Mandy didn't like baked beans, so Lizzie
ate hers, too. Mandy took little bites, and her food didn't
taste as good to her as it did to Emma and Lizzie. That
was why she was so thin, they always said.

For dessert they had a big slice of pumpkin pie and
something called 'fluff.' It had crushed graham crackers
on the bottom and a kind of spongy pudding on the top,
with whipped cream on top of that. Lizzie had never
tasted anything like it, and she couldn't figure out how
anybody could make it. It wasn't really Jell-O, and it
wasn't quite pudding, either. All she knew was that it
was one of the most delicious things she had ever eaten,
and she ate two quivering squares of it.

After their late dinner, Uncle Elis' older children arrived. Esther and Lavina were too old to be going to school, and Jesse was already old enough to be going with the youth. Emma and Lizzie did not know them very well, so they hung back shyly when Mam greeted them.

Esther was tall, with wavy light brown hair, and Lavina was smaller, with very dark brown—almost black—hair. They talked excitedly, laughing and fussing over Jason, then came to say hello to Emma and Lizzie.

Everyone was put to work after the men started unloading furniture. The girls helped arrange their bedroom, while Mam helped the aunts in the kitchen. The men carried in the living room sofa, the oak bureau, Mam's platform rocker with swan handles, and all the

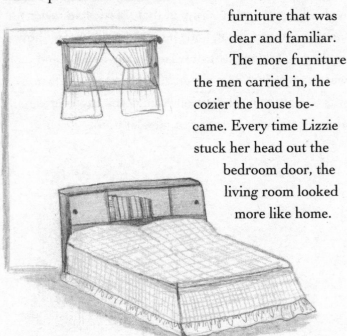

furniture that was dear and familiar.

The more furniture the men carried in, the cozier the house be-came. Every time Lizzie stuck her head out the bedroom door, the living room looked more like home.

She was busy unpacking her school things and books.
The bookcase bed went along the wall where the small
window was way up high. Their dresser with the mirror
went along the wall to the right, and the tall dresser with
five drawers stood along the left wall. The thing that was
most exciting about their new bedroom was the fact that
Mam had told them their pink chenille bedspread was
almost worn out. They had never had a new bedspread
in their life, and they were even allowed to pick a new
color from the catalog Mam had shown them. So now
they could carefully take the new bedspread from its
plastic wrapping and spread it on their bed.

Esther and Lavina helped them, exclaiming about the
lovely soft yellow color. It had tiny little loops in the fabric, and a ruffle along the border. Lizzie was thrilled. It
was the prettiest bedspread she had ever seen. Actually,
she thought there were probably a lot of English girls,
even, whose bedspreads were not as pretty as this one.
She ran her hand along the silky fabric with the little
loops in it and sighed happily. She really didn't mind one
little window way up high on the wall if they had this
beautiful bedspread.

All her books were still in good shape when she
opened the box. That was because she had packed them
so carefully. Mam had told her to stuff crumpled newspaper in the corners, where there were empty spots, so
the books would not slide around inside the box when
someone lifted it. Lizzie had told Mam if she had more
books she would not need to put crumpled newspaper in
the box—she would just fill it up completely with books.

Mam had laughed and told her she would turn into

a book soon. Then she seriously told Lizzie they would
have to see if the nearest town in Jefferson County had
a library, where you could go borrow books. Lizzie
didn't know if she liked the idea of borrowing books
or not, because you just had to take them back, which
wouldn't seem fair. Her books were so precious to her;
she read them over and over. Especially *Heidi* and *Black
Beauty*. She held them against her chest for only a moment; she was so glad to see they had come all the way
unharmed. Then she stacked them perfectly in order,
one by one, with the tallest one first, on her bookcase
bed.

Starting Anew

There was a commotion in the kitchen, and Lizzie heard Aunt Mary exclaim, "Oh, here are the school children!"

Lizzie hesitated for only a very short time before she walked slowly across the living room. Emma and Mandy followed, both eager to meet their cousins, although they felt a bit shy.

Edna threw down her lunchbox and came eagerly toward them. "Hello," she said, her brown eyes twinkling merrily. She put a lot of emphasis on the last part of the word, so it sounded like, "Hel-*lo*."

"Hi!" Lizzie said. Emma and Mandy greeted Edna warmly, while Lizzie watched the boys. Ray was smaller than Ivan, although he was the oldest. He had dark hair and his eyes were small and almost black. Lizzie thought he looked a lot like an Indian. Ivan was tall, with lighter brown hair and a lanky, wide-shouldered frame and a crooked grin. Danny was small and very thin, like Mandy, with light hazel eyes and very straight blond hair. His eyes were so light they were almost yellow. Lizzie almost giggled when he stuck out his hand with no trace of shyness, saying, "Hello, Lizzie!" in a very loud, clear voice. She liked him instantly.

"May I see your bedroom?" Edna was asking.

"Oh, yes, of course," Emma answered, and they all crowded around the doorway to see their new bed-spread. Edna was very happy, telling the girls she was excited to take them along to school on Monday morning.

"Who is your teacher?" Lizzie asked, her stomach doing flip-flops because the thought of meeting a new teacher was causing her to feel worried and nervous.

"Her name is Catherine Swarey," Edna answered.

"Is she nice?"

"Oh, yes. Well, not always. She can be really strict sometimes, but that's probably because the boys don't always behave. Ray and Ivan don't."

"Our big boys back in Randolf County didn't always behave, either," Emma assured her.

"I suppose that's just how big boys are when they go to school," Edna said matter-of-factly. Edna was very wise, Lizzie thought, because she was a lot like Emma in some ways.

Lizzie was also relieved to notice that Edna was not thin. She had a dark, creamy complexion with no blemishes or freckles. In fact, she was very pretty, Lizzie thought. She wore a bigger covering than they were accustomed to, but it was white and ironed neatly. She looked a lot like a chickadee in her coloring book, because she was brown and black and white.

After they had a tour of the house, they went out to

the barn to see Dolly. Lizzie was shocked to see poor Dolly wandering around aimlessly, seemingly at a loss to know where she was.

"Awww!" Lizzie's heart swelled with pity as she hurriedly opened the gate to her stall. Dolly pricked up her ears and walked toward Lizzie.

"Come, Dolly. Come on, poor girl. What's wrong?" Lizzie crooned, as she held her halter, stroking her ears and caressing her neck under her heavy mane. Lizzie loved to feel Dolly's neck, because it was so warm and silky underneath the soft curtain of hair.

Little Danny watched her with wary eyes. "Hey, you better watch it. That pony could bite you real easy," he said.

"Huh-uh!" Lizzie said, without thinking how arrogant it sounded. Edna watched her closely, her brown eyes still shining, as kind as always.

"Lizzie!" Emma said. "She could bite, although she never has."

Emma was so polite, Lizzie thought. She knew, and Emma knew, that Dolly would never bite either of them, but Danny was afraid of Dolly, so it wasn't nice to act too self-assured.

"Danny, come here. Dolly likes little children. Do you want a ride?" Lizzie asked.

"No!" Danny's terrified shriek almost scared Lizzie.

"Well, okay, you don't have to, Danny. That's alright," she assured him quickly.

"I don't like ponies much," Danny said, his voice as loud as ever.

Dolly's soft, warm nose nuzzled Lizzie's hand as she continued to stroke her.

"Do you have a pony?" she asked.

"Oh, yes. Her name is Sugar," Edna said.

"Really?" Lizzie was thrilled.

"She's brown and white, and so fat you'll have to laugh when you see her. We can't handle her very well. She tries to run away all the time. Ray or Ivan help us drive her if they have time. But she bucks children off and sometimes we can't hold her if we hitch her to the cart. She's just a mess!" Edna said.

"Wow!" Lizzie exclaimed.

"Hey, it's true. The last time she bucked me off, I hit my head on a rock when I landed. She ran off to the barn, and I was so angry!" Danny said, his big eyes rolling as he remembered the terror of that moment.

Lizzie pulled herself up as tall as possible and told Danny that Dat would have made him get back on and ride her again. They were not allowed to show fear of horses, or ponies, especially, because Dat told them that's why you couldn't control them. Dolly knew if Emma or Lizzie were afraid of her, and then it was harder to make her listen.

Danny watched Lizzie as she talked, his eyes never wavering from her face.

"See, Danny?" Edna said. "We'll bring Sugar here to Emma and Lizzie, and let Uncle Melvin help us train her."

"No!" yelled Danny.

"Why?"

"'Cause. Nobody's going to make me get back on
Sugar after she dumps me off."

Lizzie laughed; she couldn't help it. Danny was so
little and skinny, but his voice was so mighty, and he
certainly knew without a doubt what he meant. Lizzie
loved him. She caught Emma's eye and knew she felt the
same way. It would be fun walking to school every day
with these interesting, different cousins.

"Edna!"

Someone from the house was calling them. Edna
answered, and they all trooped back to the house, after
carefully closing Dolly's gate to her stall.

"Edna, would you go over to Marlene's house and get
some hot dogs in the freezer?" asked Aunt Mary. "The
men will be hungry and there's no reason Melvin Annie
should make supper—she's just too tired."

Aunt Mary, as well as the rest of the relatives who
lived in Jefferson County, spoke differently than Emma
and Lizzie. They all came from Ohio where Doddy
Miller lived, so their Pennsylvania Dutch accent was
completely different. Mam's speech was very nearly
like theirs, although she had lived in Pennsylvania long
enough that she didn't talk quite like they did. But
when she was with her relatives, she rolled her 'r's more
frequently, and her long 'i' sound became more of a
short 'a' sound. Lizzie loved to hear them talk, because it
sounded so cozy and warm. She never could understand
why their speech reminded her of date pudding; warm,
clean beds; smiling, friendly people; and happiness. But
it did.

Lots of words were pronounced entirely different, or they used other words that Lizzie wasn't used to hearing. Mashed potatoes in Lizzie's world were *"chtompdy groombare"* and Ohio people called them "mush." Lizzie thought they were having cooked cornmeal mush like Mommy Miller made. She thought it was awful, spoiling a perfectly good fried chicken and filling dinner with that horrible cornmeal mush with milk and sugar. But mush was actually mashed potatoes, as she found out on one of her first visits to Uncle Homers in Ohio.

When Aunt Mary said 'Melvin Annie,' she pronounced 'Annie' more like 'Ennie.' In Randolf County, the grownups all said 'Melvin sei Annie' to speak of husband and wife, which actually meant Mam was Dat's wife. Here in Jefferson County, they just put Dat's name and Mam's name together. Aunt Mary was 'Eli Mary,' and Aunt Clara was 'Junior Clara.' It seemed different to Lizzie, but she loved to hear them say 'Melvin Ennie.' It seemed as if they truly belonged here now, making her feel like they could make themselves at home.

"Can Lizzie and Emma go along over?" Edna asked.

"I guess. If Melvin Annie doesn't mind," Aunt Mary said.

So they walked across the yard, as Edna showed them where Marlene lived. The house was new, with gray siding and fancy shutters on it. The front of the house that was under the porch roof had stone laid the whole way up to the ceiling. A massive window that was shaped a bit round and had lots of small panes in it took up almost

the whole front wall. The drive was macadam, same as
the road they crossed, and the yard was mowed to perfection. It actually looked like a green carpet, not really
like real grass. There was a curving stone sidewalk that
led to the fancy front porch, with a lamp post beside it
that had a gold electric glass lamp on top.

"Why does Marlene live by herself?" Emma asked.

"Oh, she doesn't," Edna assured them. "Her husband
was killed."

"Really?"

"Mm-hmm. He worked on the railroad. I'm not sure
what he did, but he was killed one day. They lived in our
house, and Marlene was standing on our porch when
they came to tell her, so she couldn't bear to live in that
house anymore without Roger. That was his name."

"My." That's all Lizzie could say, because Edna had
stepped up on the porch and was pressing her finger on
a small, rectangular, plastic object beside the door. They
heard a faint "ding-dong" inside the house, and Emma
looked at Lizzie and raised her eyebrows.

The door opened and a tall black-haired lady smiled
from behind the storm door. She had light green eyes
and wore red lipstick, a yellow blouse, and navy blue
pants. Lizzie quickly looked at her feet, but she was
wearing warm socks and no shoes. She guessed this lady
had piles of high heels in her bedroom closet.

"Hi, Edna!" the lady said.

"Hello. Can we have some of Mom's hot dogs from
the freezer?" Edna asked.

"Sure. Come on in." She stood back to let the three

girls into a living room with soft, golden-colored carpeting on the floor. Lizzie had never walked on anything as soft and clean as that carpet.

There was a real stone fireplace along one wall, and a floral sofa and chairs with pretty pillows and afghans placed perfectly to accentuate the gold color of the rug. It was so fancy and beautiful that Lizzie could only stand and stare. She loved pretty things, and never in her life had she seen a room as pretty as this one.

"Are these the new cousins who are moving in today?" asked Marlene.

"Yes. This is Emma, and this is Lizzie," Edna said, with a little shove to their shoulders.

"Hello. How are you?" Marlene said, smiling.

Emma said they were fine, but Lizzie didn't say anything, because she was overwhelmed with awe when Marlene smiled. She was so pretty that Lizzie just couldn't speak.

"Aren't you about Debbie's age?" she asked.

"Probably," Edna answered.

Lizzie looked around the kitchen, with its beautiful cabinets, linoleum that shone like glass, and huge china cupboards that contained so much fine china and crystal that she thought it looked like gold. Everything was so spotlessly clean that it sparkled.

Marlene opened her basement door, and Edna went down the stairs with her. Emma and Lizzie weren't sure if they should go along down or stay upstairs, so they stood self-consciously in the doorway of the living room.

"Wow!" Lizzie breathed to Emma.

"I know!" Emma whispered back.

They heard them coming back up the carpeted stairway. They were surprised to see a girl about their own age open the door first. She had short, curly hair, as black as Doddy Miller's crow. It was so black that it shone blue, depending how the light shone on it. Her eyes were deep brown in color, and her skin was tanned to a deep nut brown hue. She was round and chubby, wearing a shirt that stretched tight at the buttons. She had a small, flat nose that was the cutest nose Lizzie had ever seen.

"Lizzie, this is Debbie," Edna said. "She's our age, and she stays at our house a lot, so she's used to Amish children."

Debbie looked shyly at Emma, then at Lizzie, lowered her black eyelashes, and giggled. That was all. She never said hello or asked how they were or anything like that. But a giggle rose in Lizzie's throat, and Emma smiled widely, because that's just what Debbie's giggle did. It was like a virus—you just caught it.

"Debbie, this is Lizzie and Emma, your new neighbors where Atlees used to live," Edna said, trying her best to introduce them.

Down went Debbie's black

eyelashes, followed by another infectious giggle. Now they all laughed out loud, because there was nothing else to do when Debbie laughed her little "tee-hee." Then she raised her eyelashes and looked at them, smiling, her small white teeth showing prettily. The girls smiled back, and the beginning of a true friendship began at that moment.

Edna had a few packages of frozen hot dogs and announced the fact that her hands were getting cold, so they told Debbie good-bye, thanking Marlene. She showed them to the door, and they hurried out the curved stone sidewalk.

"Isn't she cute?" Lizzie burst out. "Oh, their house is so-o fancy."

"Yes, but they are the nicest people. So common and nice to be with," Edna said.

"Does . . . does Debbie come to your house to play?" Lizzie asked.

"Oh, yes. Sometimes every evening after school. Her mom says she's allowed to stay for an hour, but it's usually longer. She likes our food. Mom makes Grandpa cookies with vanilla frosting, and she loves them," Edna said, laughing.

As they walked back across the lawn, Lizzie's heart was filled with joy. The sun was sinking lower in the sky, casting a yellowish glow across the fields. The gigantic mountain loomed to the west, enveloping Lizzie with a protective feeling.

She heard Uncle Eli's laughter ring out, which only increased the happiness and excitement of the moment.

Lizzie had never known that changes in your life could turn out to be as happy as this one. Her new beginning in Jefferson County promised to be an experience rich with adventure.

Lizzie's heart was so light that she skipped breathless little skips across the sun-drenched yard.

the end